MW00777485

Seasons out of Time

Kimberly Wenzler

SEASONS OUT OF TIME
by Kimberly Wenzler

Copyright © 2020 by Kimberly Wenzler
All rights reserved.

First Edition May 2020
ISBN 978-0-9905900-8-8 (pbk)
ISBN 978-0-9905900-9-5 (epub)

Library of Congress number: 2020907948

No part of this book may be reproduced in any form or by any electronic or mechanical means, including information storage and retrieval system, without permission in writing from the author except in the case of brief quotations embodied in critical articles and reviews.

This is a work of fiction. The events and characters described herein are imaginary and not intended to refer to specific places or living persons. The opinions expressed in this manuscript are solely the opinions of the author.

Cover image © 2020 Kimberly Wenzler
Book formatting, Cover design by *Suzanne Fyhrie Parrott*
Cover image credits:
© Ian 2010, *Sunflower*, Shutterstock.com
© matttilda, *Fall Leaves Background*, DepositPhotos.com

Seaplace Publishing
Northport, New York

BOOKS BY KIMBERLY WENZLER

Both Sides of Love

Letting Go

The Fabric of Us

Seasons Out of Time

Chapter 1

Dear Aunt Emma,

Next month, my son is leaving for college. He'll be a five-hour plane ride away, and I'm devastated. I will miss him terribly and can't understand why he wants to be so far from me. As a single parent, I do everything for this child: cook, clean, lay out his clothes. I even filled out his college applications (all the ones within an hour's drive from our house). He submitted one application – to the university on the other side of the country – without my knowing. I tried to bribe him to stay home by offering to buy him a car, but he insists on going. Can you please tell me how to deal with this life change?

~ Left in Lynbrook

Dear Left,

This is a tough adjustment for both of you. Try to embrace this next stage in your life. Your son is ready. He is seeking his independence. Be proud, let him go without bribes or guilt, and find something else to focus on.

You've devoted the past eighteen years to taking care of someone else. Now it's time for you. Join a book club. Volunteer. Get a dog. Travel. Your options are endless.

You raised this boy. Now set him free.

~ Aunt Emma

Damian pulled onto I-91E and adjusted the cruise control. We hardly spoke. The radio, tuned to the Pop Hits channel on Sirius, did little to ease the tension between us.

We passed a sign, *Amherst, 52 miles,* while our son, Charlie, slept in the back seat. Charlie got in late last night, having gone out with his friends one last time before they all separated for the semester. He'd been out a lot this summer, establishing his independence, I've been told. Somehow, it's supposed to ease the transition for this next step. I suspect it will be easy for him to say goodbye. It's been a challenging year for all of us.

I thought of the most recent Dear Aunt Emma letter I'd answered, wondering now if my strong response to the woman in Lynbrook did more damage than help. Facing an empty nest, I related all too well to her helplessness. Yet, as Charlie will be attending Amherst College in Massachusetts, which is only a four-hour drive, my pain of separation may be far less than Lynbrook. Small blessings.

"We have thirty miles. Wake him," Damian said, breaking the silence.

"Not yet. He's tired."

He sighed. "What time did he get home?"

I shrugged and looked out my side window.

"Nice, Heather. He just comes and goes as he pleases. Way to parent."

Heat rose to my cheeks. I knew exactly what time our son walked in last night. 2:42 a.m. It was past curfew, but I figured it was his last night with his high school friends who he'd spent more time with these past months than with his parents. I could hardly blame him. I was seventeen once.

"Nice," Damian muttered again.

"Why couldn't you have let me take him myself?"

His eyes cut to me before returning to the road. "Because this is a big deal, and I don't want to miss it. And he'll need help unpacking the car." Under his breath, he muttered, "God forbid you drive our child two hundred miles away."

"Says the guy who hit a car last year."

"It wasn't my fault."

"You were riding his bumper," I said.

Damian took a deep breath and shook his head. I looked back out the window. My eyes burned back angry tears, and I swallowed a frustrated scream. This was not how I envisioned today. Charlie's last morning shouldn't contain the memory of his parents fighting.

"Look," Damian said, after we covered a few more miles, "we're both emotional. It's a difficult transition for all of us. Let's call a truce."

I leaned my head back on the seat. The most difficult transition for us happened five months ago, in March when Damian packed his last bag and left the house. This, by comparison, should be a breeze. For Charlie, at least. I'd been trying to temper my emotions all week.

My baby's leaving for college.

I wrapped my arms around myself. "Can we raise the temperature a bit?"

Without a word, Damian adjusted the air conditioner, and I felt better.

"Thank you," I whispered.

Ten miles later, he reached his arm to the backseat. "Wake up, buddy. We're almost there."

Charlie opened his eyes, lifted his head, and straightened in his seat. Wordlessly, he stared out his window until we pulled into Amherst.

Cars were lined up and down the walkways throughout the campus while families unloaded trunks and carried bags, crates, and pillows into buildings. Filled with a mixture of excitement and dread, I peeked at our son.

"How are you doing?"

"Fine."

Fine. Stock answer for every emotion he won't share with me. I wanted to remove the word 'fine' from the English language.

"It's this one," I said to Damian as we pulled up to Appleton Hall, Charlie's home for the next nine months. He opened the door right away, followed by Damian while I sat inside, gathering the strength I'd need to get through this. I looked out the window at the orderly chaos around us.

Damian knocked on my window. "C'mon."

I stepped out of the car and joined the mayhem.

A small group of sweaty but enthusiastic upper-classmen helped unload our car while welcoming Charlie to campus. My son took off to check-in with the Resident Assistant and then returned with a room key. When we walked in, it appeared his roommate had already arrived. One of the beds was neatly made, and pictures hung on a small corkboard over its adjacent desk. We deposited Charlie's bags and boxes on his side of the room, filling the small space.

Students and their parents passed the open door, talking, laughing, and we stood silently, half-expecting someone to walk in to claim the other half of this space. But no one did.

Sending Damian and Charlie out to move the car, I indulged myself in one last nesting opportunity – the making of my child's bed. I was leaning over the far corner of the mattress, struggling to get the fitted sheet over the three-inch foam topper I was told to buy because college mattresses are thin when I sensed I was no longer alone.

Successfully cornering the sheet, I stood and turned to find a man watching. I pulled my t-shirt back down over my waist.

"Hi there." He reached his hand out. "I'm Cole Prue. Need help?"

I shook his hand. "Heather Harrison. It's nice to meet you." I glanced back to the half-made bed. "I think I'm good."

He took a step back and smiled. His dark brown hair was swept back from his face except for a lock that fell over an eye. The one that wasn't hidden was glacial blue. He seemed too young to be a parent and too old to be a freshman. I puzzled over his role. And then I got it.

"Ah. You must be Charlie's RA."

His smile broadened, revealing a dimple on one lightly-bearded cheek. "I'm his roommate."

Oh no. My eyes opened wide. "His roommate? I'm sorry. I thought —"

"It's okay. I've been getting that a lot today. Another parent stopped me downstairs to ask if there are quiet hours in the dorm for her daughter."

"You look older than seventeen. Well, eighteen. Charlie's a young freshman."

"That's because I am older." He walked to his desk and straightened books, appearing embarrassed. He wore a Henley shirt, unbuttoned, and I glimpsed a rock or medallion hanging from a thin leather rope around his neck, falling just below his collarbone. On his wrist was a thick, braided leather bracelet. I turned to finish my task, hoping I didn't insult him. He didn't volunteer his age, and as much as I wanted to ask, I held my tongue. I'd let Charlie get to know him instead.

I shook out the top sheet and laid it on the bed as Cole headed toward the door.

"Are you sure you don't need help?" he said.

"I'm sure. Did your parents leave already?"

"I moved in myself. They'll stop by to see me in the next few weeks. They don't enjoy chaos."

I straightened and pushed my hair from my forehead. Wearing shorts and a tee, I was still warm. "Do you mind if I open a window?"

"Allow me." He stepped to the single window between the beds and pushed it open. It helped a bit but not enough. The August air seeped into the small space, and I felt claustrophobic. My neck perspired. I slipped my hairband from my wrist and threw my thick, shoulder-length hair into a quick bun on the top of my head. Much better. I turned to Cole and shrugged. "It's always in my way."

"It's nice," he said.

I opened a garbage bag, pulled out a stack of tee-shirts, and brought it to the double dresser.

"I took the right side," he said. "I hope it's okay."

"That's perfect. Charlie is a leftie."

He laughed. He had a friendly face and a full laugh, and I felt some relief to know my son would be living with someone who offered to help make a bed or was worried about what side of the dresser he took.

"Can I ask you a question?" I said before he could walk out and I'd lose my nerve.

"Shoot."

"Why are you here if this is a freshman floor?"

He showed me that dimple again, and his neck turned pink. "I am a freshman."

I paused, decided I was over-stepping some line, and went back to the bag.

"I took some time off after high school. Decided to come back and get my degree," he said.

I kept unpacking.

"I put in for a single, but was late and told there are too many incoming freshmen, so I got roomed here. They'll let me know when a space opens. Somehow I'm not counting on it."

"So, you're…"

"Twenty-four."

"Oh." I pulled out shorts next and placed them beside the tee-shirts.

"Do you want to know anything else?"

I shook my head. "It's not my business."

"It is your business," he said. "Your son will be living with me. And you're frowning. You have concerns."

"Why not be an RA? Usually, they're older. And you'd have your own room."

"I thought about it, but I didn't want to get involved in policing students."

I pulled the last pair of shorts out.

"Anything else?" he asked.

I straightened. "Do you smoke?"

"No."

"Pot?"

He hesitated. "No."

"Drink?"

"On occasion."

"Do you have a girlfriend?"

He crossed his arms over his broad chest and gazed down at his feet. "No."

"That's okay. My husband calls them distractions. Wait. That's not true."

"He doesn't call them distractions?"

"No. He's not my husband. Well, he still sort of is… Never mind." Now, I was blushing.

Cole paused. "Well, they can be distracting. Girlfriends, I mean."

I tossed the empty bag aside and pulled another open. "I think I'm good here, Cole. If you have somewhere to be, please don't let me stop you."

"All right." He turned to leave and paused. "Mrs. Harrison, I'll be a good roommate. I'm easy to get along with and focused. Maybe it's better he's not going to live with another eighteen-year-old. They can get pretty wild."

"Another eighteen-year-old can't buy him beer."

His eyes held mine. "I promise I won't buy him beer."

Damian and Charlie walked in, and Cole stepped aside to give them room. Cole stuck his hand out to Charlie. "I'm Cole, your roommate."

"Oh, cool. I'm Charlie." He shook Cole's hand, followed by Damian, who introduced himself as Charlie's dad, and not my husband, or ex, or almost, or sort of.

"We couldn't find a spot," Damian said to me. "It's crazy out there." He began to move boxes out of the way, and Charlie stood in the center of the room, dazed.

"I'll be down the hall until you're in," Cole said to Charlie. "If you need help, let me know."

"Thanks."

Cole paused at the door, gave us a mock-salute, and disappeared.

"Your roommate seems nice," I said to my son.

Charlie shrugged and dove into a box.

"He's nervous," I mouthed to Damian over Charlie's head. Damian nodded, and we worked together until every box and bag was emptied, broken down and recycled.

Charlie agreed to have lunch with us before we left. He and Damian told me they'd get the car, which was parked in the far lot, and pick me up outside the dorm, so I stayed behind in the room to take one last look. I was pleased with Charlie's bed and his wall hangings and checked the desk one more time to make sure nothing was forgotten. Everything from here on would be up to him. I hoped we'd prepared this child well to be on his own.

I looked at Cole's desk and took a step closer to see his pictures. There were only two. One showed a beautiful young girl, big blue eyes, and blond hair, staring into the camera, daring it to capture her personality. She wanted to appear sullen, but her eyes smiled at the photographer. The other was of Cole with his arm around the shoulder of a slightly older man with a dark complexion. They didn't look like brothers. Both were mid-laugh. I stared at Cole's face. God had been kind to him. I checked over my shoulder, feeling guilty, but I was alone.

I shut the door behind me and walked toward the end of the hall. As I passed rooms with names on paper clouds taped to the doors, I was reminded of my first days at college at Brockport. I'd asked my mother to take me, but she'd needed my father to drive us. I'd bitten my nails to nubs on the drive up, trying to gauge his mood, waiting for the usual eruption from the front seat, but he remained silent the entire ride. When we arrived, I toted my crates and bags from the car to my room alone, sweating and nauseated, promising them I wanted to do it all. There were paper stars on the door, one with my name and the other, my roommate's. I dumped everything on one side of the empty room and ushered them outside before my roommate and her parents showed up. I needed to avoid any interaction between my father and my future friends if I wanted a fresh start here. I walked my parents to the car, claiming they'd hit traffic if they waited longer. The look in my mother's eyes still haunts me when I think about that day. They reflected the fear and shame I felt in public with them. She understood and told my dad she wanted to skip lunch, which we'd planned to do, and go right home. My father got into the car with nary a goodbye to me. My mother hugged me tight and whispered, "Be happy," before getting in the car with him.

My roommate and her parents showed up an hour later, smiling, tearful, and nostalgic. While I decorated my side of the room, the three of them laughed, talked and even argued about where to hang a tapestry. I cringed, waiting for the screaming, but their voices returned to normal after they figured out where to put it. They invited me to lunch with them. I declined, feeling it was a betrayal to my mother if I accepted.

I reached the end of the hall and shook the memory from my mind. Charlie wants to have lunch with us. I've done something right. There was a study room straight ahead with a large window. I went inside to see the view and was startled to find Cole lounging on a small couch, reading a textbook.

"Hey, there. You guys all moved in?" he asked.

"Yep. He's all set."

Cole stood, holding his book.

"Thanks for letting us settle in. The room's yours now," I said.

He nodded.

"We're going to grab lunch. Would you like to join us?"

When he smiled, one corner of his mouth went up. I wonder if he practiced that.

"Thank you. I'll stick around here. I have a lot of beer to buy." He pressed his lips together, trying to contain a smile.

Maybe my emotions got the better of me, the thought that my only child was heading into the next stage of his life, leaving a gaping hole in mine, or maybe it was because Cole was showing me how ridiculous my earlier statement was, implying he would buy Charlie beer, but I laughed hard, which led Cole to laugh too, clearly relieved I had a sense of humor.

I wiped my tears and nodded. "I deserved that. I'm sorry."

He shook his head. "I couldn't help it. It was nice to meet you."

The ride home was long. Damian and I had little to talk about after initially discussing our thoughts on Charlie's room and his roommate.

"He seems a bit more mature than Charlie, don't you think?" Damian said.

Charlie's thin, testosterone-hungry frame made him appear much younger than Cole's fully developed physique. Cole had a shade of dark stubble along his jaw. I wasn't even sure Charlie had packed a razor. "He's older than Charlie. He took some time off after high school. In any case, everyone matures at their own rate," I said.

"How do you know?"

"He stayed in the room while I made Charlie's bed."

Damian glanced at me.

"I asked him," I said.

"Ballsy."

I shrugged. He's right. Not my typical persona, but when it comes to my child and his safety, all bets are off.

"I hope they get along."

"He'll be fine," I said, hoping I was right.

A few miles later, we slowed down due to heavy traffic. Damian checked his watch and cursed under his breath. "I told Genna I'd be home early evening."

My cheeks burned. "Why'd you tell her that? You took your kid to college." Genna. The thirty-year-old tight body who had replaced me. "You know what's funny? She'd be perfect for Cole." I forced a laugh, knowing I sounded biting and vengeful, but I couldn't help myself. Just the mention of her name made my blood go hot.

"Nice, Heather," Damian mumbled under his breath.

It's true, I thought. They're both beautiful and young. For the sake of the long ride ahead, I kept this last thought to myself.

The traffic let up, and Damian gunned the engine. The silence in the car was stifling.

"I can't believe we just dropped our son at college," I said.

He didn't respond at first. Finally, he said, "I can't, either."

I stared out the passenger window, watching the fields along the highway pass in a blur. Damian and I were in college when we met, not much older than Charlie is now. Sometimes, it felt like only yesterday. Other times, it felt like I recalled the lives of people I once knew, who were now strangers.

Damian turned up the radio, and I closed my eyes.

Our next words were spoken one hundred miles later, right before the Throgs Neck Bridge. I broke the silence with a request to stop for the bathroom. Without a word, he pulled into a rest stop.

"I'll get gas. Don't take long."

I'll take as long as I want. Let Genna wait! Though I took care of myself through the years, there was no competing with a woman a decade younger. Genna was the antithesis of me; a tall drink of water with short, blond, wispy hair compared to my 5'4" curvy body and thick, auburn mane. He was still at the pump, staring ahead at the mini-mart attached to the garage when I returned from the restroom. Not a glance in my direction.

Today is the beginning of a new stage for me. I'd just dropped my son off at college, and I'd miss him like crazy. What I wouldn't miss, I thought as I climbed back into the car, was spending time with someone I once thought I loved, who now barely acknowledged me. Last week I turned forty-one, spent a lovely, quiet evening with my son and my sister's family, and reveled in the fact that I did not receive a gym membership or weights, gifts that reminded me I was getting older.

Damian pulled into the driveway of our house at ten o'clock and let it idle in reverse, a sign he couldn't wait to dump me and get to his new, modern apartment. Go then.

"So, parents' weekend?" he said.

I opened the door. "It's in October. I'll let you know the date. I'll go the week after."

"Fine."

He'd already pulled out and drove away before I reached the porch. Our relationship fizzled to a point where we exchanged eight sentences in four hours. I was foolishly hoping the drive would help alleviate some of the angst I felt, but it only made me feel lonelier. Did Damian not feel the same tearing at his soul as I did?

I went to put my key in the lock when I noticed something on the rocking chair next to the door. It was a bottle of wine with a note attached.

If you want to talk, come over. Doesn't matter how late. Love, D

In the foyer, I faced the dark, empty house, a colonial I'd spent years fixing up and decorating. I loved this house, its honey-colored wood floors under thick area rugs, soft fabric couches that hugged whoever sat on them, and family pictures alongside paintings I'd found at small, unknown galleries upstate, covering the walls. I'd wanted it to be homey and inviting, and here I stood by myself. Clutching the bottle of wine and note from Dottie, my neighbor, and best friend, I headed toward the fridge. In the artificial light pouring from behind the orange juice, I paused. Of course, I wanted to talk to her, and wine tastes better when shared with a friend. Still holding the bottle, I shut the fridge and walked out.

Dottie Miller answered the door in her pajamas and robe. Her short, flaxen bob was disheveled, and her makeup was washed off, which made her light brown eyes seem even smaller and lighter on her pale face. This is what a best friend does: opens the door completely stripped of protection.

I held up the bottle and tried to smile. She pulled me in and went straight for two wine glasses in the kitchen while I followed.

"Let's skip the glasses and just use a really long straw," I said, sidling up to a stool at her island.

"That bad?" She uncorked the bottle with a frown and sat next to me.

"Worse. Damian and I are strangers, it seems. It felt so uncomfortable."

"For Charlie, as well?"

I thought about it. "No, I think he was too nervous about moving in. We all were." I sipped. It was a nice red, bold. Failing to push aside the feeling of emptiness, I half-smiled at Dottie. "I don't want to be here yet. I still want him home, playing T-ball, and going to bed at 7:30. I just left my man-child hundreds of miles away."

She sighed. Fifteen years older and a widow for six years, her two adult children included one married with a baby, and the other, a successful architect living in San Diego. "Don't think of Charlie leaving as the end of a stage, but the beginning of a new life for you."

My eyes welled up. I was overtired and emotional. "I thought I had a life, Dot. I was supposed to send my child to college and face empty-nesting with my husband. When Damian and I started out, we were happy. God, I followed him around like a puppy dog. And now, twenty years later, he can't stand the sight of me."

Dottie handed me a tissue and refilled my glass. The moon shone through the kitchen window, reminding me how late it was.

"Heather, you met him when you were eighteen. You were a baby. People change."

She was right, sort of. Damian changed, no longer content with me. Once, he'd been my refuge from my parents and childhood home, a place I wanted to escape.

"If I've learned anything, it's that life has its own plan for us. I never expected to be alone in my fifties," she said.

"I'm forty-one and have to figure out my life all over again."

Dottie smiled. "And aren't you lucky?"

I snorted. "You're kidding, right?"

"Not at all. Be honest, if not for me, then for yourself. Were you happy?"

"Sure," I said quickly.

She leaned her head to the side, daring me to say more.

"Happy enough," I said. "I wasn't alone, and Charlie had both his parents under one roof."

"Is that how you want to live your life? Don't you want more?"

I thought about the past few years of my marriage, how the closeness we once shared, and the intimacy of the early years disintegrated to the point we were little more than roommates with nothing in common outside of our son. Maybe it wasn't happiness, but it was what I knew.

"I don't want more."

"Oh, Heather," Dottie said, pulling me into a hug. "Don't say that."

I don't like change, but like it or not, it was here. My husband and son were gone, and I was alone. What now?

I walked into my house after midnight. Exhausted, I climbed the stairs and went to bed.

I waited four full days before calling Charlie. When I did, he sounded happy, and his voice held no quiver of the unsureness I used to hear when he first had sleepovers at friends' houses as a child. Charlie mentioned that Cole's quiet and easy-going manner made him a good roommate and that they even shared a class together. I felt consoled hearing my son was acclimating to his new life – better than I.

Other than the one phone call, I relied on texting to communicate with Charlie – my tether to him when I needed the connection.

I was blindsided by the stillness of the house, the empty feeling left by just one person. When Damian moved out, Charlie and his friends still filled the space and made enough noise to keep the house alive. Now, I walked from room to room, not needing to straighten anything. No dishes left in the den. The kitchen was always clean. Once upon a time, amid diapers and Sesame Street, I longed for solace. Why did I long for this?

We dropped Charlie at school on Saturday. As a writer for the local newspaper, I had the luxury of being able to work from home, but by Wednesday, I could no longer stand the silence and was in the office by nine. I passed a set of empty tables, wide computer screens flashing screen-saver photos of gorgeous, exotic places I'd never been to or even imagined. It looked as if everyone had suddenly evacuated. A woman sat alone at her desk.

"Hey, Marsha."

She finished typing and leaned back. "Hey, girl."

"What are you working on?" I asked.

She scowled and pointed to her screen. "Another DWI accident. Third this week."

"It's only Wednesday."

Marsha sighed. "Keeps me employed."

I nodded to the group of empty desks. "Editor meeting? Or did everyone win Lotto?"

"Fred's sixty-two. Someone brought cake. I'm on a diet."

"You eat my cake every year."

She patted her large belly. "I like you better."

I stepped away, toward one of the spare desks in the corner and settled into my seat, logged onto my email, and started electronically sifting through letters from readers. I'd barely read through the first message when my boss, Carl Thompson, poked his head out of his office. "Heather." I looked up. He motioned me in.

"Charlie settled in?"

"More so than I am," I said as I dropped onto the seat in front of his desk.

He smiled, showing me tobacco-stained teeth. "You should take some time off. Go somewhere."

"I'd rather work. I'll wait for the next conference."

He rolled his eyes. "Get out of that house occasionally."

"I do get out. I come here, don't I?" I leaned back in my chair and clasped my hands.

Carl is like the grandfather I never knew: wrinkled forehead, snow-white hair, small friendly eyes, and surrounded by the constant odor of sweet pipe tobacco. Framed pictures of his wife, children, and grandchildren decorated the wall behind him, while photos of Carl with local celebrities were relegated to the wall near the window.

"So, what do you need, Carl?"

"Pete is retiring in the spring."

Pete Underwood ran a gardening advice column for as long as I could remember. Longer than I'd been here at the paper. As far as I knew, he loved doing it.

"That's too bad. I thought he would stick around a few more years. Want me to organize his party?"

Carl shook his head. "No. The column ran its course. He's being replaced by Google, and he doesn't want to reinvent himself. I need someone to take over his spot."

I was about to make a few suggestions when I realized where this was going.

"Me? You're kidding," I said.

"I'm too old to kid."

I leaned forward and pressed my steepled fingers against my lips while I thought about his proposal. Carl waited.

"I don't know anything about gardening."

"You've been doing the same thing for fifteen years. Challenge yourself."

I chewed the inside of my lower lip.

"Give it a try," he said. "It's extra money."

Along with the Aunt Emma advice column, I booked half a dozen speaking engagements every year. Adding a gardening column meant a more substantial workload, but I could use more money. The problem was, I really knew nothing about a plant, herb, or any other foliage, for that matter.

I stood. "Can I think about it?"

"Of course. We'll need to go with a different format. No one wants to wait one to two weeks for an answer to something they could find on the internet in seconds. I want something new."

"Like what?"

"That, I'll leave for you to decide. Oh, I saw some letters for Aunt Emma in the box downstairs. Don't forget to pick them up on your way out later."

"I can't believe people are still mailing in paper letters."

Carl looked at me. "Thank God. It's my last stubborn hold to the good days."

"Carl, what happens when people don't want my advice anymore?"

My editor smiled. "Fortunately, heartfelt and honest answers to love can't be easily found."

Back at my desk, I sifted through my emails and finally chose questions to respond to for Saturday's article. I spent the afternoon answering them and at five o'clock, decided to ponder the last one at home.

Dinner consisted of a chicken breast, a serving of steamed broccoli, and orzo. My resolve to eat healthy lasted until 9 p.m. As I lounged in the den, eating from a pint container of Heath Bar Crunch, and contemplating the emailed letter I brought home from work, the phone rang.

"What're you doing?" My sister, Trisha.

"I'm in the middle of a threesome," I said.

"With who?"

"Ben & Jerry. What's up?"

"Just checking in, making sure you aren't unconscious in a tub full of tears," she said.

"Thanks for the vote of confidence. I'm fine. Charlie is fine. Everyone is fine. My friends are melting. Can I call you tomorrow?"

"Wait! How was it?"

"The truth? I had to deal with Damian and his bitching about leaving Genna for too long."

"What's the matter? He didn't want to pay the babysitter?"

I laughed and sprayed ice cream on my shirt. Trisha was relentless about Damian's new girlfriend. "Anyway, I spoke to Charlie briefly." I blotted the mess with a napkin. "He sounds happy. I miss him."

"Oh, Boo. I'm sorry."

I sighed. "Thanks. It's an adjustment, but I'll get used to it. Went into the office today."

"Any good letters to share?" Trisha asked. She enjoyed hearing about other people's problems, often sharing her opinion on how I should respond.

"A woman is questioning her husband's behavior. She's afraid he might be cheating."

"Newlyweds?"

"Empty-nesters."

"Sounds familiar, right?"

I frowned. "Too familiar. I could write half of the letters I receive."

"Hmm. I've heard couples fall apart when they don't have the kids between them anymore. Nothing to talk about. Nothing in common," she said.

"I've heard the same."

"Tell her to kick him out."

I laughed. "I'm glad you're not Aunt Emma."

"Hey, you should talk. You gave some tough love to that 'copter mom last week."

I winced. "I know. Meanwhile, I'm all mopey, and I told her to cut the cord and get a life."

Trish laughed, then paused a beat. "Do you want to come to dinner on Friday?"

"Let me check my calendar."

"Very funny."

I spooned dessert into my mouth and let it slide down my throat. Delish.

"Heather. I'm setting a place for you. Come at seven."

"I'll bring dessert," I said.

"You don't have to. Bill is bringing dessert."

"Who's Bill?"

She paused, and I dropped my spoon into the pint, annoyed.

"It's a guy Adam works with. He wants to meet you-"

"Okay, now I'm hanging up. And I'm not free Friday," I said.

"Oh, come on! What else are you doing?"

"I'll call you tomorrow."

I disconnected the call, not in the mood to subject myself to Trisha's pity and innate need to set me up with a man. She gave me exactly one month by myself after Damian left before the calls started. I leaned back, picked up my spoon, and didn't stop until I hit the bottom of the pint.

Chapter 2

Dear Aunt Emma,

I've been married for twenty-two years to a wonderful man. We have two children who are in college and have been very happy. At least, I thought we were happy, until recently. For the past few months or so, I've noticed he's been secretive. He was never a big texter but seems to be glued to his cell phone, his thumbs moving at speeds I never knew he could manage. Now, when he leaves the room, he makes sure to take the phone with him. He used to let it lie around the house, ignored. The other night, he came in late from work, and I asked him where he was. He seemed flustered and said he stopped for a drink with his friend, Frank. I know Frank was home because I'd just talked to his wife earlier. I'm so upset, I don't know what to do. I want to confront him, but I don't want him to think I don't trust him. I'm tempted to check his phone, but I can't get a hold of it. I've never felt this way before. Can a marriage disintegrate like this after more than two decades of love and devotion? Please help!

~Almost fifty and forlorn

Dear Forlorn,

The answer to your last question is yes. A marriage can begin to fall apart at any time. Occasionally, it will seem out of the blue, though usually, there are signs of its gradual demise. Lack of communication is one clear indication that something might be wrong. Lying is an obvious red flag he's hiding something, or someone, from you.

Disagreements that escalate into arguments and lack of intimacy are other nails in the coffin of a dying marriage. Are you experiencing these? You say you don't want your husband to think you don't trust him. Writing to me that you're worried he's being dishonest or involved with someone else, is a sign you don't. You know the saying; If it walks like a duck and talks like a duck…

My advice is to speak to him and tell him how you feel. But be ready for his answer.

~Aunt Emma

Emailing several articles to Carl for review and publication during my absence, I headed to the airport on a gorgeous fall afternoon, destination: Seattle.

I enjoyed out-of-town speaking engagements, and now that Charlie was older and at school, I looked forward to them. Not only was the pay good, it broke up the monotony of being home alone. Relying on Trisha and Dottie to keep me socially engaged might no longer be enough.

Once checked into the Seattle Sheraton, I confirmed my itinerary for the conference. I'd be speaking before a group of writers about my experience and position as a female journalist and how I segued a sexist column in a local paper into a current module where women still struggled for equality. After reviewing my notes and taking a shower, I headed to the hotel restaurant for a bite to eat.

I nursed a drink at the bar, trying to stretch out the evening since it was early.

"Is someone sitting here?" asked a deep voice beside me. I hadn't noticed anyone approach, as I was texting to remind Charlie if he wanted to reach me, to call my cell.

"No. It's free," I said, still staring at my phone.

"Are you here for the conference?"

I mentally rolled my eyes, not in the mood for idle chatter. My body language must have been easy to read because he turned away from me and ordered a drink from the bartender. I put my phone down. "Sorry. You caught me in the middle of something." I glanced down the bar, saw all the available seats, and sighed.

He spun his seat to me. "No problem. I saw what you were do-ing. My fault." He wore khakis, a golf shirt, and old Nike sneakers.

I returned to my glass.

"So, yes or no," he said.

I stared at my drink. "I'm sorry?"

"Are you here for the conference?" he said again.

"Yes."

"Oh?" He shifted his body forward, and I slightly pushed back my stool. "Are you a guest? A writer?"

"I'm one of the speakers," I said.

"Ah! What's the topic?" He leaned closer.

"Journalism in a man's world."

"You're a journalist?"

"I write a column."

The man had slicked-back salt-and-pepper hair, an unnatural tan, and he reeked of cologne – a heavy, offensive musk. It reminded me of when Charlie used to practically bathe himself in Axe body spray in middle school.

"What do you write?" he said.

How to lose a barfly in ten seconds. "I give relationship advice."

He pursed his lips and nodded. "Sounds interesting. So, you're an expert on relationships?"

"Some seem to think so."

"Are you married?"

"Separated."

He laughed out loud, and I watched his Adam's apple bob under his mottled skin covered with gray stubble. Late fifties. Maybe sixty.

"So am I," he said when he recovered. "Troy." He held his hand out.

"Heather." I took his hand tentatively.

"I'm twice divorced."

"Less is more, Troy." I swiveled my chair to fully face the bar.

"I'm here for the conference as well," he said, continuing to intrude.

I nodded and sipped my martini.

"I'm an author," he volunteered, clearly ignoring my earlier advice. "I write crime thrillers mostly, and I've dabbled in some futuristic sci-fi. I'm promoting my fifth book. I'll be speaking on

Thursday. I wanted to come out early, listen to some others. Maybe learn something new."

I finished my drink. "It's always a good idea." I put my empty glass down and slid off the stool. "Well, it was nice to meet you. Good luck."

"Why don't you listen in on Thursday? I have a really insightful talk planned," he called.

I turned my head but continued to walk. "Take care."

"Heather?"

I stopped and turned. "I'm sorry, I'm really not interested."

He leaned back. "You have a napkin stuck to your pants."

I swung my hand, nonchalantly behind my butt, and pulled the paper stuck to it while trying to ignore my burning face. Nice. Right, Heather. Leaving the hotel, I headed three doors down to the quiet tavern I'm familiar with when I'm in town. I took a deep breath. Let's start this evening over.

At the restaurant, the hostess seated me at a corner table, and I was mid-bite into my burger when a familiar face walked into the pub. He was also alone. He smiled when he spotted me from the bar, and I waved him over.

"Join me," I said.

John Dixon, a friend, and fellow speaker, sat in the opposite chair and put his beer down. "I would love it."

John and I met years ago during my first speaking engagement. I was a bumbling ball of nerves the entire conference. He'd found me after my session and took me to dinner, offering tips on how to improve my delivery. He had a few years of experience over me, and I was grateful for his help. When we're lucky enough to be at the same events a few times a year, we listen to and critique each other's presentations, sharing meals and conversation.

He ordered, and the waitress left us alone.

"Don't wait for me," he said, nodding toward my burger.

"I'll eat slow. How are the girls?"

I nursed my burger while he updated me about his two daughters, one married, the other in grad school.

The waitress brought his plate and took his empty beer glass.

"How's Charlie?"

"At college," I said.

John cut a piece of his roasted chicken. "Congratulations. Welcome to the empty nest period of your life. Have you and Damian made any plans? Maybe to travel?"

I dabbed my mouth and placed the napkin on my empty plate. "Damian moved out in March. We're separated."

John put his fork down and reached his hand for mine. "I'm sorry. Do you need to talk about it?"

I looked around the restaurant and cleared my throat. "Not really." I finished my iced tea.

"Okay. Let's talk about your presentation. I saw the schedule. You're on Tuesday right before me. Do you need me to look over your notes?"

"I'm good. How about you?" I asked.

"So, the student becomes the teacher." He nodded and then chuckled.

"You've taught me well. I've come a long way in eight years."

"You have. I'm going to Pike's Place after the sessions tomorrow. Why don't you join me?" He put a forkful into his mouth and chewed.

I smiled. "You go every time we're here."

"I love the market. You would too if you ever left this street."

"Maybe," I said, knowing I wouldn't.

"One of these days, you'll surprise me and say yes."

When John was nearly finished, I raised my hand to the waitress as she passed and asked for my check. He did the same.

I dropped my money on the table and stood first. "He left me for someone else. A younger, beautiful someone else."

John looked up at me, and I struggled to push back tears.

He shook his head, left his money and his last bites of chicken, and walked out with me.

Chapter 3

I gripped the steering wheel and merged onto Route 91. This was the first long trip I'd ever taken by myself by car. I almost called Trish yesterday to be my ride-along, but I didn't want her to take over my visit with Charlie.

Amherst in the fall is exquisite. The solitary drive was surprisingly pleasant, as a vibrant, textured palette of yellow, red, and burnt orange surrounded me. It was invigorating and brought on a nostalgic sense of yearning for my own college days, before marriage and motherhood — those first years on my own and out from under my father's thumb.

Parking in a lot near Charlie's dorm building, I checked my phone as to his room number and texted him I was seconds away. The silence of the campus was calming as I walked across the grass. Nothing like move-in day where flocks of excited people crowded the lawns and sidewalks.

A student walked out of the building as I reached the door, and I slipped in. Signing in at the main desk, I headed toward the stairs. On the way, music and occasional voices drifted out from behind closed doors.

Climbing the four flights, I found Charlie's door slightly ajar. I stood for a moment to listen for sound or movement, heard nothing, and then knocked softly. No answer. I knocked again and took my phone out to text him a second time.

"He's in the Quad." I jumped when I heard a voice behind me. "I'm sorry. I didn't mean to startle you."

I turned to see Charlie's roommate, Cole, behind me. His wet hair was finger-combed back and curled at the neck. He wore a towel around his waist and nothing more. Two girls passed us then, in the hall.

"Hey, Cole," they sang in unison. The half-naked guy next to me waved to them.

"Hey," he said back, in a low voice.

"I'm sorry. Let me go and let you get dressed," I said, stepping back from the door.

"It's okay. Don't go anywhere. I'll be quick." He started to drop his towel, and I managed to turn around before I saw too much. I stood outside the door and tried to distract myself from the image of his muscled torso and hips, glimpsed before I turned. Oh, to be so young and confident.

Following a conversation with Charlie last week, I concluded that Cole must be a country club brat. Charlie had met his parents the previous weekend and told me, *"Mr. Prue is the CEO of a bank and his mother dressed fancy and wouldn't touch anything in the room."* From my limited experience with him, Cole carried himself with the confidence and ease of someone who needed very little. Life had been kind to him. We were comfortable, but far from wealthy. Our modest house on Long Island probably fits into Cole's parents' living room.

I checked my phone for a text or missed call from my son. A girl giggled in the next room, and then a deeper voice laughed with her. Thin walls. I pushed away thoughts of what went on in these rooms after classes or on the weekends.

"You can come in now," Cole said through the partially open door.

I waited an extra beat and then stepped into the room. He wore faded jeans and was slipping on a black tee shirt.

"How was your trip up?" he said as he sat on his bed.

"Uneventful." I stood near the door, feeling intrusive. He pulled on socks and walked to the closet, grabbed sneakers, and sat back on the bed. He leaned over to tie them while I stared at his hair, the way it covered his neck in a thick curl.

Sneakers tied, Cole sat up. I shifted between feet, growing impatient.

"You said Charlie's in the Quad? Do you know when he'll be back?" I said.

"No. I think he was expecting you a little later."

"I got an early start." I rechecked my phone. No text.

He pointed to Charlie's dresser, where my son's phone sat, forgotten. I sighed.

"Can you point me in the direction of where he is?"

"I'll take you to him. I'm getting breakfast anyway."

Cole escorted me down the stairs and outside into the brilliant sunshine. "I love this weather," he said as we started up the path from the dorm. "I should have come out earlier."

"Did you sleep in?" It was 11 a.m. already.

Cole put on aviator sunglasses. "Late night."

I'm sure.

A dark-haired girl in low-rise jeans and sweatshirt walked toward us. "Hi, Cole," she said, and then boasted her orthodontic work.

"Hey, Mandy."

We walked.

"What are you studying?" I said, feeling suddenly ancient on this campus.

"Quantitative Economics, like Charlie, with a dual major in Psychology."

"That's a mouthful."

He laughed softly. "My late night kept me at the library until four in the morning."

"Is 'library' code for something?" I said, using finger quotes, thinking of the three smiling and attentive girls.

"It's code for a large building with lots of books." There was no laughter in his voice.

"I'm sorry. I didn't mean to offend you."

He paused. "You didn't. No need to apologize. I have an exam Monday. Gonna be brutal."

We passed a set of brick buildings amid vibrant trees that lined the walkway. I felt proud to know Charlie studied here. Proud and responsible. Cole pointed out other dorms and paused at a building on the way to the quad. "Most of Charlie's classes are in there."

I stared at the structure until we passed it, imagining Charlie walking in with his backpack slung over a shoulder. In the blink of an eye, he went from a two-foot-tall four-year-old in nursery school to a six-foot near-man walking into this gorgeous building on a campus two-hundred and twenty miles from home.

"You okay?"

I gave Cole a slight, asymmetric smile. "Just wallowing in nostalgia."

He nodded. "I get it."

"Your mom feels the same way?"

He shrugged. "Probably. She's not overly expressive." He led me through the campus, and I felt a bit sorry my own son wasn't the one giving me the tour. "I showed her and my dad around last weekend."

"How was parents' weekend?"

He nodded. "It was fine. They met Mr. Harrison and Genna."

I stopped walking. "What?"

Cole stood beside me and winced. "Did I say something wrong?"

I swallowed. My head was reeling. Damian brought Genna here?

"Mrs. Harrison? Are you all right?"

I took a breath and faced Cole. He watched me carefully, his brow furrowed.

"Um, I'm okay." I resumed walking, and he followed.

"I'm sorry," Cole said. "I shouldn't have said anything."

I knew Damian came last week, but he didn't include this vital piece of information. Why would he bring his girlfriend unless he was considering…Oh, God. Will he marry her? So soon? They've only been living together for a few months.

"Mrs. Harrison."

"Hm?"

"I was saying the cookies you sent for Charlie's birthday were delicious. He shared them with the guys on the floor."

I couldn't muster a smile. "It's the first birthday he wasn't home. It felt strange, so I had to send something."

"He was happy. Trust me. And I went into a sugar coma." Cole stopped walking. "Here we are."

To our right, just past the Student Union, was a large field of grass almost entirely covered by students. Blankets were set down, laptops open. Some students were on their backs, taking in the sun's rays, others throwing a football or Frisbee. It was beautiful.

"This is the Quad," Cole said, "Charlie's over there. Northern corner."

I looked to where Cole pointed until I found Charlie. He was sitting, his back against one of the trees surrounding the vast expanse of property, reading.

I stepped toward the direction of my son and stopped when I realized Cole wasn't beside me. I turned to see him watching me. "Will you be okay?" he asked. His concern somehow eased the knot that had formed at the pit of my gut.

"Yes. Thank you for bringing me here."

He smiled. "My pleasure."

I crossed the field, feeling conspicuous, but no one seemed to pay attention. Midway, I turned to see Cole still watching me, I assume, to make sure I was going in the right direction. I raised my hand, and he did the same, and finally, he walked away.

Charlie looked up as I approached and jumped to his feet. "I thought you'd be here at twelve."

"I decided to leave early and made good time." I looked around the yard. "This is wonderful, Charlie."

"Isn't it? Beats the library."

"What are you reading?" I nodded toward the closed book in his hand.

"A chapter for my Microeconomics class."

"If you need to study…"

He shook his head. "I'm hungry. Let's eat."

We headed to a restaurant Charlie wanted to try for lunch. Once seated and our orders taken, I took in my son's transformation.

"You look happy. I'm relieved," I said.

"You worry too much. I'm fine."

"Okay." I sipped my iced tea. We sat near the window, which allowed us to people-watch the pedestrians outside. A man wearing a backpack and walking a dog stopped right in front of us. The pup sniffed the ground while the man stared at his phone. They were going nowhere fast, but neither seemed to mind. The man lifted his head to the sun.

"So, how was your visit with your dad last week?"

"He came on Saturday and left Sunday," Charlie said. He watched the dog lift his leg, finally.

"That's nice." I played with my napkin on my lap.

"Did Dad tell you he brought Genna?"

"No. He didn't," I said flatly.

Charlie didn't appear to want to expand on this, but I needed to know how he felt. This separation was new to all of us. As hard as it'd been on me, I know it was hardest for him to accept. Damian and I rarely fought, like other couples I knew, and Charlie was oblivious to his parents growing apart over the years. It took a lot of effort on my part to keep life at home as consistent as possible for him. Now that Damian was out of the house, we argued more.

"How did you feel having him bring her?"

"It was weird, I guess." Charlie looked away.

I had to shake off the residue of jealousy and anger that had settled on me. My ex was bringing his lover to visit my son. I show up alone the very next week, the spinster he left for the young beauty. I felt like an idiot. Charlie looked around the restaurant, biting his lip. I had to change the subject.

"Cole seems great." I tried to imagine how he must have responded to Genna. I'll bet she attracted a lot attention last weekend. I felt so small.

Charlie nodded. "He is. He mostly keeps to himself though. Spends a lot of time out of the room, walking and hiking or in the library. He doesn't come to parties with us on the weekends."

"Maybe it's because he's older than most of the kids in your dorm."

"Maybe. The guys on the hall call him 'Old Man'."

I laughed. "Does he mind?"

"Not at all. He acts old, compared to us."

"Or," I said, "he could have done all that partying during his time off and he's just more focused."

"I'm focused, Mom."

"I didn't say you weren't. I'm just saying six years is a big difference in age. At your age, anyway. Once you get old like me, five or six years makes no difference at all."

Our burgers arrived, and I kicked Charlie lightly under the table. "No, Mom, you're not old," I said, in a deeper, Charlie-like voice.

He pulled the top bun from his burger. "No, Mom, you're not old," he parroted.

"Brat."

He laughed and drowned his meat in ketchup before placing

the bun back on top. "Anyway, he's tutoring me in Calc II – the class we share. He aced the first test. Got an A."

"What did you get?"

"Not an A." Charlie said, avoiding my gaze. "This is a lot harder than high school. And the professors move fast." He focused on his burger.

"Hey," I said.

He looked at me.

"It's an adjustment."

He seemed relieved by my response, which made it harder for me to add the next thought. But I had to. "So, maybe let's focus a little less on going out and a little more on the books, okay?"

"What do you think I'm doing? I just told you Cole is helping me. It was his idea."

"Does he want money?"

"I don't know. I didn't ask." He took a large bite of the burger.

"Offer to pay him. It's the least you could do."

"Fine. Let's talk about something else."

I stayed at the hotel in town and slept fitfully, bothered that Damian and Genna were here only last week. I couldn't let it go. The following morning, I woke too early to call Charlie for breakfast, so I dressed and went for a run as the sun rose. The temperature had dipped overnight and the cool air invigorated me. As I passed unfamiliar roads mentally ticking off landmarks for my return, my mind wandered to Damian, to the first signs I realized our marriage was falling apart. They were subtle, and I must have not been paying attention, focusing my care on Charlie. The late meetings, weekend trips with clients that weren't part of his prior responsibilities. He'd been promoted, he'd explained, and this was part of the requirement of his new role. I never complained, content keeping house, being a mom, and answering letters from the lovelorn. I didn't even question our eventual decline of making love, believing that's what happens in a marriage of several years. I had no one from whom to model my behavior. My parents' marriage was tumultuous. By comparison, I felt fortunate.

I returned to the street of the hotel amid a spray of pink and blue sky feeling slightly lighter than I'd felt since arriving yesterday. As I waited at the crosswalk for the traffic light to change, I spotted

Cole with a man leaving a diner across the street. They talked, then hugged, and the man, carrying a burlap bag over his shoulder, walked away. I crossed the street, averting my eyes so Cole wouldn't think I'd noticed. I was hoping to slip into my hotel without being seen. But when I looked back his way, he was smiling and waving, so I walked over to him.

"Good morning," he said. "You run. That's awesome."

"It's a new pastime."

"Are you training for a race?"

I laughed. "No. It helps to clear my head and gets me out from behind my desk. It's cheaper than therapy."

He held on to that adorable smile.

"You're out early," I said.

"I had a breakfast date." He wore loose pants, rugged boots and a backpack. He followed my eyes and peeked down at his clothes. "I went for a hike before that," he said, as if explaining his attire. "For the same reasons as you."

I glanced up and down the street, starting to cool down and felt a chill on my back where my perspiration dried. "I'm going to head into the hotel."

"Are you seeing Charlie before you leave?" Cole said.

"We're having breakfast. I'll text him when I get back to my room."

"I'm going back now. I'll wake him."

I nodded, and was about to turn to leave when I remembered what Charlie told me yesterday. "Cole, Charlie told me you're helping him in Calculus. I really appreciate it."

"It's no problem."

"Thank you."

"You're welcome." He held my eyes until I finally turned away.

Back in my hotel room, I texted Charlie and jumped in the shower. I thought of Cole. Who was the man he met for breakfast? He was so at ease talking to me. How does a twenty-four-year-old possess such confidence? Did I, at that age? I dried myself with the thin hotel towel. *For God sakes, Heather, you're not even that confident now.* Half an hour later I was dressed, and had a better attitude to see my son.

After three texts, he finally answered me that he was awake and would be ready when I got there. Back on campus, I skipped up the four flights of his dorm to the now-closed door. Cole answered with a wink. "Hello again," he said softly. He held the door open and stepped aside for me to enter.

I walked in, relieved to see Charlie dressed in jeans and hooded sweatshirt. "Ready?"

He stood. "Yep."

We walked to the door as Cole reclined on his bed with a book. One arm rested behind his head and I could see the end of a tattoo along his inner arm, writing of some sort.

"Take care," I said.

He tilted his head and rested it on his hands. "Until next time."

We headed to the student union building on campus. I purchased two cups of coffee, two blueberry muffins and a bowl of oatmeal for myself. We found an empty table by the window overlooking the quad that boasted a handful of students brave enough to face the early morning chill.

"Not much happens here before ten, I see."

"Not on Sunday morning." Charlie bit into a muffin.

I sipped my coffee and looked around the large room, at the students yawning as they carried their trays of breakfast. A pang of regret rang through me, wanting to do college again. I forgot how much I loved being on a campus – the future mine for the taking. I'd do so many things differently.

I looked at my son. No, I wouldn't.

The October sun hadn't warmed the air yet. I could feel the chill through the window, so I pulled the sleeves of my sweater over my wrists and wrapped my hands around the warm coffee.

"How are things at home, Mom?"

"How do you mean?"

Charlie shrugged and gazed out the window. "Without me home, it's just you now. Are you okay? Lonely?"

I put down my mug and rested my hands in my lap. "I miss you, but I'm perfectly fine. I have my work and I've been away since I last saw you. I have three more conferences this year, Aunt Trish calls me constantly, and Dottie came over for dinner right before I left."

He took another bite of his muffin.

"Charlie, I promise. I'm fine. You worry about yourself. Get high grades so you can graduate and make a respectable living. One that gives you choices. If you do that, I'll be the happiest woman you've ever met." I smiled wide while my heart throbbed. I didn't want my child to worry about me. Worrying was my job.

"Have you thought about dating?"

I dropped my smile. "I'm not ready."

"Okay."

"Why the sudden interest in my life?" He didn't express these concerns at dinner last night.

He shrugged. "I don't know. Cole was asking and it made me think…"

"Well, don't think."

He chuckled.

"Do you know Carl asked me to take over the paper's gardening article? Pete Underwood is retiring."

Charlie's eyes flew open. "Does your editor know you can't keep anything alive in our house?"

"I kept you alive."

"Because I can talk."

I laughed. "I don't think they care. I also don't know the first thing about giving advice on relationships, and I've been fooling people for fifteen years."

"Good point," he said.

I left my son with a hug and his promise to call next weekend. Driving home, a jumble of thoughts ran through my mind: Damian and Genna walking around the campus last week with Charlie and Cole, Cole and his breakfast date so early on a Sunday morning, and Charlie, trying to figure out his way. I'm so proud of him. I am determined he grow up feeling more loved and confident than his mother did.

Chapter 4

Dear Aunt Emma,

I'm recently divorced and looking to date but I don't like to go to bars. My friends are trying to convince me to join a dating site but I'm afraid. I've heard horror stories about them. I work in a very small office so there's no chance of meeting someone there. What should I do?

~Alone & Wanting

Dear Alone,

Dating sites are popular and there are reputable ones out there if you do some research. Keep in mind, many of those who sign up are in your shoes. If you're still not comfortable with that option, try something new. Consider taking a dance class. You don't need a partner for line dancing. It's good exercise, and you'll have fun. I guarantee you'll make friends. Who knows what will lead from there? Baby steps.

~Aunt Emma

As I answered Alone & Wanting, I tried to think of all the people who weren't writing to me, the happily married couples who have no need for Aunt Emma, but my optimism was still strained.

At home, I sat at my desk and stared at the computer screen when my sister called.

"What are you doing?"

"I'm working," I lied. I spun my chair around to look out the window. "What do you need?"

"I need you to take off your chastity belt and try one date with Bill."

"Who?"

"You know, the guy I told you about. The widower," she said.

I exhaled. "Trisha, you have a listening problem. I told you, I'm not interested right now. Leave me alone about this."

"It's one date. Damian left seven months ago."

"So?"

"So? You're not getting any younger."

"And you're not helping your argument by insulting me."

"He's sweet. And not bad-looking. Please."

"I don't want to."

"You have to."

"What are you talking about?" I said.

Trisha hesitated. "I need to ask you a favor."

"Oh, God, what did you do?"

"I kind of invited Bill to your house for Thanksgiving."

"Un-say it."

"I can't. His son is skiing in Colorado that week and he's completely alone."

I squeezed my eyes shut, feeling a headache coming on. "Don't make me do this."

"Make you do what? He'll come as our guest and you just have to feed him. You love feeding people."

Silence.

"Come on," Trish continued. "You always say no one should be alone during the holidays. Dottie's coming."

"Dottie's my best friend."

"Okay. Please. I can't un-invite him."

"I'm going to live to regret this."

Relief filled her voice. "Thank you! He's bringing pecan pie. He's a baker."

"Wonderful. Trish?"

"Yeah?"

"This is not a date."

"Okay. You won't regret it."

"I already do. I have to go. I'm on a deadline."

"I'll call you next week. I'll bring dessert and wine."

"I have wine."

"You never have enough."

Because you drink all of it, I wanted to say. But I swallowed my words.

I hung up the phone and returned to the screen, where I had started my profile on a dating site I found doing research for my last letter.

Describe yourself: Single mother of one. Looking for someone to talk to, spend time with, and make memories.

Someone jiggled the front doorknob. I ran to my bedroom to put on a bra under my ratty sweats, and threw my messy hair in a bun before I went downstairs as Damian let himself in.

"What are you doing?" I said.

He looked up to see me on the stairs. "I wanted to drop off the payments and pick up the mail."

I met him in the foyer. "I forwarded you the mail yesterday. You'll have it tomorrow. You have to stop walking in as if you still live here."

He stepped by me, and I detected a cologne I didn't recognize. Probably a brand Genna bought him. I used to love the way Dior smelled on his skin. It used to be the only cologne he wore. Now an overpowering floral scent filled my nose and turned me off.

I followed him into the kitchen where he pulled a carton of orange juice from the fridge. He poured himself a healthy amount in a glass he took from the cupboard, and sat at the table.

"This is still my house," he said.

"Please leave."

"Why? Am I interrupting anything?"

"I'm working."

He snorted and drained the juice in one swallow. Then he looked around from where he sat. "I wanted to see how your trip to Charlie went. You brought Trisha, I assume."

"No, I went alone."

He spun the empty glass on the table. "Wow. How brave of you."

I flushed. "It was no big deal." But it was. I did consider bringing my sister, and it bothered me that he knew it.

"Did Charlie tell you I met his roommate's parents?"

"Yes. Why did you bring Genna?"

"Why not? She wanted to see the school."

"Is she thinking of applying?"

He glared at me. "She's not *that* young. And I think she and Charlie got along well."

"Says who?"

"I saw it. Why? Did Charlie say otherwise?"

"He didn't say anything. I'm sure it's not easy for him to have us separated, but really, Damian, that was pushing it."

"Calm down."

"I am calm!" I took a deep breath and crossed my arms, still standing across the kitchen.

"This Cole's got a lot of money," Damian said. "His father's some CEO of a bank."

"I heard."

"And the wife. She's something. Gorgeous. Covered in Louis Vuitton and Gucci. Genna made sure to point that out."

"I'm sure you didn't need Genna to point that out."

He rolled the glass back and forth.

"So, what about it?" I asked.

Damian shrugged. "Nothing. Was interesting is all." He stood. "I'm going."

"Thank you."

"What are you doing for Thanksgiving?" he said.

"Why?"

"I thought I'd see if Charlie wanted to go to dinner."

I felt myself heat up. "He's spending Thanksgiving with me and my sister. You cannot ask him. Don't even think about it."

Damian stared hard at me. "Don't you think it should be his choice?" He walked out of the house, leaving me seething in the kitchen. I heard the door close behind him, and then walked past the table, past the dirty glass, and back upstairs.

Returning to the computer, I stared at the screen for a long time. *Describe yourself.* I pressed the delete button until everything was erased.

Chapter 5

Charlie was coming home for Thanksgiving, and I was exuberant at the thought of seeing him. He called on Monday to check in
and I reminded him his father was going to pick him up. Freshmen
weren't allowed to have a car on campus without special permission.
I had asked Damian to get him, thinking it would give them some
time to spend together and he wouldn't be tempted to try to woo
Charlie away for Thanksgiving dinner.

"So, you're all set. Make sure you're packed and ready by noon
on Wednesday," I said.

"Okay." He sounded distracted.

"Charlie, what's up? Everything okay?"

He hesitated, and my heart skipped a beat. "I have two exams
this week, and I'm just a little nervous," he said.

"How's it going with that class that you're having trouble in?"

"Calc. That's one of my tests. Cole's been working with me
every day. I got an A on the last exam but that only brought my
average to a C."

"That's good!"

He sounded cautious. "We'll see. This one will be harder."

I closed my eyes. If Cole was spending time with Charlie, was
his own work suffering? I felt a stab of guilt.

"He's clearly helping," I said.

"For sure. Without him, I don't know what I would do."

"Well, good luck, babe. I can't wait to see you Wednesday."

"Mom?"

Oh no. There was something else.

"Cole's parents are on a cruise. He was going to stay on campus
for the weekend, but I was wondering if I can invite him home
instead."

I set up the spare bedroom between Charlie's room and mine, for our surprise guest.

Trish called on Wednesday before the boys arrived. An upside to Cole joining us was that he was one of those freshmen with special permission to have a car and offered to drive Charlie home, saving Damian the trip.

"When is Charlie due home?" Trish asked.

"They should be here around dinnertime."

"They? He's bringing a girl home already?"

"No. His roommate, Cole, whose parents are away during the holiday," I said.

"Do you remember when I brought home my roommate freshman year?"

I winced. "How can I forget? She called her mother in the middle of the night to pick her up because she was so afraid of Dad. The woman had to drive over an hour and a half to get her."

Trisha paused. "I don't know what I was thinking, letting her come."

It didn't take much to send our father on a tirade. At fifteen years old, I had still responded the same way, hiding in my room, sweating it out until he left the house or ran out of steam and locked himself in his room.

"At least you got to go back to school. I had to deal with them by myself."

Trisha sighed. "Why do you think I transferred home?"

"You told me you failed out."

She didn't answer for a minute. "I couldn't leave you alone with them any longer."

The boys pulled into the driveway in a pickup at dusk, and it took all my effort not to run out and hug my kid tight. Instead, I waited, peeking through the window, as they grabbed their duffels from the trunk and walked up the path to the door, where I met them in the foyer. Charlie dropped his bag and allowed me to grab him. When I finally let go, I acknowledged Cole, standing with his bag still over his shoulder.

"Cole, I'm glad you could join us." A partial truth. I really wanted alone time with Charlie.

"Thank you for having me, Mrs. Harrison."

While Charlie took his roommate upstairs to put away their bags, I tossed the spinach salad and heated up the chicken Marsala, Charlie's favorite dish. Choosing an informal setting, we sat to eat in the kitchen. I listened to discussions of mid-terms, professors and girls in their classes. Charlie talked about one he'd become friendly with, Kate, he said. At first, they started the semester on the wrong foot and didn't really like each other, but a little time appeared to have changed that.

"Many relationships start that way," I said, adding to the conversation. Cole was quiet as Charlie talked about Katie.

"Cole, anyone catch your eye at school?" I asked.

He grinned. "I don't need the distraction."

"Which is why he'll make Dean's list," Charlie said.

I held my tongue, knowing how worried Charlie was about his own grades.

I was used to Charlie's friends talking loudly over each other, slaying each other with crude, insulting remarks that I learned quickly was their way of bonding. They were gregarious and immature, a contrast to this quiet, reflective young man. Country-club upbringing, perhaps? Prep-school training? Whatever it was, Cole was easy company to have.

"Who's coming for Thanksgiving?"

"Aunt Trish, Uncle Adam and your cousins, and Dottie."

"No one should be alone on a holiday," Charlie explained to Cole. "Dottie is our neighbor next door. Her kids live out west, so Mom makes her come here."

With that comment, I decided not to tell him about Bill.

"Her children will be home for Christmas. She's my friend," I explained to Cole. "She's not a charity. We've been close for years, and I'd go to her if I were alone."

"No, you wouldn't," Charlie said. "You have Aunt Trish over for every single holiday. Her house is small, and she's not a good cook. She'd rather sit at the table, watching you make dinner while she drinks."

I glared at my son. *Don't disparage my sister or friend.* This was Damian's behavior peeking through, and I abhorred it.

"I'm sorry," I said to Cole, "my son is being rude. It'll be a nice day tomorrow. My sister is fun. So is Dottie."

Cole nodded. "I look forward to it."

I stood and brought my plate to the sink. My back was to the boys as I took out Tupperware to store the uneaten food.

Charlie brought his plate to the counter. "Thanks, Mom. Cole, come up when you're done. I'm jumping in the shower." He left the kitchen, and I was acutely aware of being left with his roommate. I washed a pot, placed it on the draining mat, wondering how long he'd sit here with me.

I turned around. Cole was in his seat finishing his meal.

"So, your parents are away?" I said.

"They're on a Mediterranean cruise for two weeks."

"What a trip."

"They do it every year."

"That must be nice," I said.

Cole nodded. "It is. They took my sister."

"You have a sister?"

"Gretchen. She's thirteen."

"You chose to stay home alone instead of going to Greece?"

"I've been there several times. The next time I go will be on my terms with my chosen company."

Of course. It's just another trip for this kid. My empty passport sat in my desk drawer, ignored and racing toward its expiration date. I picked up a pot and towel and started drying. "You're okay with not seeing your family for Thanksgiving?"

"I can't miss classes."

"Well, I would've gone to Greece," I said. "No. I would go to Paris if I could."

"Have you been?"

I shook my head. "Never been out of the country."

"You should go. It's amazing. When the Eiffel Tower is lit up it's awesome."

"I'm sure it is."

"How about now that Charlie is in school?"

"Ah, but you see, that's more reason for me to stay home and work." I kept a light tone in my voice, wanting to make sure I didn't come across as complaining. I was happy and proud to work so my son could go away to college.

I leaned against the sink, trying not to focus on the small pile of pots and dishes left to do and the big dinner to prepare for tomorrow.

"Thanks again for helping Charlie with his class," I said.

"It helps me study so it works both ways." He returned to his food. I watched him. I'm sure it's not helping him at all. In fact, spending extra time with Charlie is probably holding him back. He lifted his head, and I got caught up by his eyes. It was the first thing I noticed about him when we met. They were so blue, like an incandescent summer sky.

"What?" Cole said, smiling.

Yikes. I'm staring.

I shook my head. "Your eyes. They're…beautiful."

He laughed. "Thanks."

My whole face heated in embarrassment. "I'm sorry. You must get that a lot."

"I don't."

"Oh." I ran my hand over my thick ponytail, trying to figure out how to finish this conversation. "Do either of your parents have blue eyes?"

"My dad," he said, "though everyone says I look like my mom, but with darker hair."

Right. Damian mentioned Mrs. Prue was gorgeous.

"I'm sorry I haven't met your parents, yet. Charlie mentioned your father is the CEO of a bank. What does your mother do?"

Cole blinked, as if I'd brought him out of a trance. "She runs the house. And when a cause suits her, organizes fundraisers."

She runs the house. How big is this house?

"Are you finished? I'll take your plate," I said.

He stood and carried his dish to the sink. "You're a great cook. I loved it."

"Thank you."

He left me alone taking an electric charge with him. I stood in the empty room and started scrubbing.

I was up at six the following morning, rolling out the pie dough I'd prepared last night. The apples were sliced and ready to pour into the pie dish when Cole appeared in the kitchen with a sleepy, tousled look. His hair fell in his eyes, and when he raked it back, his blues were still at half-mast.

"Smells awesome. Like cinnamon," he said.

"Apple pie. It's Charlie's favorite dessert."

He said nothing and leaned on the door frame, wearing a faded pink tee, and flannel pants that hung low on his hips. I said a silent prayer of thanks for remembering to put on a bra this morning. Amazing how a few weeks of empty-nesting channeled my inner seventies, braless woman. I'd hoped to have a few hours to myself, but I remembered Cole being out early when I visited their school last month. Charlie was a late riser.

"You're up early."

"I don't sleep a lot." He tapped his head. "Thoughts keep me awake."

"Thoughts? What could you possibly be thinking at seven in the morning? And at your age?"

He tilted his head. "People my age don't have thoughts?"

"I'm sorry. I'm used to Charlie's buddies. Sleep like rocks. No cares in the world."

"Must be nice."

"You're telling me."

He stayed at the door. "I really like this kitchen."

"You do?"

He nodded. "The big sink and chunky table. If I saw a picture of it, I'd think it would smell exactly as it does now."

I laughed. "It was ultra-modern when we moved in. Sleek, black cabinets, a white counter and white tile floor. I ripped everything out and replaced it with refurbished woods and the farm sink. I like the country-style."

"I see that."

My eyes swept around the familiar surroundings, taking in the mess of dishes and half-prepared food covering the butcher- block counter, on top of blue wood cabinets with copper pulls. I loved this room.

"So, pie for breakfast?" he said.

"I wanted to prep for tonight, so I'm not doing everything when people show up. Helps me enjoy my company."

"My mother relies on a small network of people to pull off a dinner party."

"Well, it's just me. Keep that in mind when you sit down later. Some dishes will be warm and others cold."

Cole pulled himself straight, stretched his arms over his head and yawned. "Can I help you with something?"

"Thank you. I think I'm ready for another cup of coffee. Can I get you one?"

"Sounds great."

He sat, and I brought two mugs and joined him at the table.

"So, Charlie told me you spend most of your time at the library," I said.

He sipped quietly and put his cup down but said nothing. Right. I didn't ask a question, did I?

"He talked about a girl named Kate last night. Is this someone he likes?"

"I think so. They spend a lot of time together."

I stared into my cup.

"She's a sweet girl."

"What about you?" I said.

He shrugged.

"There's got to be someone who intrigues you."

He leaned his elbows on the table, put those baby blues on me and nodded.

"Oh." Lucky girl.

I finished my coffee and stood to get back to the tasks at hand, more to get away from the intense way he looked at me. What did he see, I wondered?

"Are you sure I can't help you?"

I thought a bit and turned to him. "How do you feel about peeling potatoes?"

He stood. "I live for it."

Cole and I prepped in the kitchen for three and a half hours. He helped me set the table, dress the turkey, make mashed potatoes, and wash and peel Brussel sprouts. He was easy to talk to and made me laugh as he playfully mimicked his mother doling out instructions for each minute detail of a party. *"Manuela, por favor, re-fold the dinner napkins. I'd like the corners inward and up. Get it? Inward and up."* I played the stereo low so as not to wake Charlie, and as I walked past Cole to the sink, I heard him humming.

"You know this song? It's so old."

"I do. I learned to dance to this."

"You dance?" I said, looking up at him. He had more than six inches on me. I guessed him to be six feet.

"Mom used to make me practice with her. She loves to dance, and my father worked long hours."

I thoroughly enjoyed Cole's company, forgetting for the morning that I was cooking with my son's roommate. "I don't think I've ever had this much fun preparing a holiday dinner."

He stood next to me, close enough that our shoulders touched, while he dried dishes. "I'm glad."

Charlie walked into the kitchen at eleven. "Breakfast," he stated, his eyes still sleepy. I went to my son and hugged him, so happy to have him home.

My sister, her husband, Adam, and their two girls, Amanda and Allison, showed up at three. With Cole and Charlie's help, the table was set, with most of the food prepped and in the oven. When Dottie arrived a half-hour later, Trisha was on her second glass of wine. Cole, Charlie, and Adam were in the den watching football along with my teenage nieces.

"Look at them," Trisha said from the kitchen door, peering into the den. "My girls are staring at Cole, like puppies waiting for scraps of attention to fall toward them. I don't blame them."

I basted the turkey, which was turning a beautiful golden hue. Dottie, sitting at the table, smiled at Trisha's statement.

"They're too young for him," I said after the bird was securely back in the oven.

Trisha walked into the kitchen and poured herself another glass before taking a seat next to my neighbor.

"Isn't he adorable?" she said to Dottie.

Dottie agreed. "He is a cutie. There's something about him. A quiet confidence."

"I know what you mean," I said.

"He's hot is what he is," Trish said, her voice rising.

"Shh! He'll hear you," I hissed.

Trisha rolled her eyes. "Who cares?"

"I care. Let's not embarrass Charlie today, okay?"

"Please. If he wasn't so young, I'd have a go at him."

"Trish! My God. Stop!" I looked over my shoulder, thankful we were alone. "Adam might hear you."

My sister blinked and focused on me. Dottie stood. "I think I'll watch some football if you don't need any more help here."

"Thanks, Dottie. I'm good. We'll be eating soon," I said. I waited for her to leave the room and turned to Trisha. "Lighten up on the wine today."

Trisha sighed. "Adam wouldn't care."

"I care. Besides, I thought you guys were getting better. Why don't you try counseling?"

"You didn't."

"You can't compare *my* marriage to yours. I wasn't given a choice. Besides, Adam is different."

"I'm not so sure."

I sat down next to her. "What happened?"

She shrugged. "We had sex this week. Finally."

"Well, that's good, right?"

"There's something missing."

I put my hand on hers, knowing how gut-wrenching it was to not feel desired.

After a few moments, Trisha pulled her hand away. "I don't want to talk about it today. Let's talk about Bill. I really hope you like him."

"I still can't believe you sprung this on me." I stood and returned to the counter to finish the salad.

"You're doing a nice thing. Besides, you need a man. You need to show Damian you're moving on."

"I'm not going to date a guy to get even with Damian. I don't care if he thinks I'm alone. I don't care."

"Well, I do." The doorbell rang, and Trisha smiled. "Here he is. You can thank me later." She finished her wine and stood at the entrance to the den, as we heard Adam greet his friend and co-worker at the front door.

"Dottie is squeezed between my girls on the couch." Trisha said. "No one likes the knitting chair. You really should replace it. Get something comfortable so she doesn't have to wedge herself between them."

I ignored her. I'd bought a stiff-looking, upright chair when we got the comfy couches for the den. Damian and I argued over it, and it made me want it more. I'd thought it added another dimension to the room, a compliment to the couches. Now, it sat alone, unused, and the butt of family jokes. I didn't mind. Normally, I didn't have enough people in the house to warrant more seating.

My sister was slurring by the time I placed the sliced turkey in the center of the table. Nine of us squeezed around the dining table. Charlie and Cole sat to my left, and Dottie immediately to my right, buffering me from Bill, who seemed rather shy. He was nice-looking in a pale doughboy way. He brought me flowers, which sat on the credenza below the mirror, a home-baked pie, and a bottle of wine, which my inebriated sister had opened.

Plates were passed back and forth across the table. I watched, enjoying the spectacle after so much work.

"This looks amazing, Mrs. Harrison," Cole said.

"Thanks to your help this morning," I said.

"Thank you for having me, Heather," Bill said. "This is a far cry from the leftover Chinese dinner I was planning."

"Oh, she couldn't wait to meet you, Bill," Trisha gushed from the other side of the table. Her voice had risen by decibels throughout the afternoon. The more she drank, the louder she got. We had now reached "concert-worthy" levels.

"Isn't that right, Heather? I hardly had to convince you at all." Trisha punctuated this with an unmistakable, over-exaggerated wink that quieted the table. Adam put his hand on his wife's arm. She yanked it from him and then took another drink.

We settled in to dinner, and conversations started again. Charlie chatted with his cousins about college, Bill and Adam discussed work, and Dottie told me of her upcoming holiday plans with her children in December. Out of the corner of my eye, I watched my sister stare at Cole. Oh, no.

"Cole," she said louder than necessary. Cole, who had been listening in on my conversation, ignored her. "Yoohoo!" He caught my eyes and held them before turning his attention to Trisha. "Why are you here?"

Everyone quieted. My nieces looked down, their shoulders slumped in unison. Charlie rolled his eyes. Bill found his stuffing fascinating and kept eye contact while eating, and Adam leaned back in defeat.

"I'm sorry?" Cole said.

"You don't spend the holiday with your family?"

Cole placed his fork down. "I have. My parents are away this time of year."

"Where did they go?" Bill asked, trying to temper the tension that had formed. I looked at him in gratitude.

"Greece. Santorini," Cole replied softly.

"It's beautiful there," Bill said.

"You've been to Greece?" I asked Bill.

"I have, many years ago."

"Well, maybe you can go back," Trisha interjected. "Take Heather with you. She never goes anywhere. She's a lonely home-body." Trisha leaned over, jabbing a finger uncomfortably close to Bill's face. "You should take her out."

"Trisha!" My stomach rolled. She was slurring heavily, and I knew she'd passed the point that I could stop her, any more than I could stop a freight train that had gone off the rails.

"Oh, come on! Admit it. You stay home every day. You need a man to shake things up. A better one than that ex of yours."

I glanced at Charlie, who was whispering something to his roommate. Cole's eyes never left mine. Bill stared down at his plate, again, and Adam pushed his plate away. Dottie placed her hand over mine.

"Trisha," Dottie said, "Let's leave Heather alone. She made us a beautiful dinner."

Thank you's were murmured around the table, but that freight train hurtled toward me.

"Oh, Dottie, lighten up. You're another one who could use a man. I'm just saying seven months is enough time to wait. Bill here is the perfect solution for my sister. Don't you agree, Bill?"

Bill didn't answer. He looked at my sister, but his expression was unreadable. Probably shock.

Adam grabbed his wife's arm. "Trish. Stop it!"

"Fine!" She looked at me, her glassy eyes trying to focus. "I'm just trying to help. She'd be so much happier if she got lai-."

"Enough!" I jumped up from my chair and it rocked back, falling to the floor. "No more." The table was quiet. "Excuse me," I whispered and walked upstairs, taking refuge in my bedroom. I listened to Adam wrestle his wife and girls out the door as tears of humiliation and anger stung my eyes. Our mother used to drink to excess. An outburst at Thanksgiving or Christmas dinner was the norm. Our parents were gone now. The cycle continued.

After calming down, I forced myself to go back downstairs. My upturned chair had been righted and returned to its place. Cole and Bill were helping Dottie clear the table and Charlie was MIA. I stepped onto the porch embracing the cold air. Sitting on one of the rocking chairs, I stared into the night. Bill stepped outside.

"I think it's time I leave," he said.

I stood. "I'm sorry." It was all I could think of to say. How do you put into words a lifetime of family issues? To a stranger, no less?

"Don't be. Despite the interesting conversation, I'm happy I came."

"You are?"

"We met once. You don't remember."

I stared at him, speechless.

"Adam and Trisha hosted a company dinner party a few years ago. I was with my wife at the time and you arrived late with your husband. We spoke only briefly. I asked you about your job."

"And then you asked me when was I going to write a story."

He smiled. "That's right. And do you recall what you said?"

I shook my head, barely remembering the conversation in the first place. I do, however, remember someone asking when I was going to write a book. I thought it an odd question at the time. I still do.

"You said, I'll write one when I have something to say," he said.

"I didn't realize I was so ridiculous."

"Hardly ridiculous. Anyway, it was a wonderful meal tonight. I hope to see you again."

I exhaled. "You're not making a strong case for yourself. Any sane person would run as far as possible from me."

"Maybe you just need some more time."

"How long has it been for you?"

"Elaina passed away three years ago."

"I'm sorry."

Bill's face showed nothing. He was probably sick of hearing that. "When you wake up more lonely than sad is when you'll be ready," he said.

What I wanted to tell Bill was that I've been lonely far longer than these past seven months. And it wasn't so much sad, as angry. Instead, I said, "Thank you for…Well, thank you."

I watched him walk to his car and then drive away. After the taillights disappeared, I sat back down on the chair and wrapped my arms around myself. It was cold, but I wasn't as numb as I wanted to be. The door opened and I braced myself for Charlie and his disappointment with my sister, but it was Cole with Dottie.

She bent over and hugged me tightly. "Ignore everything she said. It meant nothing. I'll call you tomorrow. We'll have dessert then."

I nodded.

Cole walked Dottie home and when he returned, he placed his jacket around my shoulders and then sat down next to me.

"Are you okay?" he asked.

"Yes." I pulled his jacket tighter around me. "Just embarrassed. I'm sorry about all that. I love my sister, but sometimes she's hard to take." I took a deep breath. "I'm sure you're wishing now to be with your own family."

He ran his fingers through his hair and stared into the sky. "Every family has issues. It was the liquor talking. We knew it."

I closed my eyes. "Do you want to know what's sad? What she said is true. All of it. I just wished she wouldn't have said it in front of Charlie, I —" I shook my head. When Cole didn't answer, I looked at him. "I don't know why I just admitted that to you."

"I'm easy to talk to."

"No. That's not it."

He emitted a low laugh, and I grinned. We were quiet for several moments.

"So," Cole said, "Bill."

"It was supposed to be a blind date."

"That's an interesting first date."

I blew out a frustrated breath.

"He seems like a nice guy."

The sky was a deep, rich black, dotted with stars. "Not for me," I said.

We sat longer, rocking.

"I'm glad I came," Cole said.

"The highlight of my day was preparing with you." I didn't care how it sounded saying it to him. It was true.

He rubbed his hand over his mouth but his smile showed through. "For me, as well."

Charlie stuck his head outside. "Are you guys coming back in? It's cold out here."

I stood, and Cole followed me back in the house. "Where were you?" I asked my son.

"I escaped downstairs to play videos. She's nuts," he said.

"That's my sister you're talking about."

"Mom. She insulted you in front of the whole table, and you're defending her. I told you she'd drink too much. Amanda is fed up with her. And Allison already drinks at parties."

"She's only fourteen!" My mouth dropped open. Dear Lord. Not my sweet niece too.

Charlie shrugged. "Like mother, like daughter." He turned to Cole. "Let's go. My friend is having people over."

Cole looked at me and then back at Charlie. "Tonight?"

"Yes. He just texted. Some people are there. It's close. I'll drive."

"I'll drive," Cole said.

"Whatever. I'll just change my shirt, and we'll go."

Cole turned to me. "Do you mind?"

"No. I'll finish cleaning, and I can't wait to pass out." He placed his hand on my arm, sending a pulsing through my entire body. Slipping his jacket from my shoulders, I handed it to him. "Thanks," I said.

"Anytime."

I climbed into bed shortly after they left and fell immediately to sleep, but not before fantasizing whether there would be a next time.

Chapter 6

Dear Aunt Emma,

I was married for thirty-five years and have been separated from my husband for almost one. My friends try to set me up with men, but I have absolutely no interest in dating, and I'm starting to worry I will be alone for the rest of my life. I'm fifty-nine years old. What should I do?

- Don't want to be alone, or do I?

Dear Don't,

Anything you want, my dear. One year alone is not a lot of time. You've been with someone for more than half of your life. Give yourself time to adjust to this change. It's okay if you don't want to date. There are no rules, and no partner, saying what you must do.

You'll know if and when you're ready to let someone into your heart. Feelings will surface when you least expect it and when you're not looking for it. Trust yourself. Until then, enjoy singlehood.

-Aunt Emma

I was still mentally hungover the following morning from yesterday's catastrophe when I answered this question. Too many of us, unfortunately, are going through the same experience. I responded to the question from Don't as I would want to be answered. I'll have to remind Trisha to read it when it publishes. If, and when, we speak.

Cole walked into the den while I was on the couch, working on my laptop. The television was on. My favorite movie had just started.

"Morning," he said. "What are you doing?"

"Some work," I said. "The thing about working from home is you can do it around the clock."

In flannels and the faded tee, he sat down on the other end of the couch. "You work from home?"

"Yep." I shut my computer and put it on the coffee table. "Occasionally, I stop into the office, but primarily, I stay home."

"What do you do exactly?" he said, his voice gravelly. It sounded…nice.

"I write an advice column."

"About?"

"Relationships, mostly."

Silence.

"I know. I can't keep my own, but I still advise others. Cruel irony. If my readers ever found out, they'd probably stop writing in."

"Why did you and Mr. Harrison break up?"

I smiled at the simple term, 'break-up,' as if we were kids just dating. Cole's face showed no hint of humor, so I stifled my amusement. I guess he's not so far off.

"We couldn't live together anymore."

"Did you fight a lot?" he said.

"No." You need passion to want to fight. What we had was indifference.

Cole watched me, waiting for more.

"It's complicated."

He frowned. "Is it?"

I shook my head. "No. It's simple actually. But I don't want to share." I was still trying to scrape my ego off the ground.

"Fair enough." He looked around the den. "I'm sure it wasn't your fault."

"It takes two to break a marriage."

"Does it? Anyway, it hardly disqualifies you from giving advice. I think people just want to vent about their problems and get a stranger's opinion." This from a twenty-four-year-old with his life barely begun.

"Why would you think that?"

He rolled his neck and stretched his arms over his head. I stared at his lengthening triceps, trying to see what was written across the smooth, pale stretch of skin along one muscle, but the tattooed words remained half-hidden beneath his short sleeve. "For one, my mother is in therapy, and she told me it feels good to talk about something the therapist knows nothing about."

"Oh."

"What's the name of your column?" he said, dropping his arms.

"Ask Aunt Emma."

"Sounds like an old woman."

"People want advice from someone with life experience."

"How old are you?"

"Forty-one."

"So, you've experienced enough life to dole out advice?" he asked.

"As far as they know. What's worse is I started in my twenties when I knew nothing."

We sat in companionable silence.

"What are these?" Cole put his hand on a small pile of books between us. "Doing some gardening?"

"I was offered another column, though I don't know why. I kill everything. I managed to kill a cactus Charlie gave me for Mother's Day years ago. Seriously. How can you kill a cactus? They're pretty hearty and live in a desert."

Cole chuckled. Standing, I gathered up the books and placed them on the shelf. "Would you like some breakfast?"

"I'll wait for Charlie. You can keep working. Don't let me distract you."

Too late, buddy. "I'm finished for now. I've been up for a while."

"What are you watching?" he asked.

"*The Way We Were.* It's an oldie. I can change it," I said as Robert Redford swayed at a bar on the screen while Barbara Streisand stared.

"No. It's fine." He watched the screen. "Just fill me in on where we are, and I'll follow."

I caught him up on the few minutes he missed, and we settled on opposite ends of the couch to watch.

More than halfway through the film, I felt Cole readjust himself on the cushion. I turned as he leaned toward me, appearing ready to say something when Charlie walked into the room.

"Dude, don't you sleep?" Charlie said.

Cole stood and stretched again, and I glimpsed his hip bones above his low flannels, his flat stomach, the faint trail of hair leading down to... I looked away.

"What're you guys watching?"

"*The Way We Were*," I said.

Charlie rolled his eyes. "How many times have you seen that?"

I stood and shut off the TV. "Not as many times as you've seen *The Hangover*. How about French toast?" I went into the kitchen before they could answer and turned on the oven.

They devoured breakfast. The key to my French toast is orange zest and brown sugar, a recipe I perfected over the years. Charlie often requested it on Sundays growing up. I had bought a loaf of sourdough bread from the bakery and sliced it thick.

"What are your plans today?" I asked.

Charlie looked at Cole and seemed uncomfortable.

"What is it, Charlie?" I had a brief, panicked thought that they'd want to head back to school early. I wasn't ready. I wanted him home longer.

"I told Dad I'd hang with him today."

"Oh." I sighed with relief. "Okay, sure. Will you be joining him, Cole?"

"I don't think so. I thought I'd take a ride and explore a bit. Charlie said there's a hiking trail not far from here."

"Yes, two miles west. It's got some beautiful areas to stop and take in the view of the Sound." It's the trail I run often, I almost said.

Charlie stood. "I'm jumping in the shower." He kissed me on my cheek. "Thanks, Mom. Breakfast was awesome."

Cole stood slowly and brought his plate to the sink. "What are you doing today?"

"Me?" I asked, startled by his interest. I had no plans this weekend. Not that I ever had a full calendar while Charlie was in school. I realized after Damian left how few friends I had that weren't part of a couple. People spend time with their spouses on the weekends. Separation is a lonely affair.

"Mrs. Harrison?" He cut into my thoughts.

"Oh. Sorry. I'll probably stick around here."

"Would you like to take a hike with me?"

The offer was tempting. I've never hiked with anyone. Cole watched me, waiting for an answer. I decided it made more sense not to start now. "No thanks. You go. Enjoy."

He ran his hand through his hair and scratched the back of his head in thought. The muscles in his arms flexed with his movement, and I caught a whiff of musky scent.

"Okay. See you later," he said. At the kitchen door, he turned around. "How does it end?"

"Huh?"

"The movie. How does it end?"

"Oh, they break up even though they love each other. They're two different people and they can't make it work. At the end of the movie, they see each other again, and it's obvious the feelings they still share. They have a daughter he never met. It's quite devastating, really."

Cole nodded in thought and then walked away.

After the boys left, I decided to clear my mind and went to the gym, since I couldn't very well go to the same hiking trail as Cole, especially after turning down his invitation. It was Black Friday, the busiest shopping day of the year, so I had my pick of parking spots out front and treadmills inside. Jumping on a machine, I picked up speed until hitting a comfortable pace where I stayed for forty-five minutes. Since the split, running helped release my pent-up frustration – with myself, my worries, loneliness. Exercise became an effective antidote. Usually. Because of all this angst, I have never been in better shape.

I stepped off soaked in sweat, wiped down the machine, threw on my sweatshirt, and headed home. My answering machine blinked in the bedroom and I hit Play before peeling off my Lycra shorts, sweatshirt, and tank top. One message from Trish wanting to apologize. I deleted it.

I pulled my sticky sports bra over my head and tossed it with my undies in the hamper. My naked body prickled against the cool air in the room. I made the bed while the shower water heated. Then I pulled off my hairband and crossed the room to put it away. Passing by the open bedroom door, I froze as Cole walked across the hall. He glanced toward me when I gasped.

Holding his shirt in his hand, perspiration clung to his chest. A lock of wet hair fell across his forehead above those bright blue eyes that connected to mine. It lasted only a moment, then Cole averted his gaze with a soft "Sorry," as I awkwardly covered my nakedness and slipped into the bathroom.

Under the hot spray, I leaned my head against the tile and fought a rush of humiliation. I stayed in the shower until the water turned cold. If I could, I would stay here until Monday, until this boy was out of my house and I could avoid him for the rest of my life. But my hands were pruned, and my skin was covered with goosebumps.

I dried myself, stepped out of the bathroom, and gently closed my bedroom door, locking it. Cole was in the shower in the hall bathroom, giving me time to dress and get downstairs, but I'd only put on my bra when he shut the water off. I sat on my bed in my underwear and listened to him open the curtain over the tub. Then silence. *Is he waiting too? Is he as horrified as I am?* I took a deep breath. You're being ridiculous, my inner voice said. Just get up, act like it never happened, and move on. He'll probably handle this more maturely than you will. Either way, I can't hide here all weekend. Throwing on jeans and a flannel shirt, I combed back my hair, took a deep breath, and opened the door.

The hall was empty, the bathroom dark. I had to pass the guest room to get to the stairs. *Please be looking away.* I had just put my foot on the top step when he appeared at the door. Shirtless and in those damn faded jeans.

"Are you hungry for lunch?" I couldn't look at him. I stared down the steps and considered throwing myself down them.

"Mrs. Harrison."

His voice was soft and low. My eyes met his. "For God's sake, Cole, call me Heather at this point. There are no secrets between us."

His baby blues didn't flinch. His eyelashes looked darker, almost black, still wet from the shower. Nature had been kind to this boy. No, not a boy. I kept referring to him as if he was my son's age. He's nothing like Charlie, matured in such a way that Charlie hasn't done yet. Or is it I can't see my child past his bruised knobby knees and baby face?

"Heather," he whispered, rolling my name on his tongue. Somehow, it made me feel less ashamed. "I'm sorry. I didn't see anything."

"I should apologize. The last thing you need to see is a naked woman twice your age. I hadn't heard you walk in. I guess I got used to not shutting my door with Charlie out of the house. I'm sorry." My mind imagined him comparing me to the hard bodies that walked around the campus, the tight beauties waving and smiling to him, trying to get his attention.

"You're not twice my age," he said.

I pressed my lips together but maintained the gaze we held.

"I picked up sandwiches for us," he said, finally.

I looked away, my heart thundering through my shirt. I'm going to have a heart attack right here on my stairs. *Woman dies while kid tries to get out of naked exposure.* God, I so wish I could do today over again.

"Fine." My voice came out a whisper. I cleared my throat. "Fine. I'll meet you downstairs." I walked away, leaving him in the doorway.

He came down twenty minutes later wearing a hooded sweatshirt, and I placed a salad I'd made on the table, along with the turkey clubs he'd bought.

"Did Charlie say what time he'd be back?" he asked.

I shook my head. I had no idea, but it couldn't be soon enough.

"I'm sure he'll be home for dinner," I said. "What did you have planned for the afternoon?"

"I have some reading to do. The next few weeks are going to be intense."

"Did you always work this hard at school?"

"Yes. We were reading early, my sister and me. It was a quiet house. Serious house."

I stabbed lettuce with my fork. Charlie and I used to lie on the floor watching cartoons on Saturday mornings. I was younger than Cole when I had Charlie. A kid, raising a kid.

"My parents lost a daughter, my sister Brynn, when I was five," he said.

"Oh! I'm so sorry to hear that. What a tragedy."

"She was hit by a car. My mother was waiting to cross Main Street in town and ran into someone she knew. Brynn pulled her hand from Mom's to cross the street." He looked at me. "She loved dogs. There was a German shepherd on the other side and…well, my mother couldn't catch her."

"That's horrible." My heart pained at the thought of the poor woman losing her daughter, of seeing her get hit and not be able to save her. "Where were you when this happened?"

"I was holding my mother's other hand."

At my intake of breath, Cole dropped his eyes and fixed his napkin on his lap. "I don't really remember it happening. They say I stopped talking for a while, but I don't remember. Not that I try. Anyway, five years later, they had my sister, Gretchen, but they were never there. I think they thought they could replace Brynn. But you can never replace a child."

"How old was Brynn?"

"Three."

I reached out and put my hand on his forearm. "Thank you for sharing that with me," I said.

"I don't usually share much about myself."

"Why not?"

He picked at his food. "I don't want to be judged on my past."

I felt the same way. I kept my hand on his arm. "Thank you for the sandwiches."

He smiled. "You're welcome."

We ate the rest of our lunch in silence, and he stayed with me to clean up. Considering what transpired since I woke up this morning, even with the horrific mistake earlier, I felt a connection to him.

When we were finished, he said, "I'm going to hang in the den."

"Okay. I'll join you. I have some work to do as well."

I sat on the club chair with my laptop. Cole took his spot on the corner of the couch. We sat for an hour. I stole a few glances his way, watched him absorbed in his book, his dark hair curled over his forehead and against his neck, his jaw clenched slightly, his fingers, long and elegant, touching the page, fiddling with the corner, waiting to turn. I wondered what kind of childhood he had after such a tragedy. His parents must have been devastated. It might explain his maturity at such a young age.

He lifted his head and caught me staring. Again.

"Do you need anything?" I asked.

He held his page, watching me as if he could read my mind. "I'm good." He didn't return to his book.

My cheeks burned, thinking again of what he saw upstairs. I

needed space. I moved my laptop to the side and pulled myself from the chair. At the doorway, I turned to him.

"I'm going upstairs until Charlie gets home." Trying to come off light and airy, my voice sounded unnatural to me.

"Did I do something?"

"No!" My response came out forceful and quick. I breathed. "Just make yourself at home in the kitchen if you get hungry."

Upstairs, on my bed, I picked up the phone to call Trish before remembering I was mad at her. I hung up and grabbed a novel from my nightstand. Cole doesn't need me hanging around him all day, and Charlie will be home soon. I sighed and leaned back on my pillow. I really needed to get out more.

Two hours passed when Charlie texted me at three o'clock. *Dad, Genna, and I are grabbing dinner in the city. Cole won't answer his phone. If he's there, can you ask him if he wants to join us?*

I reread the text. Charlie won't be home for hours. I should have realized Damian would want to spend the entire day with him. Why shouldn't he? But with Genna? The idea unnerved me. I went downstairs, but Cole was not in the house. His truck was in the driveway, so I looked out the living room window into the backyard where he was on the patio lying on the lawn chair next to the covered pool. I slipped into my army jacket, went outside, and sat on a chaise next to him. His eyes were closed. He was handsome, even in repose. His strong jawline beneath the shadow of his beard, the way his hair curled at the base of his neck…

"Did you have a nice nap?" Cole asked, his eyes remaining shut.

"I was reading," I said. *Did he know I was watching him?*

"Anything good?"

"Yes. I have a few go-to authors I love. They provide a great escape from my daily existence."

"That's George R.R. Martin for me. He's a genius."

"Didn't he write *A Dance With Dragons?*"

Cole opened his eyes and turned to me. "I knew I liked you."

I laughed. "I'm a reader."

"A reader lives a thousand lives before he dies. George R.R. Martin." Cole watched the swaying trees, the gentle breeze playing with his hair.

"I don't expect a twenty-four-year-old to quote an author," I said.

"Do you know many twenty-four-year-olds?"

I slowly shook my head. "You seem the more outdoorsy type than a reader. Did you play sports in High School?" I thought of him out hiking before breakfast that morning when I visited Charlie. He had a nice build, not quite football material, but not thin either.

"I played some ball for a while but stopped."

"Why?"

He closed his eyes and didn't answer me.

The sound of rustling leaves surrounded us. The crisp air and soft wind soothed me, and I felt rested and peaceful. I gasped when my phone vibrated in my jacket pocket. Charlie had texted four times.

Mom? Did you ask Cole? We're leaving soon!

Is he there?

Are you there?

I cleared my throat. "Charlie invited you to dinner with his father."

"Did he?"

"He said he texted you. Would you like to go?"

He paused, and opened his eyes. "No."

I'll never admit, not to anyone, least of all to this young man next to me, but I was glad he didn't want to go. I found his company comforting.

"Can you let him know?"

Cole took his phone from his jeans pocket and texted Charlie. "Done," he said and then put his phone down. He looked around the yard. "You have a great property. The trees are beautiful."

I followed his gaze. We lived on half an acre, surrounded by towering maple and elm trees. "I love them. Unfortunately, I don't spend as much time out here as I should. But on the rare occasions I do, I listen to their leaves rustle in the wind. I imagine the wind and the birds as the orchestra and they're dancing."

He looked at me. "I love that."

"Thanks." I blushed. I never express these thoughts. The affirmation felt nice.

"My sister loves jumping in the leaves. She has me make her piles and piles in the fall and spends all day racing back and forth, rolling around the lawn, leaves in her hair, stuck on her clothes." He laughed at the thought.

"You're the perfect older brother. Do you really make piles for her?"

He stopped laughing, but his face still smiled. "I'd do anything to make Gretchen happy."

I breathed the crisp air in deeply and crossed my arms. I like him, this boy who takes care of his sister.

"I can't remember jumping in the leaves with Charlie. Or, ever, come to think of it. Isn't that strange? That I don't remember doing it?"

He pursed his lips and then stood. "I'll be right back."

He walked across the grass to the shed, pulled out a rake and started to gather the leaves into a mass.

"What are you doing?" He is so not going there. Cole ignored me. I watched him work amidst a gorgeous sea of burnt, vibrant colors. He is, isn't he? He's making a leaf pile. I was about to suggest he retire the rake and come back to sit, but I enjoyed watching him. He was amused with his task, and I couldn't contain the giggle inside. Sure enough, twenty minutes later, he stood in front of a huge leaf pile. He dropped the tool and held his arms out in triumph. I clapped my hands and waited for him to jump in. But it seemed he had other plans. He reached his hand to me, beckoning me to join him.

"I'm too old to play," I said, but I stood and walked toward him.

Without a word, he took my hand, turned my back to the awaiting pile, stood next to me and asked, "Ready?"

"No."

"One, two, three!" He dropped back onto the pile and landed with a soft thump. I watched him sink into the leaves. I turned, wondering to myself what the hell I was doing and followed. The mound was so cushioned, my landing was silent.

We got up and pushed the pile together again. Cole took a running start and jumped in the center, and for a moment, he disappeared in a wave of orange and yellows. I stepped back several paces and then followed him in, sinking into the earthy mound. The sound of crackling and the odor of dry leaves surrounded me. Over and over, we pushed the pile together and jumped in. Each time, I laughed harder. It was so much fun.

We lay on top of them and stared at the darkening sky, watching the clouds glide overhead. It took a few minutes for me to catch my breath. I heard him struggle, too. We looked at each other and started laughing again. I felt giddy.

"God, I miss that," I said.

"I thought you never jumped in the leaves."

I shook my head and looked back at the sky. "No, not that. I miss the sound of my own laughter. It's been a long time." My throat constricted.

Cole didn't say anything, and I was glad. He picked up a large, red maple leaf from his chest and held it up. "This is my favorite season."

"Is it? Not summer? Warm weather, no school, no stress…"

"No, for me it's now," he said, twirling it by the stem. "You know, when the leaves turn color, it means they're dying."

"That's sort of sad," I said.

"Why is that?"

"The idea of being your most beautiful right before you die." I felt his eyes on me and turned to him. "What?"

He grinned. "Nothing."

"For someone so serious, you do smile a lot."

He picked up another leaf and turned it in his fingers. "I'm happy."

The sun descended further, and the temperature dropped. I zipped my jacket and then stood. "Would you like something to eat?"

He pulled himself up and stretched. "You like to feed me."

"It's what I do."

"You feed people?"

I nodded and brushed my clothes free of lingering leaves.

"You do more than that," he said.

I didn't answer. What did I really do? Write columns. Keep a house. Feed the family. I associated good cooking with keeping people happy. When I made dinner on those nights my mom was too drunk to do it, was when my father was most placated. I learned to make his favorite dishes to keep him happy and to keep him from going after her.

Cole and I started to walk back toward the house. He paused and focused on a patch of grass near the corner.

"What?"

"You should grow a garden. You have plenty of space, and I'm thinking this area," he motioned to the west side of my property, "gets ample sun in the summer."

"How could you possibly know this?"

"Well, there are no trees over it, for one."

I laughed. "So, common sense tells you."

He dropped his head in mock defeat. "I was hoping to come off as more intelligent, but yes, fewer trees usually means more sun."

I stared at the space in question. "I have no right planting a garden."

"Why not? What's the worst that can happen?"

"I'll fail."

"So?"

"I'm afraid to fail." My father had no patience for mistakes. My behavior was baked in.

Cole paused, then said, "It's a good thing Graham-Bell and Franklin weren't afraid to fail or we'd be sitting in dark houses with no phones."

"Would that be so bad?"

His head swiveled to me. "Maybe not."

"Anyway," I said, "I told you, I kill things that try to grow. It wouldn't be fair to seeds to take away their chance at becoming someone's salad."

"But it will help authenticate your gardening articles."

"I'm most likely not going to take that, either."

We surveyed the land in the dying light. I'd never in my life desired to plant a garden. Thinking of the work that went into it only to have the plants get a disease, or fail to produce fruit made it not worth the effort. Writing about it was even less desirable.

"Do you have plans tonight?" Cole said as we walked into the kitchen.

"Why do you ask?"

"I was wondering if you'd take a ride with me to the mall. I want to buy my sister a birthday gift."

Chapter 7

My phone dinged as I locked up the house. Trisha left another voice message, followed by a text.

I'm not 100% sure what I said. I only know Adam is also not talking to me (nothing new) and thinks if you accept my apology, then you're a saint. Since I already polish your halo, I have hope. Please call me back.

I ignored it and climbed into Cole's idling truck.

Inside the mall, we stepped into the first clothes store we came upon. I perused the clothes alongside Cole, who eventually stopped at a table covered with soft fleece sweatshirts. He lifted a pastel pink one and held it for me to see. Remembering the photo on his desk at school, I thought the color would perfectly compliment Gretchen's gorgeous blue eyes and blonde hair. I nodded, and he draped it over his arm. On our way to the cash register, he picked up a lavender long-sleeve tee, too.

I waited outside in the mall corridor while he paid, enjoying the passing crowds of shoppers and holiday music piped through overhead speakers. Across the way was L'Occitane, an expensive skincare store Trisha loved. I took a step toward the store, thinking I'd pick up that crème she always talked about when I remembered I was still angry with her.

Instead, through the window, I watched Cole at the register, chatting with a young salesgirl who rang him up. Bag in hand, he stepped away from the counter. She followed him, ignoring the next patron on line. They chatted as he took small steps toward the door. She continued to talk, touched her hair, smiled brilliantly, inched her waif-like frame closer to him. I laughed inwardly as I watched the exchange. Cole took one large step to distance himself from her before he turned to point toward the corridor where I stood. He saw me, and his face immediately eased into a grin as he rolled his eyes.

When we left the mall, the sky was dark, though it was only approaching seven o'clock. In the pickup, we listened to a country station. Garth Brooks sang my favorite song, "To Make You Feel My Love." When he reached the last verse, "*I could make you happy, make your dreams come true,*" I filled with a longing to be young again, to want to fall in love and have it be reciprocated the way the song described. I thought about the salesgirl in the mall, wanting to be with Cole. He was appealing, but more than his beautiful face, he possessed a quiet confidence that would have pulled me to him had I been twenty years younger.

Then I thought about my reaction when he saw me waiting for him outside the store. His expression lit up at the sight of me. It made me feel heady for a moment until reality set in and brought me back to earth.

I shook my head.

"What?" he asked, breaking his gaze from the road to look at me.

"I think we set a record for speed shopping back there," I said, and pointed left.

"I hate shopping. I'd much rather be doing anything else." He followed my direction, turning onto a side road that gently wound through a maze of tall trees and brush. I often used this route as a cut-through on my way back from town, as a way of avoiding traffic lights and speeding cars on the main street. During the day, it was a gorgeous ride – when sunlight sifted through the leaves, creating dancing lines of light. Tonight, the branches reached toward a dark sky like skeletal limbs, surrounding us in a ghostly aura. Winter was near.

"It's not that bad. That salesgirl was cute, no?" I smiled.

"Who? The one in the store just now?" He appeared confused.

"Yes. She didn't want to let you go."

"She's not my type."

"So, what is your type?" I asked as Cole accelerated around a curve.

"Someone who turns me on."

"How would you know if you don't give her a chance."

He looked at me. "It's a gut feeling. I react, and I know—"

I saw the buck before he did and screamed, "Cole!"

It seemed to have materialized out of nowhere, catching us by surprise as it dashed across the road in front of us. Cole slammed on the brakes. The tires locked, screaming in protest, but we couldn't avoid the animal. There was a loud thump, and the truck jolted to a stop. My body was thrown forward, but the seatbelt held me back. Cole's head snapped forward. I heard it connect with the steering wheel before he fell back against the seat.

Then everything went quiet. We sat for a moment, stunned. Cole's breath came out in gulps, the same as mine.

"Are you okay?" he asked and reached over to me.

"Yes," I said, clasping tightly to his offered hand.

My heart beat against my ribcage, and my hands shook. Somehow, the impact wasn't hard enough to set the airbags off. In front of us, the large animal pulled itself up and ran, maimed, into the woods bordering the road.

"Crap, Heather. I'm so sorry."

"I'm fine. Are you okay?" I turned to look at Cole and gasped. "Your head."

A thin trickle of blood oozed from above his eyebrow.

I pulled the door handle, hopped out, and rushed around the back of the truck to get to him. I opened his door. "Look at me."

He turned to face me. There was blood over his eye and dripping down the side of his face.

I dug into my pocket, pulled out a travel pack of tissues, and mopped up the blood as best I could.

"It looks bad," I said.

He touched his head and brought his hand away, bloodied. I handed him the tissues.

"I'm fine. It's a scratch. The head bleeds a lot."

"It's more than a scratch. You need to have that looked at. Move over. I'm driving. You might have a concussion."

"I don't."

"Get out of that seat and let me in." My tone left no room for negotiation. He lumbered out of the cab and walked around the front, stopping to assess the truck before getting into the passenger seat. I climbed in behind the wheel.

"We got lucky." He tossed the bloodied tissues on the floor and put his seatbelt on. "The front headlight is smashed, and the corner bumper is dented, but otherwise, no damage."

I ignored him and put the truck into drive. "It's a quick visit to the ER. They'll make sure you're okay and maybe stitch that up."

"I'm not going to the ER," Cole said. He sat straight, staring at me with his hands on his legs, as if we'd just pulled over to chat and didn't just slam into a large antlered buck, leaving him with a gash, growing uglier by the minute as we wasted time with this silly discussion.

"Yes, you are." Despite the way my legs still shook, I eased on the gas and pulled onto the road.

"You're making a big deal over nothing. I don't need a doctor. I'm fine."

"Don't be ridiculous." I turned the truck around and headed back toward the main road when he reached over and grabbed the steering wheel, forcing us to swerve aggressively to the side.

"Stop the truck!"

Shocked by his outburst, I hit the brakes, pulling to a sudden stop.

"What's your problem?" I yelled back. I threw the truck into park. I thought I was angry, but the look on Cole's face usurped me. His eyes blazed, and his hands were in fists.

"Heather, I need you calm down and just take us home," he said through tight lips. "There is no way I'm going to the hospital for something as minor as this."

"It's not min-"

"I said, no!" He took off his seatbelt and threw the passenger door open. "If you're not going to listen to me, I'll walk back. Either way, I'm not going to the hospital."

I half wanted to wring his neck, and half wanted to beg him to listen to reason.

"Okay." I pushed back in the driver's seat with a sigh. Even if he was my son's roommate, I couldn't force this decision on him. He was a grown man. "I'll take you home."

When he faced me again, his anger was gone, replaced by remorse. "I'm sorry. I didn't mean to yell at you. I promise if I feel concussed, I'll let you know."

"Your eye."

"Do you have a bandage? That's all I need." His voice was low. He managed a smile. A truce.

I stared at his bloodied face, trying to understand his reaction. What was he afraid of? "Fine. I'll drive the rest of the way. But if a bandage won't fix it, I'm going to have to get tough and throw you back in the car."

"Deal."

We rode the rest of the way without speaking. Charlie wasn't home yet when I pulled into the driveway. We walked into the house and directly to the kitchen.

"Sit down." I pointed to the table. He sat.

Cole looked pale, and I couldn't see past the bloody mess above his eye. I moved to him and leaned over, bringing my face close to his wound. He sat stock-still. I couldn't even detect his breath. I lifted my fingers and then paused.

"May I?" I asked, and when he nodded, I carefully pushed his hair back and took a closer look. "Don't move." I ran upstairs, grabbed bacitracin, cotton, a washcloth, which I ran under warm water, and a box of bandages.

He was in the same place when I returned minutes later.

"Okay, let's see what you have here." I pulled a chair in front of him.

He closed his eyes. I blotted the moist cloth over his eyebrow until I'd cleared the blood, exposing a small gash. A bump had already formed. He kept his eyes closed, his jaw clenched.

Pulling the cloth away, my eyes caught on his face, his square jaw, the muscles beneath his light beard working hard to contain whatever it was he was feeling. I tried to ignore the fluttering in my gut, telling myself I was still nervous and upset from the incident. He opened his eyes, and they locked with mine. I pressed my lips together and shifted my focus to his temple. Gently, I brought the cloth back to his skin and rubbed it along his cheek down to his chin until I'd cleaned the line of blood that had begun to dry.

He cleared his throat. "Well?" His eyes bore into mine. Unexpected heat rose along my neck. There was a palpable energy about him, a wave of untapped anger beneath his stoic exterior. Nonthreatening anger, unlike my father's unbridled wrath. Instinctually, I knew that. This was something different.

It was alluring.

I swallowed. "You may need a few stitches. Doesn't it hurt?"

"I have a high tolerance for pain."

"Clearly. I'm queasy just looking at you."

"I get that a lot."

I exhaled a laugh and tried to calm myself. I felt his eyes on me as I searched my bandage box for something to cover the wound. "We can go to the walk-in clinic and get this stitched up. It's easy."

"Enough."

I paused.

"Please," he said in a calmer tone. "Let it go."

"Fine. Your call." I refocused on my task of finding a bandage.

"Do you think he's badly hurt?" he asked, his eyes following my movements.

"The buck?" Cole nodded. "I'm not sure. His adrenaline enabled him to get up and run, but he's compromised. We definitely clipped his hindquarters."

"I hope he's okay."

"Me too." His concern for the deer pleased me. I went back to my search. "Ha. Victory." I held up a butterfly bandage. "Stay still."

I applied bacterial medicine onto the bandage. My hands shook as I brought them to his skin. With two fingers, I pushed the gash closed. His breath hitched, and I went to pull back when he grabbed my wrist and held it in place.

"It's okay," he said. He held my arm an extra beat before letting go.

I nodded, again pulled the skin together as best I could, and affixed the bandage over it, the heat from his hand still on my skin. Our knees touched, and I could feel his breath now against my neck as I stretched up to make sure the bandage was secure. His hands rested on his thighs. There was no denying the charged air between us. I wanted to stay here longer, but at the same time, I wanted to run away.

"I hope this works," I said softly. "If not, this handsome face is going to be scarred."

He shrugged. "No biggie."

"If it does scar, it'll be partially hidden by your eyebrow." I finally leaned back to assess my work, trying to ignore the way his eyes clung to me. Warmth enveloped me as our knees remained connected. His hands never moved from his thighs.

What is happening? I stood and pushed my chair back. "For someone who avoids medical assistance, you're a good patient."

"You're calm under pressure."

I exhaled. "A first for me."

"A first for me, too."

Color had returned to his face. His stomach made a loud rumbling sound, and we laughed. Lunch seemed a distant memory.

"I'm hungry too. I'll make some pasta," I said.

He stood and carefully pulled his sweatshirt over his head. "Sounds great. Thanks."

While I filled one pot with water and poured the sauce into another, Cole headed toward the bathroom to inspect my bandage work. He returned and leaned against the kitchen opening.

"Thank you."

"You're welcome. If that leaves a mark, you'll never forget me."

"Not a chance." He said it so quietly, I almost didn't hear it.

Except, I did.

I busied myself with taking out plates and the strainer for the pasta while he stood at the doorway, watching.

"Heather, would you do something else with me?"

"Why? Wasn't shopping, hitting a deer, and splitting open your head not enough?"

"I promise, it's a very safe request." He motioned to the den. "I saw Scrabble on the shelf. I love the game. Will you play with me?"

"You want me to play Scrabble with you? Did we just travel back to the seventies?"

"I also play a mean game of Call of Duty, but I sense that's not your thing."

"You sense wrong. You happen to be looking at a Prestige One, level thirty-two player."

He raised one eyebrow. The other was restricted by the bandage. "I'm impressed."

"It comes with the job of being a mother to one. Helps with communication."

"So, would you like to play COD?"

"I don't think you should be playing videos right now." I pointed to his head. "How do you feel?"

He frowned. "Please don't ask me that. I'm fine. I'm good."

He wanted no special attention. Okay. "I don't have a Scrabble partner, so I'd love to play."

We sat on the rug in the den with the coffee table between us, and ate our pasta while playing. He started to ask questions as we sorted and counted our tiles and occasionally forked our penne.

"How do people reach Aunt Emma?" he asked.

"Mostly email, with occasional snail mail, which I prefer."

"Do the letters get sent here?"

"I have a post office box. My editor and I share it."

"Do you read every letter?"

"Every one. I try to read every email too, but that's harder."

"Do you answer them all?"

"Unfortunately, no. But there are many similar problems. If I answer one, I'll usually satisfy a bunch of others."

"Do you like what you do?" He paused, fork over the bowl, waiting for my answer.

"Sometimes."

"Have you ever thought about doing something else?"

"Only every day." I smiled. "I just don't know what I want."

"Why don't you try to figure it out?"

"I'm not good with change. This is easy, comfortable."

He looked in my eyes. "Change is growth."

"Yes, I got that same fortune cookie, once." I was joking, but he wasn't. "You ask a lot of questions," I said.

"I'm interested." He put a large forkful in his mouth.

"I have a question." I looked at the bandage, now partially covered by his hair.

He chewed, swallowed, and leaned back.

"Why are you afraid of the doctor?"

"I'm not afraid."

"You refused to address your-" I pointed to his head without finishing my sentence.

A grin played on his lips. "I had more fun having you take care of it."

Heat rose from my neck to my cheeks. "You're embarrassing me."

"I can see that."

"You're difficult." I smiled.

"So, I've been told."

Empty bowls to the side, the Scrabble board lay half-filled. He studied his tiles while I risked watching him for an extended period.

His fingers touched one tile, then another. His hair fell over his forehead. When his eyes popped up to look at me, I moved my gaze. Staring at my own tiles, I heard a rumble as he held a laugh inside.

"You're slow," I said.

"I'm concussed."

"What?" My face went slack.

He winked. "I'm kidding."

I breathed out and shook my head. "Don't scare me like that."

He laid his tiles down. HYMN.

"That's what I can't stand," he said.

"What?"

"The worried look. You had it back at the truck too. I don't like it."

"I can't help it. You were hurt. I was concerned. Anyone would have reacted the same way."

"I know," he said. "I don't like it."

We stared at each other over the table. I smiled. "See? This is me not concerned."

"Much better. It's your turn."

I studied his word against my hand.

"Have you talked to your sister yet?"

Without taking my eyes from my tiles, I said, "No."

I laid down a word, PITH, added up the points (a mere nine), and picked replacements from the pool.

"I'm not ready," I said, when it was clear he was expecting more of an answer. "I will, though. I mean, she's my sister."

"So?"

"It's complicated. I need her in my life, even if she makes me crazy."

He tilted his head in question.

"Growing up, she was a good older sister. I won't forget that."

"How so?"

"Trish protected me from our parents as long as she could."

He stared at me.

"It's hard to explain. My parents had issues. It wasn't easy to live in that house."

"Why?"

I held up my hand. "That, my friend, is for another Scrabble game. I've already said more than I ever have about it."

"Well, I'll look forward to the next game then. In the meantime," Cole laid down an eight-letter, triple point word, MAXIMIZE, "I'll be here, claiming victory."

I clapped, impressed, as he counted his points. "I see your strategy. Get her talking and she'll let her guard down." I manipulated my tiles, my eyes darting back and forth from the board to my hand. When I looked up, he caught me.

"This is nice. I'm happy to be here with you," he said.

"Me too." Should I have admitted that?

He leaned back on his hands and gazed at the board. I tried not to stare at his collarbone, exposed in the V-neck Henley he seemed to like wearing. The leather string holding his hidden pendant lay against his smooth skin.

"What's the pendant you're wearing?" I said.

He pulled it from inside his shirt. "It's not a pendant. It's a stone."

"Does it mean anything?"

His fingers played with it. "To me, it does. It was a gift." He left it at that, and I didn't press, thinking a past girlfriend gave it to him.

"I like it," I said.

He grinned and I focused again on the game. I put down the word ZEST and noted my points.

The front door opened just then, and Charlie walked into the room. He grimaced at the sight of the game board and shook his head.

"Who's winning?"

"He is."

"She is."

We answered simultaneously and laughed.

Charlie didn't join in, and I realized how it must look to see your mother playing a board game with your roommate. I stood. "How was dinner?"

"We went to Nobu," he said and pointed to Cole's head. "What happened?"

Cole stood. "A deer jumped in front of my truck earlier. I hit my head on the steering wheel."

"Crap. How's the truck?"

"Drivable. I was lucky. The buck was a six-pointer."

"Damn. That's scary. Did you get stitches?"

Cole shook his head while I sat there, mute. "Nah. I put this on it. It'll do fine."

Charlie looked at me. "Was it bad?" I started to shake my head when he said, "Never mind, I know you couldn't look at it. You can't stand the sight of blood." He chuckled. "My mom gets queasy with just a scrape."

Cole smiled, saying nothing.

"Hey, tomorrow, let's go out. A few of my friends are getting together. I'll introduce you," Charlie said, moving from the subject.

Cole nodded. "Sounds like a plan."

"Perfect. Mom, I'm heading up. See you in the morning." He leaned over for a half-hug.

"Goodnight, babe." I hugged him back.

Cole and I stayed in the den, listening to my son ascend the stairs to bed.

"You didn't tell him I was with you," I said.

"No."

Thoughts whirled through my mind as I stared at the space where Charlie stood minutes ago. Cole tilted his head toward me. "Not everything you do needs to be shared."

I started to shake my head in disagreement and then thought about his response when he saw me from inside the store at the mall and the tension between us in the kitchen earlier. Was I overreacting? Reading into innocent behavior? Cole watched me consider his statement. No, it wasn't innocent. Nor was it appropriate.

I stepped away from him, keeping a proper distance between us.

He lied to my son. And by staying silent, so did I.

Chapter 8

Charlie came downstairs the following morning.

"That's a first," he said when he saw I was alone in the kitchen, sipping my coffee. "I'm up before Cole."

I had been lost in the view through the window on the last few leaves clinging on to the branches before giving up and letting go.

He poured himself a glass of OJ and joined me at the table.

"Cole told me about his day yesterday. Did he tell you?" Charlie said.

"Tell me what?" I clutched my mug, thinking I'd spent almost the entire day with Cole and my son knew nothing. I should tell him we had lunch and then went shopping, that I was in the car when we hit the deer and I took care of Cole's head. But then would I admit to feeling pangs of want for someone completely inappropriate? In hindsight, over my coffee, the whole day seemed innocent and I knew I was making too much of nothing.

Foolish woman.

"He met some salesgirl at the mall. Said he got her number and wants to see her again." Charlie smiled. "All these available girls at school and he finds one near my house."

"Let's talk about you. You mentioned someone the other night. Kate, is it?"

"Oh. I didn't realize I talked about her."

I chuckled and then took another sip. "Where does Kate live?"

"Right outside of Boston. Almost two hours from school."

I nodded, understanding my future with my child returning home after graduation may be dependent on the girl who steals his heart.

Charlie looked up and raised his eyebrows. "Hey, sleepy."

Cole entered the kitchen unshaven, scrubby and hair messed. He offered a slow smile and my mouth suddenly felt dry. I drank the last of my coffee and jumped up to put the tin of French toast in the oven, more to cover my unexpected reaction to how sexy he looked than to feed them. I busied myself with laundry while they talked in the kitchen. When I smelled the intoxicating aroma of brown sugar, I took the toast out of the oven and placed it on the table.

"Mom, join us," Charlie said as I began to walk away.

"That's okay. You guys talk."

"No, I haven't seen you that much."

Pleased and hungry, I sat at the table.

Charlie dominated the conversation. He spoke of Damian and Genna, how strange it was to be at dinner with his father and someone else. "Dude, that's why I wanted you with me. To act as a buffer," he said to Cole.

Cole glanced at me and I looked away, feeling flushed. He was quiet this morning. "I had some shopping to do," he said.

Charlie laughed. "Right. Shopping." He winked at me. "Anyway, at first it felt so awkward. But then it turned out okay. She's nice. I don't mind her. She was trying hard to find things to talk about."

I ate my food, trying not to think of Damian and another woman out with our son. It's a picture I'll have to get used to. Finished, I left them to talk and make their plans for the rest of the day. I was in my bedroom when they both showered and left in Charlie's car. Restless, I decided to stop over at Dottie's for a visit. She answered the door in khakis and a sweater.

"I'm meeting my friend from work later, but come in. I just made myself a coffee. Would you like some?" she said.

"No thanks. I'm not even sure why I came over. I just didn't want to be home." I followed Dottie into the kitchen.

She took her steaming mug from the counter and brought it to the island. "Come to the movies with us."

I dropped onto a stool next to her and put my head in my hands. "I don't think I can sit through a movie right now."

"What is it?"

"Oh Dottie, I'm still trying to get used to my situation while Damian is taking our son out with his young girlfriend. You're the only person I'll admit this to, but I feel like the frumpy old maid who doesn't leave the house. I feel like a loser."

She put her hand on mine. "Don't ever compare yourself to

anyone else. What you're feeling is normal. It's a tough situation. Believe me, I was in your place a few years ago."

"Not really. George didn't want to leave you. He died."

"Death doesn't make it easier. It's just a different way to be alone."

I felt my shoulders slump further. "I don't agree. If Damian died, I wouldn't feel so…unlovable."

"You're plenty lovable. And you're a knockout. How many forty-one-year-olds have your figure?"

I laughed, but it sounded hollow to me. "Did I tell you what Damian said when he told me he was leaving?"

She paused mid-sip. "You might have. You shared a lot those first weeks."

"I didn't share everything. I was too embarrassed. I still am, but I don't want to hold it in anymore."

"What did he say?"

"He said he was tired of living with the incredible shrinking woman." God, it hurt so much to hear it again.

"What does that even mean?"

"I thought a lot about it, and I think it means there was so little of me left, there was nothing to hold onto."

Dottie bit her lip.

"Do you know what's even worse?" I said.

"I can't imagine."

"I agree with him. I don't even know who I am anymore. Yesterday, Cole asked me if Damian and I fought a lot."

"Cole? The roommate?"

I nodded. "I told him no, which was the truth. We never fought, Dottie. Do you know why? Because I fear conflict and gave in. All the time. To keep peace. Damian wants a fighter."

I stayed with Dottie for an hour, ended up helping her flip her mattress, and left so she could meet her girlfriend.

Back at the house, I changed into sweats and drove to the hiking trail I sent Cole to yesterday. The day was overcast and cool. I passed a few other hikers along the way, but for the most part, enjoyed the gorgeous traipse through the woods alone. I had spent hours here after my separation from Damian. This was a challenging transition for me. I'd never been alone. I went from my parents' house to school to Damian and never had to share my own company. It was time to get reacquainted with myself.

Feelings of loneliness were exacerbated by the two people who were spending the weekend at my house. My son's presence painfully reminded me of his absence, and it hurt knowing he was leaving in twenty-four hours, not to return for three weeks. Our relationship was changing as he grew older.

Cole reminded me that it felt good to laugh and feel at ease with someone who wasn't Dottie or my sister or a new date.

I reached the pinnacle of the hike - the spot that overlooks the glorious sky and forest below. I released a sigh. I need to start living my life, though I'm not sure what that is. These are times when I miss talking to my sister.

I returned to the empty house, and remembering this time to lock my bedroom door, showered, got dressed, and called Trisha, asking her to go out with me. She readily agreed and we decided to meet at a centrally-located restaurant at seven. I felt ready to see her, and once again, get past this hurdle.

Charlie and Cole walked in as I came down the stairs, wearing snug jeans, boots and a turtleneck. I had straightened my natural waves, and wore my hair loose, letting it fall past my shoulders.

"Where are you going?" Charlie asked.

"I'm meeting Aunt Trish for dinner."

My son shook his head. "I hope there's no bar where you're going. Maybe you should meet her at AA."

"Charlie, be respectful."

"It's hard to respect her, Mom. I can't believe you're even talking to her."

"Watch the tone, Charlie. She's my sister. I owe it to her to forgive."

"Sorry." His cheeks flared slightly. "We're going to eat quick and head back out to meet the gang at Jessie's. OK?"

Cole stood quietly with his hands in his pockets.

"There's leftover pasta and sauce in the fridge. Help yourself," I said.

Charlie gave me a quick hug and kiss on my cheek and walked to the kitchen.

Alone in the foyer, Cole and I looked at each other. "You look really great," he said.

I shifted my gaze from him, not knowing how to respond, when he whispered, "Good luck."

"Thank you," I replied, and watched Cole walk into the kitchen.

Trish was waiting at the bar when I arrived. A half-drunk martini sat in front of her. I slipped onto the saved barstool.

"I was beginning to think you'd never talk to me again," she said.

"The thought had crossed my mind."

The bartender placed a napkin in front of me, and I ordered a Coke. I wanted to scream at my sister for having the nerve to drink a martini after what she did, but bit my tongue instead.

Trisha winced and stared at her drink. "I'm sorry. I'm sorry for what I said at dinner. Adam told me."

"The fact that you don't remember scares me. And the fact you're having *that* scares me too." I pointed to her cocktail. "You have got to get control of yourself. You're becoming just like her."

Trisha's head jerked up and her eyes widened in surprise. "No."

I nodded. Our mother got so bad, our father eventually stopped going out with her in public where he might see someone he knew. Business functions were forbidden after she vomited on his boss's shoes at a ritzy awards dinner. Trisha and I made sure to water down the bar before holiday gatherings. When I finally left for college, Trisha stayed home. I remained at school, even over breaks, and latched onto Damian.

"I don't do it a lot," my sister said. "It's been getting worse between us. Adam has been coming home later and later from 'work.'" She used finger quotes when she said work.

"Do you think he's cheating on you?"

Trisha shrugged and her eyes filled.

"Not everyone cheats. Not everyone is Damian," I said.

Trisha stared into her drink and then pushed it away.

"Have you asked him?"

"No. I don't want to know," she said.

"You have to know."

She looked at me. "Why? It won't change anything. I wouldn't leave him."

"You don't have to leave him. But at least you'll know what's going on."

She sniffed.

"Do you love him?" I asked.

She nodded and wiped her nose with the semi-moist napkin from under her glass.

"Then you must talk to him and fix this."

"I don't know if he wants me." A tear dribbled down her cheek.

I put my arm around her shoulder, all too familiar with what she was feeling. The difference between us, though, was how we handled our fears. She turned to drink, and I turned inward. Both behaviors were destructive.

"Well, we don't have to figure this out tonight. But please, I beg you, try to control yourself. Do you want your girls to go through what we did?"

She gasped and pulled away. Then she slid off the stool. "They won't go through what we did, because Adam is kind," she said. "Come on, I'm hungry."

I stepped from my stool and wrapped my arms around her before following her to our table.

Charlie's car was in the driveway when I pulled in after midnight. The house was dark, and I tiptoed up the stairs. I paused outside of Charlie's room, heard deep, methodic breathing and continued past the guest room toward my bedroom. As I stepped, the floorboard creaked beneath my foot.

"Good night, Heather," Cole called softly.

I hesitated, turned, and then stood at the guestroom doorway. I could barely discern Cole lying in bed with his hands behind his head.

"You're home early," I whispered.

"Not early enough."

"You don't like Charlie's friends?"

"They're fine. They sit around, drink beer, and watch YouTube."

I leaned my head against the door frame. "And this doesn't interest you?"

"No. Have you and your sister made up?"

I sighed. "Until next time."

"Interesting relationship."

"It's a sister thing. I need her. She holds up the mirror I refuse to see."

"And what is your mirror telling you?" he asked.

I gazed into the darkened room, at his silhouette, thankful he couldn't read my mind.

"That, I won't share."

"Maybe someday."

"No. Good night, Cole," I said, and walked to my bedroom.

They left the next day and I conquered the following hours by cleaning the entire house trying not to dwell on the tight hug Cole gave me before he walked out behind Charlie. He'd given me an extra squeeze and soft kiss near my ear followed by a whispered thank you. In that moment, it felt warm and masculine and made me want him to hold me a bit longer.

Stripping the bed in the guest room, I tried unsuccessfully not to inhale Cole's scent on the sheets before putting them into the washing machine. One final sweep of the guest room uncovered his tee shirt tucked between the bed and the wall. I folded it, unwashed, and placed it in my pajama drawer.

Chapter 9

Dear Aunt Emma,

I recently divorced after a ten-year marriage, and I've been trying to date. The problem is, I am comparing all my dates to my ex-husband. He left me and is now in another relationship, but I still want him. I think the men sense this because I've been on a lot of first dates and no second dates. I'm trying to be open-minded, and have allowed my friends to keep setting me up, but I'm getting frustrated with my hook-up failures. What do you propose I do?

~ First dates only

Dear First,

Have patience. You're comparing all men to your husband because you've been married to him for a decade. Until you come to terms with the divorce, perhaps don't force another relationship. Give yourself time. Try a new hobby instead. Get involved with an interest group where you can make new friends or learn something new. You'll know if someone is right for you when you react to him physically and emotionally. It will happen, and when it does, embrace it. It is a gift. Good luck.

~ Aunt Emma

If only I felt as confident as I sounded on paper. When I took over for the original Aunt Emma, I tried to emulate her style and incorporate her personality for a smoother transition for our readers.

Eventually, I worked in my own sense of style. The person who wrote this advice could be my alter ego. I've never joined an interest group nor even a book club. The overused but relevant cliché, *"Do as I say and not as I do,"* is never more prevalent than with my column.

Two days after Charlie and Cole returned to school, my son called to tell me he scored a 96 on the Calculus exam he took before Thanksgiving. His level of excitement was evident, and I filled with gratitude toward his roommate, who might very well have saved Charlie's semester. Charlie then said that he worked out a study/tutor schedule with Cole for the remainder of the semester, and he was confident he could get at least an A- in the class.

With the house empty again, and Christmas a month away, I jumped into my work with a fervor. When I wasn't working, I was running, lately at the gym to escape the cold, trying to exhaust myself and to try to forget what transpired over Thanksgiving break: the fight with my sister, our conversation days later, the disastrous blind date, and even the surprising highlight of spending time with Cole. The exertion also helped diminish my desire for sex. Lately, it occupied my thoughts, and I started every day in a frustrating heat. Something opened within me that had been closed for so long. I decided to call Trisha.

"Can you text me Bill's number?"

She paused. "Holy crap. What flipped your light switch?"

"I don't know. I didn't really give him a chance at my house."

"This is so great. I'm sending it now."

I pressed the button, disconnecting the call, and wondered if I was making a mistake. Trisha's text came over within seconds. Before I could change my mind, I dialed the number and reached Bill's voicemail. As I listened to his robotic voice instruct me to leave a message, I paced the living room, chewing on my thumbnail, second-guessing my actions, when the beep suddenly sounded in my ear. I left a quick message, included my number, and hung up.

Did I make the right call? Not that Bill was a bad person. In fact, he seemed rather nice. Plain and nice. No mystery with Bill. I wandered around the house, flip-flopping on my decision to satisfy my carnal urges when the phone rang in my hand, startling me.

It was Carl. "Have you given any thought to Pete's article?" he asked without preamble.

I sunk onto the knitting chair. "I'm not sure, Carl. I've been reading some gardening books, but I'm not really feeling it."

Silence.

"I'm afraid I'll be terrible," I added. "I'm not comfortable with it."

He heaved a frustrated sigh in my ear. "I'll give you 'til Mother's Day weekend to decide. Then I'll have to give the slot to someone else."

"Fine." I should've told him then to give it away, but I was in no mood to hear his disappointment.

Over dinner, I thumbed through one of the gardening books I bought, stifled a yawn, and tossed it aside. Enjoyed another threesome with Ben & Jerry, and as I climbed into bed, Bill returned my call, and we made a date.

Bill picked me up promptly at seven on Friday night. I stepped outside as he reached my porch. He wore corduroy pants and a sport jacket over a button-down shirt that accentuated his slightly protruding stomach. His short hair, more salt than pepper, was combed back. He looked nice.

We walked to his car, and I pulled my wrap tighter over my dress as the cold air snaked up my legs. It had been so long since I'd gone on a date, I wasn't sure what to wear. My goal was to appear elegant yet casual, sexy, but not slutty. I finally decided on a simple black wool dress that fell to my knees and left a rumpled, discarded pile of clothes on the closet floor.

"I'll put the heat on," Bill said as he started the engine. He pulled off my street, and I pointed the way to get to Main Street. "I didn't expect to hear from you so soon."

The warmth through the vents felt good against my chilled skin. "You expected I'd call?" I asked.

He glanced at me and back to the road. "No."

We laughed.

"I didn't either," I said.

A full mile passed before he spoke again. "Why the change of heart?"

"I'm trying to keep an open mind."

"That's a good thing."

We drove in silence. I tried to think of something to say that wouldn't bring us back to our previous disastrous meeting. *Do you remember when my sister announced to the family that I needed to get laid? What are your thoughts?*

I watched the bordering brush off the road and glimpsed a deer, her head down looking for food. What was I thinking? I'm not ready for this. I opened my mouth to suggest that we abort this before we were both even more sorry when he said, "I thought we'd go to Suprianis. Have you ever been?"

"No. That sounds great."

Once seated, the waitress handed us menus and a wine list. "None for me," I said when Bill suggested a bottle. I didn't want to compromise my judgment, and I wasn't feeling festive. Just a bit regretful.

"You're sorry you came," he said after our orders were taken.

"Why do you say that?"

"I'm getting vibes." He smiled. He had a sweet smile. Full lips in a round face.

"I'm sorry. I haven't had a first date in…Well, forever," I said.

He sipped his water. "Technically, this is not our first date."

"I'm not counting Thanksgiving. In fact, let's strike that from our memory, shall we?"

He paused and then reached his hand across the table. "Hi. I'm Bill Ellimen. Widower, grandfather to one and one on the way, Pisces, love mystery novels, hate reality television. Very happy to be here."

He let go of my hand and waited for me to speak. He was really trying. We were here. At least I should make an effort too. I caught our waitress's attention. "We'll take that wine list."

Over dinner, we each spoke about our work, our reluctant transitions to singlehood, even touched on a childhood memory or two (his, not mine). I was nearly finished with my pasta when I admitted I'd never been set up.

"I have. Twice," Bill said.

"How did they work out?"

"The first one went pretty well. I married her, and we had twenty-seven good years together before cancer took her. And the second…" He shrugged and looked down, "started a bit rocky." He looked back up to me. "But I made it to a second, first date."

I found Bill to be self-deprecating and funny, but I detected an underlying sadness about him. This man was in love with his wife, who passed away only three years ago. When he talked about her, his eyes shone, and his cheeks pinked, and I filled with envy.

We pulled into my driveway at eleven o'clock. Bill glanced at his watch. "Four hours. Didn't see that coming at eight o'clock."

I laughed. "I had a nice time."

"Me too."

We both looked through the windshield.

"Can I call you again?"

"Sure," I said.

The easy camaraderie at dinner dissipated during the ride home. Now, we sat here, in awkward silence after what should have been a clean ending. He faced me, leaned over, and I turned my head, expecting him to kiss my cheek. Instead, his lips brushed my jaw. He pulled back and focused his hands on the steering wheel, as embarrassed as I was, I'm sure. I wanted to jump out of the car and run into the house, but I felt compelled to fix this first.

"Bill?" He turned to me. I leaned over and my lips met his. He put his hand on my hand on the center console. I hadn't kissed someone in a long time. Damian stopped kissing me during sex, and then he cut us off altogether during our last year, so I was surprised at how little I felt here with Bill. The one thought that went through my mind while our lips touched was: No more.

I pulled away and opened the door. "Thank you for dinner."

Chapter 10

With a week left before Charlie came home for holiday break, I busied myself with work and shopping, buying gifts for Charlie, Trisha, my nieces, and as always, trying to pick up something special for Dottie. After George passed away and since my separation, she and I had grown even closer. For the past several months, she'd been unsuccessfully trying to convince me to take line dancing lessons with her. *"It's one dance where you don't need a partner."*

At the mall, I found a pair of pink leather cowboy boots and bought them for her. I smiled all the way home, anticipating her reaction when she opened the gift.

I pulled up to the house to find Damian's car parked at the top of my driveway like he'd been doing it undisturbed for the past seven months. My ire rose within me. He wasn't in the car, and I knew he'd let himself into my house. I entered through the garage door to find him standing in the kitchen looking through the mail.

"You could wait until I'm home and knock on the door." I contemplated walking over and grabbing my mail from his prying hands.

"We're having dinner out tonight, and I wanted to get these first. I didn't know how long you'd take," he said, tossing unwanted items on the counter, not bothering to look up.

"Why can't I just text you the amounts and you can send a check? Or, do you want me to have the bills mailed to you directly?"

"I don't mind it this way."

I do, I thought. *I mind when you walk in like you still live here and yet you make sure I know you have a dinner date with your perfect girlfriend.* The words in my head wouldn't come out. Instead, I said, "Stop treating this house like it's still yours."

He finally met my eyes. "This is still mine." He emphasized with a sweep of his mail filled hand.

"But *I'm* living here."

He shook his head and then smirked. "But *I* pay the bills."

"Not all of them."

"Anything in there for me?" He pointed to the packages still in my hand.

"Please go." I sighed, defeated, and put the bags on the table.

"That's why I want to see the bills."

He leaned against the counter for an extra beat knowing it would get under my skin. Half of this house was mine. My own blood, sweat and tears went into the refurbishing and re-construction, but we both knew Damian paid financially for almost all of it, and he never let me forget it. I stared at him, trying not to breathe too heavily or show him his presence gnawed at me.

"You're picking Charlie up?" Damian asked.

"Yes. I took off work and I'll get him Friday. You can see him on the weekend."

He nodded, and having nothing else to say, pulled himself straight and then strolled out of the house. Immediately locking the door behind him, I then carried my packages upstairs. My heartbeat was erratic, and I paced the floor. I'd considered changing the locks, but I wasn't ready to face the finality of what that meant, so I pushed the thought from my mind. I threw on layers of workout clothes, covered by a sweatshirt and wool hat, and went out for a run.

An hour later, spent and sweating despite the cold, I walked back into the house. I was still angry and hurt, but no longer feeling as charged.

I told Dottie what happened over coffee the next morning. She listened while I reiterated my conversation with Damian. When I was finished, she frowned.

"You shouldn't let him get away with that."

"He owns the house."

"He should respect your privacy. He's blatantly mocking you," Dottie said.

"I know. I feel powerless to stop him. We're only separated, so I don't know what the rules are. His name is on the deed."

"Did you buy the house as a couple?"

"Yes."

"Then it's yours, too," Dottie said. "He's bullying you."

I lowered my head, frustrated.

"Does he do this when Charlie's home?"

I thought about it. "No."

"You can stop him, you know. I think you allow him to do this."

I pushed my coffee mug away. "You know, Damian left me once before."

Dottie's eyes flew open. "What? How do I not know this?"

"Because it's not something I include in most conversations. Especially being left twice. I've never told anyone. Trisha obviously knows, but that's it. Charlie was seven. Damian packed his bags and moved out for two months."

Dottie remained stunned. "I'm sorry. I didn't know. What a creep."

I exhaled. "I felt so inadequate that I couldn't make him happy. I had cooked a nice dinner every night, doted on our son, basically reverted to a 1950s Stepford wife. I tried to be everything my mother wasn't."

The new revelation of what I just said shocked me. Is that what I did? Tried to meet Damian's needs so he wouldn't be disappointed in me, a feeling I lived with my whole childhood?

"It wasn't enough. That was clear. We married too young, and he still needed to experience other women," I said.

"Needed, Hah! Don't make excuses for him, Heather, and don't convince yourself it was your fault."

"But it was, Dot. He seemed to be growing and changing, and I felt like the same needy teenager he married."

"What made him come back?"

"Charlie. He cried a lot, begging his daddy to come home. So, Damian did."

"My God. What was it like then?"

I stared at a small chip on the rim of my mug. "We never really talked about it. I just continued as if it never happened." I looked at my friend. "How can someone leave for work in the morning and then walk back in at the end of the day with nothing to say? More than the sex, which I could live without, I missed having someone to talk to."

Dottie was quiet. Speaking about our earlier separation out loud made me feel even more ashamed than I already was. But it was also a relief to share it with her.

"So," she finally said, "by allowing him to walk back into the house at will, are you thinking one day, he'll walk back in with his bags and stay?"

I started to shake my head, denying it, when I realized maybe that was exactly what I was doing. "I don't know," I said.

"Do you want him to come back?"

"He won't. The last time, he stayed on a friend's couch. He's living with someone else now."

"That's not what I asked," Dottie said.

"I don't know what I want. I think that's always been my problem."

From the small radio on the kitchen counter, Michael Bublé sang us a song, low and smooth.

Standing, Dottie picked up the coffee pot. I held up a hand, declining a second cup. She refilled her own mug and sat back down. "It would explain why your sister is so desperate to set you up with someone."

I snorted. "Yes. Trisha hates Damian."

As the song played in the background, we let our conversation sink in.

"When does Charlie get home?" Dottie said.

At the mention of my son, the tension in my shoulders eased somewhat. "Friday. His last exam is Thursday and then he's home for five weeks. I can't wait."

Dottie smiled with me. "Tommy and Cheryl are coming next week. I've convinced Cheryl to leave the baby with me for a few days, so she and her husband can stay in the city and have a mini getaway."

"How old is the baby now?"

"Almost one. The holidays are still hard for me without George. The baby makes missing him hurt a little less."

"What happened to that nice guy you went out with a few times?"

Dottie sighed. "I've been avoiding his calls. He got needy."

"You don't want companionship?"

"I enjoy my own company far more." She sipped her mug thoughtfully before replying. "I refuse to settle. I don't have to. I had a love. I'm fulfilled."

I thought of Bill, who clearly loved his wife, how he was searching for another.

"Listen," Dottie said, "if Prince Charming comes knocking at my door, I'll let him in. But not until then."

"Do you think there's a Prince Charming?"

She rested her chin on her palm. "I do. Mine came in the shape of a pear with ear hair and a perfectly round bald spot right here." She reached toward the top back of her head. "He may have been a little messy, occasionally flatulent, but he was the love of my life."

"I don't feel fulfilled, Dottie."

She grabbed both mugs and stood. "No, I don't suppose you do."

Weighted by my admission, I followed her to the sink to help.

"I did go on a date last weekend," I said.

"Oh! How did it go?"

"It was with Bill. From Thanksgiving. It wasn't bad. But he's not what I'm looking for."

"That's too bad." She stared out her back window. "He might be a little old for you."

I stood beside her and looked out the window too. How many afternoons did we spend in her yard talking about life over a cup of coffee?

"What is the right age for me?" I said, taking the clean mug from her to dry it.

"You're young yet. Find another forty-year-old."

"I'm sure it's that easy," I said and then laughed. "The problem is, forty-year-old men want thirty-year-old women." Like Damian.

Dottie turned to me. "So, you go get a thirty-year-old, too. Why not? There are no rules. But keep in mind, you must leave your house to find him. They don't just come knocking at your door."

Charlie called me two days before I was due to pick him up.

"I'm all set for Friday," I told him. "I'll leave by six and be there at eleven-ish." I was so looking forward to having him home again, I'd been thinking of little else all week. I'd prepared lasagna for the weekend.

"Mom, there's been a change of plans."

I carried the phone, pacing from room to room. Change of plans? Did he want Damian to pick him up? I'd offered because my work schedule is so flexible, and Damian readily agreed. In fact, I'm sure he was relieved not to have to make the trip.

"I'm not coming home on Friday. I'm staying up an extra few days to spend with Kate."

I dropped onto on my living room loveseat, feeling gut-wrenched. "Charlie, doesn't the school close for the holiday?"

"They close on the twentieth, but I'm only staying in the dorm until Sunday. Then I'm going to Kate's house for a few days."

I stared out the windows at the trees that only weeks ago held onto their last leaves. Now they stood bare, naked in the cold.

"Mom? Are you upset? I'll be home next week, the latest, still in plenty of time for Christmas. Is it okay?"

Was it okay? I didn't pace. All the energy was sapped from me. I looked at the empty corner of the den, waiting for the tree Charlie and I were supposed to pick out. "Of course, it's okay," I lied. "So, I should pick you up when?"

"Well, here's the good news. Since Kate lives close to Boston, I'm going to jump on the Amtrak train to Penn Station and then take the train to you. You just have to pick me up at the station in town." He sounded happy. That's all I wanted.

"That *is* good news," I said.

"So, you're okay with it?"

"Of course. Have fun. And Charlie, be a good guest in her parents' house."

"Will do. Thanks. Love you." He hung up.

I placed the phone down, disappointed by the call, took the prepared lasagna from the fridge, and moved it to the freezer.

Trisha called as I shut the freezer door. "I just wanted to give you a quick ring before we left."

"You're still going?" Every year Trish and Adam took the girls to Florida to spend time with Adam's parents before Christmas. Since she and Adam hadn't been getting along these past months, I thought Trisha would honor her threat of not going.

"Yes. Because I have no backbone and the girls want me with them."

"Okay. Did you stop the mail?" I asked.

"Yes. We'll be back on the twenty-third."

"Have a wonderful time," I said.

"How wonderful can it be? I'm staying at Adam's parents'. We have a love/hate relationship. They love my kids, and they hate me."

I laughed. "Please, Trisha, don't drink while you're down there. Don't get yourself in trouble."

"I don't need your advice, little sister." She hung up without saying goodbye.

I slept in on Friday since I was no longer driving to get Charlie. Now I had a whole day to myself without a plan. Trisha left for Florida. Dottie was busy preparing for her son and daughter's visit in a few days, and I'd written extra Aunt Emma letters in advance, to give myself some time off. The day was cold and overcast, so I stayed in my flannels and a tee-shirt, deciding against a run. Instead, I lay on the couch and indulged in sappy, but fulfilling, holiday stories on Lifetime. The only thing missing was a pint of Ben & Jerry's Heath Bar Crunch.

The doorbell rang as one movie ended. I discarded my blanket and answered, slightly embarrassed to still be in pajamas. It was Rob, the UPS driver, smiling and waving through my side window-pane by the door.

"Hi, Rob. What do you have for me today?"

"Mrs. Harrison." He nodded his greeting and lifted a square package. "Sign here, and it's yours."

Scrawling a chicken-scratch signature on the hand-held device, I thanked him with a tip, and closed the door. I checked the return address to see Carl's name and the newspaper's address. I opened the box, and on a small pile of letters was a note. "Got more this month for you. We have room for extra letters in the next publication. Holidays are tough for people. Thank God. Talk to you next week. Carl."

I put the box on the dining room table and returned to the couch to start the next tear-fest. The doorbell rang again an hour later. This time I was unsuccessfully trying to suppress my emotions as I wiped my eyes while walking to the door. I somehow knew Dottie would pop over. She was baking and probably forgot an ingredient.

My heart thrummed loudly as I saw not my neighbor on my welcome mat, but Cole. I inhaled, and my hand went to my chest, as if it could control the erratic beating of my heart. I took a breath and opened the door.

"Cole. What are you doing here?"

He stood with his hands in his jeans pockets, wearing a fleece jacket and a skull cap. I took in his blue eyes, the curl of his dark hair under his hat. He looked devastatingly beautiful.

"Why are you here? Charlie's—"

"I know. He told me about his plans." He looked down at his shoes and back up to me.

I flushed and stood stock still, not sure what to do.

"Can I come in? It's a little chilly out here."

Wordlessly, I stepped aside, and he walked past me to the foyer.

"What are you doing here?" I asked again.

"I'm not sure. I got in the truck and started driving south. Every exit I passed, I thought, I should turn around, but I never did. And then I crossed the bridge, and well," he shrugged, "here I am."

"You came here to see me?"

He nodded.

"You drove all the way here on the off-chance I'd be home?" I couldn't comprehend what was happening.

He nodded again.

"What if I had plans?" I said.

He pulled off his cap and eyed me up and down, noting my pajamas at 2 p.m. "Whatever your plans are, they're very casual."

My hand went to the messy bun on top of my head. Then it touched my blotchy, makeup-less face. "You shouldn't be here."

"Maybe, but I am."

"You can't be here," I said.

His eyes held mine.

I took a deep breath, swallowing my panic. "Is there another person you're on Long Island to see?"

He shook his head and unzipped his jacket.

"Cole..."

He took a step closer to me, forcing me to tilt my head up to see his face. "Please don't send me away." It was a soft plea.

I stepped back. "This is crazy. I can get arrested."

He smiled and that dimple taunted me. "For letting me in? I don't think so," he said.

Tears threatened, so I bit my top lip hard. "Go," I finally breathed. "Please."

He stepped back. "Do you mean that?"

I didn't answer. I wanted to say yes. But seeing him here, I couldn't.

"It's a long ride back. I'll leave tomorrow, if you don't want me here. I promise."

My lip tingled with pain while my brain whirred. I'm supposed to tell this kid he shouldn't be here alone with an older woman who happens to be his roommate's mother. But he knows that. And he came anyway.

"What do you want?" I asked.

"I want to spend some more time with you."

"I shouldn't have let you in."

"You're wearing my shirt," he whispered.

My cheeks singed. What was I going to do? Turning away, I waved him to follow me into the den while I decided how to approach this unprecedented situation. I gestured for him to sit on the club chair across from the couch, where I sat. After draping his jacket and hat on the upright chair near the corner, he dropped casually into his seat.

"Heather, I have a question I want to ask."

I braced myself. A bead of perspiration dripped down my back.

He leaned forward. "Do you ever sit in that chair?" He pointed to the upright chair and I exhaled. Cole smiled.

"Not really. When we bought it, it seemed like a good idea at the time. Charlie calls it the knitting chair because it looks like it belongs to an old lady who knits mittens."

Cole seemed at ease sitting in my den with me. I'd give anything for an iota of his self-confidence.

"What are you thinking?" he said.

"I admire your bravado, walking in here like you knew I would let you."

His face lost all humor. "It's not bravado. It's hope. I've been thinking about you. Every day since I've been here."

"You have?"

He touched the bandage still above his eye. "Yes. I like spending time with you. You're easy to be with."

I put my fingers on the base of my throat. The feeling was mutual, but I wasn't going to admit that to him.

"I didn't know what to expect coming here, and I'll understand if you ask me to go. But I've learned that life is too short not to try. I felt a connection when I was here last, and unless I read this all wrong, I think you did, too," he said.

My face burned, and my legs trembled. Our conversation over Thanksgiving break, the tension between us as I took care of him after hitting the deer, and the way he'd looked at me, did not go unnoticed. But I thought I'd overreacted and that Cole was simply showing kindness to his friend's mother. Maybe having a little fun. "Cole, no matter what you think or how I feel, we can't just hang out." I pointed between both of us. "I'm old enough to be your mother."

"Sure, if you had a baby at seventeen." He grinned and then grew serious. "But you're not. You're a woman. I'm a man."

I exhaled a laugh. "A twenty-four-year-old man."

"It's just a number."

"It's an important number."

"To whom?"

I stood. "I don't...I can't..." Walking into the kitchen, I leaned against the counter, and took a deep inhale.

I felt him behind me, so close I could feel his breath in my hair. He put a hand on my arm. "It's okay. I promise I'll respect your wishes. But I'm here, and you're here, and no one else is. I'm not here to seduce you. I'd like to get to know you."

Seduce me? I turned around. "I don't know how I feel about this." We stood in the kitchen, not moving. He waited for me to say more and in my mind, I went through several ways to tell him to leave. My stomach growled, reminding me I hadn't eaten yet today. "You're here and drove a long way." I sighed. "I'll make us something to eat."

He moved back to give me space, wearing a victorious grin and kept me company while I made us chicken cutlet heroes. We ate in the den, while he told me about his finals, and about the boys on his and Charlie's floor. Then he turned the conversation to me, asking about my Christmas plans, how it was going with Trisha since we'd made up, and about my column.

We started to watch a movie, leaving our plates on the coffee table. By the middle of the story, we had abandoned it and started talking, falling into a natural and comfortable dialogue. Cole delved into my life as if trying to know every aspect of the forty-one-year-old Heather.

"I was married at twenty-one, having Charlie two years later. I was scared out of my mind, but I loved Charlie more than anything.

"I studied graphic design at Brockport but then decided I had a knack for writing. So, I switched my major to English, thinking maybe I'd be a teacher or a journalist. I didn't know. Anyway, after Charlie, none of it mattered. I stayed home with him."

"And then you became Aunt Emma," he said.

"Yes. Damian worked long hours. At first, when he was home, he talked about work and I had nothing to contribute. We had little in common outside of our son. So, I started part-time at the paper doing administrative work and eventually took over the column. I was glad for the job."

It took some time for me to grow comfortable with talking about myself. Eventually, I flipped the discussion, and soon we were chatting back and forth through two more movies playing on the TV in the background.

"I don't remember much right after Brynn died," Cole said almost reverently. "I do remember spending a lot of time with my nanny, who was young and fun. My parents were reserved and very quiet. My father worked all the time. He was always out. And my mother kept to herself. She still does."

Poor Mrs. Prue. My heart ached for her, having to bury a baby. I don't know that I could have survived it. Cole turned to the television while I watched him, wondering what it was like for him as a young boy having to deal with that loss in the family. He doesn't remember it, but it had to have shaped him.

Considering his mother, I asked, "Cole, where do your parents think you are?"

Those blues remained focused on the TV screen. "They know I'm here."

"What?" My heart dropped down to my feet. What could they think of this, of me?

"They know I'm visiting Long Island to see someone I like and want to spend time with," he clarified.

"When do they expect you back?"

"They don't keep tabs on me. You won't either, when Charlie is older."

I picked at my blanket.

"When do *you* think I'll be back?" he asked.

I stopped picking and brought my eyes to his. Though I knew it was wrong, I wanted him to stay. I enjoyed his company last month, more so than Bill's or anyone else's. I shouldn't. Everything about him being here was wrong, but there was something about this man.

He waited, biting the inside of his lip.

"Let's play it by ear," I said.

We talked into the evening and we were hungry again. I made scrambled eggs and toast which we ate in the dark kitchen under the single light over the table. Time flew and we filled the hours with conversation and laughter until finally, I faced the moment I needed to say goodnight.

"Heather, I'd like to get my bag from outside." He watched me carefully, looking for a sign of regret or hesitation, I think. I showed nothing.

"Okay. I'll make up the bed in the guest room."

He stood. "Don't. I'll do it. Don't wait on me."

I stood in the foyer while he went to the truck to get his bag, hugging myself when he let in the cold air. Following him upstairs, I filled with nervous dread, fearing an awkward lingering near my bedroom door, and an uncomfortable rejection. Instead, Cole gave me a small wave and disappeared into the guest room.

I laid in my bed reviewing the day, wondering what would become of this, knowing Cole would go home in a day or so, or possibly even tomorrow, with no more than he came. As I rolled over, I clutched the tee-shirt covering me – the one he'd forgotten during his last visit. I'd been wearing it lately, enjoying his lingering smell.

Why, Heather? Now that he's seen it on you, he knows.

Chapter 11

Cole wakes early. I knew that. I was downstairs at six-thirty and wasn't surprised to hear him walk down at seven.

"Morning," he drawled, with that gravelly voice I like. He poured himself a cup of coffee with the mug I'd put out for him.

"How did you sleep?" I said.

He sat down across from me. I could see day-old growth on his jaw in the weak winter sun through the window. His hair was tousled and shone in the same light. This guy could walk out the door and have a line of women waiting for his attention. Yet, he's sitting here with me. I sipped my coffee.

"What is going on in that head of yours so early in the morning?" he said.

My cheeks heated. "You go to school with thousands of young, single girls. Yet, you're here. I'm sure any one of them would want to be sitting at a table with you in the morning, looking like you do."

He sighed and ran his hand through his hair. "You don't get it. Look past my face, Heather. Look at me."

I did. I looked at Cole sitting at my table, wanting to be more to me than what I told him he was. And when I did, I no longer saw the beautiful face, the sun-dappled hair, or the glint on his chiseled jaw. I saw the soul of a man reaching out to me. Saw a person who all his life got attention for the wrong reasons. This was why he connected with me. Girls his own age couldn't get past the surface, which he had no control over.

"Okay. I see you," I said.

His shoulders relaxed. "I have a question."

"You have lots of questions."

"Why don't you have a Christmas tree?"

"It's too heavy for me to bring home and set up by myself. I thought Charlie would be home yesterday."

"I'll help you," Cole said. "Where do you get one?"

"Home Depot." I sipped my coffee.

He frowned.

"What?" I said.

"I was hoping you cut down your own."

"Who's got time for that?"

He looked incredulous. "Everyone." He leaned forward, pushing his mug out of his way. "If you don't have time to spend an afternoon choosing a tree, then you're doing it wrong."

"Doing what wrong?"

"Life."

I laughed out loud. "Right. Most people get their trees from a store, or a pop-up lot along the Expressway. You're in. You're out. You're done."

He stood. "Let's find a tree farm, pick one out, and cut it down. It's a beautiful day and we should spend it outside."

I stood too, put my mug in the sink, and started for my bedroom. "I'm an indoor cat, except when running," I said, passing him.

"We're going to change that," he said behind me on the stairs. "I'll meet you downstairs."

Bundled in boots and sweaters, we drove an hour out to a farm in Mattituck on the North Fork of Long Island. I'd insisted on driving since I was familiar with Long Island and knew how to get to the farm based on glimpsing the map. We chatted easily about past holidays, traditions, and expectations for the future. I admitted my fear that Charlie might settle off Long Island.

"So?" Cole said.

I squeezed the steering wheel. "So, it would be difficult if he didn't come home. I'd miss him."

"The world is a small place now. You can have a constant connection with just about anyone, including your son."

"It's not the same. To be able to see Charlie in person, to touch him. You'll see when you have your own. There's nothing like the unconditional love and constant inner fear you feel for your child. It's terrifying. I highly recommend it."

Cole didn't answer.

"Nothing to add?" I smiled in his direction.

"No."

"Don't you want to have children someday?"

"I don't."

"You'll change your mind," I said.

I pulled into the farm lot, and we started down a row of trees, circling each one before continuing. The day was cold and clear, and the farm seemed to go on forever, though the website said it covered only twenty acres. Every tree was beautiful. I enjoyed myself so much and wanted the experience to last, so I kept finding reasons to keep looking. After an hour, Cole started to laugh.

"What?"

"Either you're picky, or you're having fun," he said.

I smiled and pulled my hat further down over my ears. "I'm not picky. The first tree we saw was perfect."

"Ha! I knew it," he said.

"Show off."

He laughed, and I watched the plume of his breath dissolve in the air.

"So, this is something you do with your parents?" I said.

"Believe it or not, I've never done this, either."

I lightly punched him on the shoulder. "Hey! Then why did you guilt me into this if you've never done it?"

"I've always wanted to try it."

We rented a saw and decided on a tree. It took us thirty minutes to finally take it down. Not because it was so thick, but because we couldn't stop giggling. The tree fell onto a soft bed of pine needles, and I wished Charlie was with us to experience it. The deep cologne of pine and the bright blue sky filled me with joy.

"I can't believe this is the first time I've ever done this," I said.

We followed a worker to the car, and Cole helped him secure the tree to the roof.

"It's never too late to try something," he said.

We drove back the way we came, stopping, at Cole's suggestion, at a winery, where we sat wrapped in coats, sipping wine and noshing from a cheese board on the small outdoor patio.

"Are you sure you don't want to sit inside?" I said.

"I love it out here." He lifted his head toward the sky and closed his eyes. I allowed myself the luxury of looking at him, unable to deny he did something to me. I'd never act on it, of course, but I couldn't deny it.

"I'm happy to be here with you," he said.

"Why?"

"Because you're fun, and beautiful, and easy to talk to."

I closed my eyes, tilting my head up, as he did, and visualized things that should never be.

We arrived home at dark and dragged the tree into the house. While I held the base, Cole lifted it into the hole, and together we tightened the screws into the soft trunk. Then we stood back and admired our choice.

"It's perfect for the space," he said.

"I agree." I turned to him. "Thank you."

He offered a half-bow. "My pleasure, ma'am."

He helped me string the lights, telling me how his father hires someone every year to decorate the house, inside and out. It has to look perfect to keep up with the standards of the neighbors. As a child, he never decorated his tree.

"It's one of my fondest traditions with Charlie," I said. "He used to jump around at my feet, impatiently palming the orna-ments while I did the lights. When he finally put them on, they'd all be clumped in one area, low enough for him to reach, and the rest of the tree would be bare." I loved my memories and felt sadness for a boy who didn't have them.

Cole smiled. "I can see Charlie doing that. He's a happy guy."

"And you're not?" I said.

"I am. We have different temperaments, is all."

No, I thought, there's something about this young man that tells me he was never really an exuberant, innocent, happy child. Perhaps, because of his sister's death, his parents didn't engage. I felt the urge to hold him, but of course, squelched the desire. As we placed the last lights along the bottom branches, he stared at me with an expression of tenderness. He wants to ease my pain, as well, I thought.

I cleared my throat. "I hope you don't mind, but I have to leave the ornaments for Charlie."

Cole blinked. "Of course."

I crawled into bed at midnight, exhausted from all the fresh air, but tossed and turned the entire night, confused, wanting, self-re-criminating, as Cole slept in the next room. I climbed out of bed early and sat in the den, contently watching the sun rise through the trees.

When Cole came downstairs, I had pancakes sizzling on the griddle.

"I want to take you somewhere today," he said as we sat across from each other at the table, eating.

"Okay," I said.

Five hours later, we stood at the corner of Tillary and Adams Streets on the Brooklyn side of the bridge, satisfied on prosciutto pizza and Brooklyn Beer from Ignazio's. The weather was cold and cloudy. I buttoned the top of my down coat and turned to my walking partner.

"Ready?" he said.

"As I'll ever be."

When Cole told me where he wanted to go, my first instinct was to say no. I'd never had the desire to walk across the Brooklyn Bridge, or any bridge for that matter, especially in December. But I had nothing else planned, and he waited, poised over his pancakes, for my answer, so I agreed.

We started on our journey across the 5,989-foot bridge amid a thick crowd of pedestrians. He'd never been to Brooklyn nor walked across the bridge toward Manhattan either. It was a first for both of us, which made it sweeter. Halfway across, Cole stopped, and I knew why. The view of the Manhattan skyline was spectacular.

He looked at me. "A bucket list check-off for sure."

"Absolutely."

We continued and paused again by an extensive collection of padlocks along a fenced area.

"What's this?" Cole said.

I used my phone to Google the meaning behind the padlocks and read it to him. "They're called love-locks. Couples leave their padlocks and throw the key into the river as a show of everlasting love."

He stared at the padlocks and then to me.

"Corny," he said.

"Totally," I agreed.

Laughing, we moved on. When we reached the Manhattan side, he turned to me and gave me a quick hug. "Thank you for coming with me."

His cheeks were rosy, and his eyes shined. His face brought a rush of warmth to my heart. We were an hour's drive from my house, and I'd never done this. How could I have missed this all these years?

"Okay, now I can show you something." I led him through Chinatown to Little Italy. Eventually, I found a small café I had been to once, years ago, and was happy to see it was still in business. We walked in from the cold, savoring the warm air. He grabbed a round table for two while I bought what I believed to be the world's best hot chocolate and scones. We sipped and picked at our snack, giddy from the day.

"You look happy," he said.

"I am," I admitted. "I had a wonderful time today."

Cole reached for my hand and held it. "Me, too."

I looked down at our joined hands, and my smile faltered. I pulled mine away, turning to see if anyone saw. When I did, I glimpsed a woman at another table who I recognized from work. Oh, God! How does this look?

"Heather." He appeared hurt. "I'm sorry. I just wanted to hold your hand."

"You can't." I cannot, under any circumstances, hold hands with a young man like this in public. I looked down and suddenly wished I hadn't come.

"Why?"

I shook my head slightly and glanced again at the woman at the table. I'd made a mistake. She wasn't who I thought she was.

"It's not a crime," he said. "What's the matter?"

I glanced around us. "Don't."

"Why?"

"It's wrong."

He stared at me. "To whom?"

"To everyone."

"Who cares?" he whispered.

"It's wrong to me."

He leaned forward and crossed his arms on the table. "If there was no one here and it was just you and me, would you hold my hand?"

I didn't answer.

"If I were forty-five, would you hold my hand?"

"You're not forty-five," I said. "And there are people here."

"Do you enjoy my company?"

I nodded.

"Do you…find me attractive?"

I blushed. "Not at all."

His lips twitched. "So, it's just my age that bothers you."

"It should bother you, too."

"It doesn't. I don't care what other people think. I care how I feel."

He was right. I shouldn't care what strangers thought. Not at this point in my life. But I did. I cared very much.

His face softened, and I wanted to reach over and touch him, but refrained, fisting my frustrated hands under the table. We were nearing a dangerous line here. I'd intended for us to remain casual and friendly. He was pulling me toward that line, and I had to send him home.

"Never do things for other people." He sipped his cocoa.

"There are rules."

"You're not breaking any rules, Heather. You're only putting off the inevitable."

The inevitable? I loved the idea of what he mentioned. My entire body tightened at the thought of being with him. But there was no way I could let it happen. What then, am I doing with him? I lifted the mug to my lips. The aroma of rich, creamy chocolate wafted in my nose. "I don't know what I'm doing here."

"I think you do."

"Why don't you spend time with girls your age?" I said.

"I have. Plenty. But I've never responded to anyone this way."

I chewed on a piece of scone.

"You're interesting,'" he said. "And sexy."

I averted my gaze, wondering if anyone could hear him. When was the last time someone thought I was sexy? When was the last time I felt sexy?

"Yet, an unsure girl peeks out from time to time," he continued. "It's intoxicating."

"Have you ever been in a long-term relationship?" I asked.

"No."

We finished our drinks and left the café. The sun had gone down, and the sky was quickly getting dark.

"Where to now?" he said.

"Let's go home."

Two hours later, we changed into sweats and watched a movie, sitting on the couch, but still not too close. Cole was respecting the space I needed. I felt calm and not threatened, but after our earlier conversation, I was more confused and intrigued than ever. At midnight, he stood up and said goodnight, leaving me on the couch to watch him walk away.

Chapter 12

Dear Aunt Emma,

Two years ago, I got out of a painful, three-year relationship. I thought it was love until my boyfriend trampled all over my heart, leaving me a pulpy, depressed mess. Since then, I have avoided getting romantically involved with anyone else. However, I met someone recently who asked me to lunch. Though I am interested in him, fear prevents me from pursuing anything. I can't handle another toxic relationship. The last one left me in tatters, feeling unworthy of love. My ego is destroyed, not to mention my self-confidence in the bedroom. Is there hope for me to find someone who'll finally make me happy?

~Knocked down

Dear Knocked,

Okay, you've been knocked down and beaten up, emotionally. It's tough to get over that, believe me, I get it. The good news is, everyone is not your former boyfriend. There are some gems out there. Accept the date, and get to know your new friend. It's only lunch. Try it. If it leads to another meal, then take it in stride. Stop looking too far into the future. This one may peter out before it begins. He may also be "the one." But you'll never know if you allow your fears to prevent you from taking a chance.

Take what you've learned from past experiences and apply them to new ones. Know that yes, you are worthy of love by someone who will raise you up instead of tear you down.

~Aunt Emma

I woke up at nine the following morning to the music of a sizzling stove and the odiferous allure of bacon. I found Cole in the kitchen, cooking breakfast.

"Good morning, sleepyhead," he beamed.

I leaned against the counter. "I can't believe I slept in. I haven't done that in ages."

He went back to the eggs and slid them from the pan onto two plates.

"Did I have bacon?" I asked as I poured myself a mug of coffee and sat at the table. He set two place settings and brought our plates over, setting them down before joining me. Are we playing house?

"No. I went to the store while you were sleeping."

He'd made eggs over-easy with English muffins. I took a bite and a sip of coffee.

"This is a little weird," I said.

"What?" He dug his fork into his food and ate half of his plate in one shot.

"This. Making breakfast for me like we're a couple."

"Or, I could have made two people something to eat who might be hungry."

I continued to eat.

"Stop labeling everything. Just enjoy a meal prepared for you. When's the last time you did that?"

I couldn't remember.

"There you go. Relax. Enjoy it. No one needs to know."

I envisioned how this scenario might look to anyone else. But there were only two people here. And neither of us seemed to mind what was going on.

He finished first and watched me.

"What?"

He smiled. "Nothing. What did you have planned for today?"

Today, I was going to finish my holiday shopping and start my menu for Christmas dinner. And I was hoping to spend some time with Charlie.

"Not much. You?"

"Just going with the flow. I'm a feather on a breeze," Cole said.

"A hard concept for a planner: To go where the wind takes you. I've never been that relaxed."

"It's too bad. Some of my best memories were unplanned."

I swallowed my last bite of eggs. "What was your last best memory?"

He thought a bit and rested his elbows on the table. "Twenty-one, traveling through Taiwan. I'd joined a group a few days earlier and decided one morning in Taipei that I was ready to leave them and be by myself again. I headed to a small town I'd read about, called Juifin.

"It was awesome. I stumbled onto Old Street, which is a step back in time. I ate black pork, tofu, and tea and walked for hours until I found a small temple in a village. I don't remember the name, and I dropped my backpack and sat in the center of it. There were no walls, a statue on a small pedestal, and me. I tried to pray, but couldn't. I abandoned that and focused on breathing. Just breathing. In. Out. In. Out." He stopped and looked at me. "It's harder than you think. It took a long time, but when I emptied myself of thoughts, it was life-affirming. My mind was empty, but I felt full if that makes sense." He paused again and stared out of the kitchen window as if seeing himself in his story.

"I knew then, no matter how bad it got, I'd be okay. One way or the other."

"How bad what got?" I said.

"Life." He stood and brought our plates to the sink, leaving me wondering how a kid who could take a few years off to backpack, with parents so wealthy he'd never worry for money, could have it bad.

We cleaned up our breakfast mess, and Cole said he'd take a shower if that were okay.

"Of course. You know where everything is."

"Think of something you'd like to do today. I'm up for anything." He came downstairs half an hour later. "Where to?"

I didn't have the heart to or the inclination to stick with my pathetic list of errands. Instead, I blurted out the last thing I'd expected to say. "I haven't seen the Christmas tree in years. Have you ever been?"

"To Rockefeller Center?" He smiled. "It's been years for me too. I'd love to go."

He waited in the den while I showered, and we drove into NYC. We found an open parking garage fifteen blocks from the most tourist-driven scene in the world and meandered down Seventh Avenue. We ignored the bustling pedestrians around us while we talked.

"What made you go backpacking alone at twenty-one?"

He wore his skull cap and scarf around his wool coat. The air was cold but not uncomfortable.

"I left when I was twenty. I needed to be out from under my parents' thumb. I craved space."

We walked while I pondered this. "It would have bothered me if Charlie felt like I was smothering him."

"You didn't?" he said.

"No. He had plenty of his own space. Even after Damian left, I made sure to be available if he needed me, but let him go out, see friends, work.

"That's why he may not need to escape," Cole said.

"Were your parents okay with you going?"

Cole looked up at the buildings and then to me. "They understood. I think we should turn here."

The Christmas tree at Rockefeller Center made me nostalgic for lost days. We took Charlie here many times when he was young. Still, he lost interest in recent years, and Damian only complained of crowds and parking, walking, and inflated prices. I loved the whole materialistic mess of it. If I could bottle up the fragrance of roasting chestnuts mixed with taxicab exhaust, I would.

My sister first brought me here when she was sixteen, and I was thirteen. I was utterly overwhelmed and enamored by the assortment of sights, sounds, and smells of the city. It was another world from our humble little house in Suffolk County. My eyes welled with the memories.

Cole and I stood next to an angel, gallantly holding her trumpet in the air as we gaped up at the tree. The crowd was dense, and someone shoved between us to get past. He grabbed my hand. "So, I don't lose you," he said. "Don't pull away."

We watched the skaters below and kept returning to the tree. But mostly, we talked.

We found an Italian restaurant that suited us in Greenwich Village and ate pasta and fish. I ordered a glass of wine, and Cole ordered lemon water.

"You don't drink?" I said.

"I do. Just not often."

On the subway uptown, he asked what my plans were for the gardening article.

"I told Carl I most likely won't do it."

The train stopped, and we stepped off. On the street, Cole pressed me. "Why won't you?"

"I don't want to jump into the unknown. I'm not a risk-taker. I have never been."

He pulled his scarf tighter around his neck. "Maybe it's time you step out of your comfort zone."

"I'm already out of it. I'm here with you, aren't I?"

"And how does it feel?"

I faced forward. "Terrifying."

Cole put his arm around me. "Being scared is okay. It means you're alive."

I let him keep his arm on my shoulders, though I was aware of people passing us, watching for their reactions

"I have to feel scared to be alive?" I said.

"You should feel something. Safe isn't always the best way."

"Cole, I spent my formative years living in fear. Safe is okay. For me."

He slowed his pace, and I matched it. I felt his eyes on me. "My father had an unpredictable temper, and my mother drank too much, her way of dealing with him, and because she was afraid too. That left my sister and me to fend for ourselves. It was exhausting." We walked another block in silence. I wanted to say more. "My sister brought me to see the tree when I was thirteen. It was my first time at Rockefeller Center. She pulled me out of the house and onto the train to Penn Station, and we spent hours staring at the twinkling lights and watching the skaters, surrounded by sounds and music and angels."

"Where were your parents while you were here?"

"When we left, my mother had locked herself in her room, and my father was kicking the door, trying to get at her." I peered up at Cole. "That's why Trisha got me out. She didn't want me to see or hear anymore."

He looked at his feet and shook his head. "I'm sorry. God, that must have been hard."

"It was. But I had Trish. Some people aren't that lucky."

He tightened his arm around me. "Thank you for sharing that." I leaned into him. It felt good. *He* felt good.

We passed the street where the car was parked because we were so involved in a conversation and not paying attention. By ten p.m., we were home and changed into sweats watching television in the den until finally, Cole yawned and checked his watch. His eyes caught mine and held them. "I'm heading to bed. Thank you. I had a great day."

He left, and I listened to him climb the stairs, use the bathroom, and when I could no longer hear him moving, allowed myself to breathe. If anyone saw me spending the day with this kid, they'd think I was crazy. Happy, but crazy.

I got up, feeling restless, not sure what I wanted to do. I walked into the kitchen and saw the box of letters I'd put aside three days ago on the dining table in the adjoining room. Was it only three days ago? Resigned to waiting for sleep, I took the box and brought it to the den. I poured myself a glass of wine and started reading. The first several letters were the typical complaints of husbands not performing or intruding in-laws – the same problems year after year. I sifted through the pile, picking random envelopes, trying to find one or two that might be different or interesting – anything that would spike the responses of my readers.

I finished two full glasses of wine and realized an hour had passed. I scanned twenty letters, all monotonous, and wondered how much longer I should keep up with this line of work. Maybe I should make a change in my life.

Mid-yawn, I picked up the last envelope. I pulled the letter out, and as I read, the blood drained from my face.

Chapter 13

Dear Aunt Emma,

Please help me. I am attracted to a wonderful woman. I've never reacted to someone this way. She is beautiful and kind. In a flannel shirt and jeans, with her gorgeous hair in a careless ponytail and minimal makeup, she is the sexiest woman I've ever seen. And she doesn't know it. She is unaware that her beauty comes from within and radiates out to the world, warming me like the sun I've been missing my whole life.

This is my dilemma: She is older. She won't allow herself to act on her feelings because society tells her it's wrong for a woman to be attracted to a man almost twenty years younger. Her heart tells her otherwise. I can see it written on her beautiful face, in her smile when she thinks I'm not looking.

Can you help me? Can you tell this amazing woman that I want nothing more than to spend time with her? Can you please tell her that the heart doesn't discriminate by age but by desire? Because I don't think she knows. I think she believes in rules and self-denial. And that's no way to live.

-Student of life

I read the words over and over and rested my head back on the couch. When did Cole send this? I looked at the postmark date and saw that it was a week after he and Charlie went back to school after Thanksgiving weekend. Did he think I didn't acknowledge it? He hadn't mentioned sending it. We spent the past three days together, and this letter was never brought up. I thought of his questions when we spent that Friday together weeks ago. *Do you read every letter? Yes, every one.*

I re-read the words. "...her beauty comes from within..."

He showed up at my door, uninvited. And I answered wearing the shirt he left for me to have. A tear trickled down my cheek. It was a done deal the minute I let him in. He knows it too. He was waiting.

I placed the letter back in the box, put the whole package in the bottom drawer of the credenza, and went upstairs.

I stood at the entrance of the guest room, in complete darkness, wanting to go to him, wanting to ignore my reservations. I listened for the deep breathing of sleep but didn't hear anything. Then, he spoke, startling me.

"How long are you going to wait, Heather?"

"Did I wake you?"

"No. I've been waiting for you." His voice sounded warm in the dark.

"How did you know I'd come?"

He turned the blanket back and moved off the bed toward me. "I hoped."

I stood in place, braver because of the wine, but still frightened. I'm out of practice.

"Come here," he whispered and took my face in his palms. He leaned down and kissed me so tenderly, tears formed again, and one escaped. His thumb grazed my cheek, and he kissed my moist eyes closed.

"Don't. Please relax. I won't hurt you." Words he would say to a young virgin, unsure of herself.

He pulled the bottom of my sweatshirt up. I lifted my arms obediently, and he dropped it to the floor. I wore a cami underneath, a thin, silky piece of material that couldn't hide my reaction to him.

The room was lit up only by the hall light outside. Very slowly, he took the cami off me, dropping it onto the sweatshirt. He lowered himself to his knees and kissed my breasts, taking each one in his mouth, and I wanted to fall onto the floor right then with a hot need I'd been repressing since we met. He pulled my sweatpants down. I leaned on his shoulders and stepped out of them. His fingers were at the waist of my undies when I put my hands on his, stopping him.

"Cole. Wait."

He looked up at me, and his blue eyes shimmered in the dark, small pools of light, wanting me.

"I don't look like the girls you've seen."

He started to pull down my underwear, and I put my hand under his chin, forcing him to see me and hear me. "I had a baby."

He took my hand from his chin and kissed my palm.

"Please," I said.

He stared up at me and then pulled himself to stand.

"I don't know about this." I stepped back.

He frowned. "Are you attracted to me?"

"That's not the point."

"It kind of is the point."

I shook my head and crossed my arms over my breasts.

"No?" he said.

"No. Yes. Cole, please." My voice cracked.

"What's wrong?"

"Everything."

He stared at me, waiting for more. I exhaled. "I haven't done this in a long time."

The corner of his mouth lifted. "It's like riding a bike."

My face burned in the dark. "I was never very good at it."

Cole closed the gap between us. He put his hands on my face and kissed me. His lips felt warm, and his tongue played with mine as heat stirred within me. Just a kiss and my insides were on fire.

"You've been riding the wrong bike," he whispered in my ear. My head dropped back, and he nibbled my neck.

"Stop," I managed.

He did. I opened my eyes, trying to ignore my disappointment.

"I have an idea. Let's play a game," Cole said.

"A game?"

He nodded. "Close your eyes."

"No."

"Trust me. Please." It was a whisper.

We held each other's gaze until finally, I closed my eyes.

"Imagine tonight is a gift where you can do anything you want, and then it would be wiped clean." He paused. "If that were true, what would you want to be doing right now?"

I kept my eyes closed and thought about the question. I inhaled and felt calm. Then I opened my eyes.

"This."

Cole's face opened, and he smiled. "Well, then."

Kneeling at my feet, he slowly pulled my undies down my legs. His hands shook, and somehow it made me feel better. I stepped out of them.

He sat back on his heels and gazed at my body while I remained rooted to the floor, hoping my knees would hold me. He ran his fingers along my calves and thighs to my hips, leaving a trail of shivered skin in his wake. He kissed my hips, holding me firmly with both hands and stood. Without a word, he lifted me and laid me down on the bed.

Standing over me, Cole slipped off his boxers. His body was young, robust, virile, and I tried to absorb what was happening. I'd waited so long for someone to make me feel this way, to make me want. He climbed over me, his knees on either side of my legs and leaned over my face. "You're not like the girls I've seen before. You're much more, Heather. You're beautiful."

I covered my face with my hand, embarrassed, ashamed, excited. When he spread my legs and moved down my body, I let him, and my emotions took over, spilling tears of fear and longing onto the pillow. He was gentle but thorough and my thoughts turned from *I shouldn't be doing this* to silent screams of *please don't ever stop*, until my relief poured out in loud cries of ecstasy.

He wouldn't stop, over and over, until I could take it no more and pulled his face up to mine. His lips and chin were moist from my body, and he gave me a small smile. I pulled his mouth to mine and greedily pushed my tongue to his. Cole held me tight, kissing me hard, bringing out a hunger in me alien to anything I'd ever known until finally, we were one.

Wrapped around him, I lost my inhibitions, clutching him, moving in perfect harmony with his body, his beautiful, smooth, muscled, flawless youth, bringing me to life after a long, dull slumber.

We lay side by side. Cole's body glistened with sweat, and I watched his chest rise and fall with his breath. We didn't speak for some time until he rolled over to face me and rested his head on his hand.

"Are you okay?" he said.

"Are you kidding?"

He chuckled low in his throat, and the sound stirred a tingling deep in my belly. He pushed my hair from my forehead and kissed it. "You are everything I imagined you'd be."

I put my hand on his. "You imagined this?"

He nodded. "When I opened the door of my dorm and saw you there. That very moment. I wanted you."

"You told me you just wanted to spend time with me. You said you weren't going to seduce me."

"It's the only lie I'll ever tell you. I promise."

"I'm too old for you."

He picked up my hand and kissed the tips of my fingers. "You're perfect for me."

I pulled my hand away. "This was amazing. We must never mention this happened. Ever. You are going to have to go. Tomorrow."

"I don't understand."

"Cole, this will never work."

"It seemed like it worked pretty well to me. I think you agree."

I didn't answer.

"Do you really want me to leave tomorrow after we just learned we're so compatible?"

I turned to him. "I have a feeling you're this compatible with any woman you'll bed."

He frowned. "I wasn't referring to what just happened. The past days with you have been wonderful. I love your company. I enjoy our conversations." He lightly ran a finger down my nose, over my lips to my chin. "Have you been enjoying my company?"

"More than I should."

He pressed his lips together and pulled his hand from me. "I'd like to stay." He rolled back and faced the ceiling. I nestled myself in the crook of his shoulder. He wrapped his arm around me and held me to him. I closed my eyes and sighed. I wanted him to stay, too.

"Why don't we take each day as it comes and not worry too much about everything," he said.

"That's the first time you've shown your age," I said.

"How so?"

"Young people don't worry about the consequences or the future. But when you get to be my age, it's all you do. Everything leads to something else."

He said nothing at first. "So, what you're saying is the older I get, the less spontaneous I'll be?"

"Yes. You'll have to weigh courses of action before you do anything." I breathed deep. "Of course, do as I say, not as I do."

"Sounds horribly mundane," he said.

"It's not that bad."

"Then I won't get old." He moved his head to look me in the eye. "I wish I would have done this a month ago."

"I'm glad you didn't. I would have pushed you away."

He leaned over and kissed me. "Are you sure?"

I laughed. "So confident. Must be nice."

"No risk, no reward." He smiled. "The rewards can be life-affirming."

"You're full of clichés, aren't you?"

He ignored my remark and moved his fingers to trace my collarbone beneath my skin. Then he kissed my neck and whispered in my ear. "I'm going to show you my age again."

In one fluid motion, he flipped me onto my stomach, and soon I was lost once more.

We went downstairs at dawn, ravenous. I wore his tee-shirt, and he wore boxers. Cole forced me to sit at the table while he made me a feta cheese and tomato omelet. We ate in silence, looking at each other and looking away, a flirty game that made me feel at once shy yet wanting.

"What's with the wicked smile?" I said.

He stood and pulled me up to stand. Then he bent down and lifted me by my legs so I straddled him. He walked into the den and sat me down on the knitting chair beside the Christmas tree we'd cut down only days before, still so fragrant with pine, still waiting for ornaments. On his knees, he spread my legs, so I was completely open and vulnerable to him. Holding my thighs, he said, "This is the purpose of this chair."

It didn't take long before my head fell back, and my ankles were clasped around his shoulders.

We slept intertwined until midday, waking up in the guest room where we started earlier. I opened my eyes to find him looking at me.

"Why didn't you bring me to my bedroom?" I said.

After the knitting chair and the next stint on the den floor earlier, he'd walked me back upstairs. I was so exhausted and spent; I could barely keep my eyes open.

"Have you ever made love to anyone in this room?"

"No."

"That's why."

"I'll let you in on a secret. Before you, I've only been with one man my whole life, and we weren't very adventurous."

He took my hand in his and kissed each of my knuckles.

I covered my eyes with my free hand. "I'll never look at that chair the same way again."

"I hope not. I want you to visualize what I did to you every time you walk in that room."

"I don't need a chair to do that. Or to be in that room for that matter." I looked at him, all humor gone. "It will be something I hold onto."

Cole kissed me.

"You've given me something I've been missing for a long time. Maybe something I've been missing my whole life. I'll always be grateful," I said.

His face darkened. "Don't talk like this is a one-time thing."

"I'm afraid it has to be."

"And I'm sorry to disappoint you, but you're wrong."

"Listen to me." I sat up to face him, no longer concerned I was wearing no clothes. We were so beyond that at this point. "You have your whole life ahead of you. Years and years of experiences. You're young. You're beautiful. And I'm not referring to this." I touched his cheek and gestured to his body. "You're going to fall in love with someone more suitable for you, and you're going to see this for what it is."

He clenched his jaw. "And what is it?"

"This, what we did, was a brief, wonderful exploration of the unknown – for both of us. A taste of taboo. That's all."

He climbed over me and stepped off the bed.

"You know so little about me, Heather. I don't think this is taboo. You're not some dare or conquest I needed to make." He took a breath. "My heart bursts at the sight of you. At the mere thought of you. I have no control over that. I can't turn it off. And I don't think you can, either."

"You have to."

He shook his head. "No. And I don't want to."

"You're only twenty-four. How could you possibly know what you want?"

"When did you meet your husband?"

"That's different," I said.

"How?"

"For one, look where I ended up."

I wanted to deny it, but I hadn't been this happy in a long time, and I wasn't referring to the sex, which was incredible and re-awakened me. It was all of him. It was my disbelief that something so amazing could happen to me. It couldn't last. Nothing this wonderful ever lasts. And…we're at two different points of our lives. It will never work.

He was at my side, pulling me into him. I rested my head on his shoulder, letting my frustrations and fears for what just happened, and what would happen, go unsaid.

"I promise. It's okay," Cole said.

I pulled back. "No promises."

He cupped my cheek with his hand. "Okay."

"What are we going to do?" I said, and by saying this, he knew I was admitting to him that this was not a one-night experience for me, either.

"We're going to shower and get dressed. I'm going to take you to a movie and dinner. And we're going to take each day as it comes. Let's not know now. Let's just be."

We showered together, a quiet, sensual caressing cleanse that ended wrapped in a towel on the bathroom floor. Cole couldn't feed my hunger, it was bottomless, and he was insatiable, answering my needs, filling me over again.

We dragged ourselves out of the house and inhaled a huge tub of buttered popcorn at the movie theater. I couldn't repeat the plot of the movie we saw; he consumed me. We found a restaurant on the opposite shore of Long Island, to prevent any chance of seeing someone I knew. How would I explain what I was doing? We ordered steak, mashed potatoes, and creamed spinach.

Cole nodded toward the wine list. "Do you want a glass of wine or a cocktail?"

I shook my head. "Do you?"

"No."

"Beer?"

"No."

I winked. "Bad experience?" I had my share in college.

"You could say that. Don't let it stop you, though."

"Being with you these past few days has given me a high I could never get from alcohol," I said.

His chin rested on his hand, and he stared, as if in a trance. "I've been looking everywhere for something. Now I know I was looking for you." It was a whisper, but it heated through me like a blaze.

"Take me home," I said.

As we walked through the small dining room after dinner, I caught the disapproving stare of a woman we passed and had to turn away.

We slept in the guest room again. In his arms, I asked him how long he was planning to stay. He paused before answering. "I'll leave before Charlie gets home. I have to see my sister."

It felt so natural wrapped within him. He woke me from sleep, and I responded to his need with my own. My body was experiencing feelings dormant for so long. Either my memory failed me, or I'd never enjoyed this intense, satisfying lovemaking in all my years of marriage. How could anyone ever make me feel this way again? This was a fleeting affair for him. If he didn't know it yet, he would.

In the morning, I went to the bathroom to brush my teeth and returned to bed as Cole woke up. He opened his arms, and I fit myself to his frame.

"Morning," he said and kissed my nose.

"Morning sleepyhead. What do you want to do today?"

He yawned and let me go so he could climb off the bed. He put his finger up and disappeared. A few minutes later, he returned smelling minty. I sat up, and he sat next to me, giving me a full kiss.

"Better," he said.

I giggled, feeling young and vibrant. Until I looked in a mirror, I felt twenty-years-old again. Cole pointed to my heart. "I want to do you today. Nothing more."

He pushed me back and lay on top of me. Propped on his elbows, he looked down, his thumbs caressing my temples. I let out a quiet moan and closed my eyes. When I opened them, he was watching me.

"What?" I said.

His eyes circled my face, and I followed his gaze until they were back on mine. "You take my breath away."

"Please." I snorted.

"Hey. You do," he whispered.

My hand moved from his face, grazing the bandage above his eye to his shoulder. I touched a scar near his collarbone. "How did you get this?" I said.

"A fight."

"A fight? You're a fighter?"

"When I have to be."

"I don't think Charlie ever fought," I said.

"He's a lucky boy."

I lifted Cole's arm and touched his elbow, running my fingers over a rough, jagged line across the bone.

"How did you get this?"

"This one was from a bike accident. I was seven and was skidding on dirt for fun with my friends. Wiped out and walked home bloody."

I shivered.

"Are you monitoring my scars?"

"I'm just curious. I've seen a lot of you, and I wanted to know."

He lifted off me and bent his left leg. "Did you notice this one?" He pointed to a long, thick line down the inner calf.

"Of course."

He laid back over me, and I held him close.

"I kicked my leg through the storm door window. Blood everywhere," he said.

"Why?"

"I was angry."

My hands ran through his hair, and it fell back over his forehead. "You must have made your parents crazy."

"You have no idea." He kissed me deeply. "You have no scars?"

I shook my head. "I've been careful my whole life."

"That's not good."

My hands traveled down the corded muscles of his back, and he rested his head on my shoulder. "Do you have any more?" I said.

"None that are visible," he answered into my skin.

I gently bit his shoulder, and he writhed.

"What does your tattoo say?" I said.

I referred to the scripted ink along the inside of his left bicep in a language unfamiliar to me.

"It says, let's play a game."

I punched him lightly on his shoulder, and he laughed.

"Seriously. Tell me."

"It translates to: Don't dwell in the past, don't dream of the future, concentrate the mind on the present moment." He held my eyes, and I understood that *Let's play a game* carries the same meaning. Don't think about tomorrow or yesterday. Today is what counts.

"Who said that?"

"It's a Buddhist saying."

"It's good," I said.

He chuckled. "No tats for you?"

I shook my head. "I used to want one, but I never had the nerve. I'm afraid."

"Afraid of what?"

I thought about it. "Choosing one. The permanency. The pain of getting it. Regret afterward. Everything."

"You worry. It's just a tattoo."

"I know."

He closed his eyes, and I watched him, wondering what kind of past he'd had that already, at this young age, he curtailed his drinking and had scars from fights and angry outbursts. He didn't act like a violent person. I used to live with one, so I had experience. Maybe he was an alcoholic? So young? His eyes opened, and he caught me staring. Wordlessly, he pulled me close and hugged me. *You're a complex man, Mr. Cole Prue.*

I didn't want to leave the bed, this oasis from my life, but I'd exerted so much of myself physically, my stomach screamed with hunger. I'm sure Cole had to have felt the same way, though he never voiced it.

I finally pulled myself from his side and stood at the door, wearing nothing but a smile. He lay in bed, propped up on pillows, his chest smooth and tantalizing.

"Do you shave your chest?" I said.

"We're not a hairy people."

I didn't go further. Cole didn't have much hair on his body. His legs had some, and his pelvic area, but the rest of him was marble. "I have to eat," I said, leaning my head against the door. "Do you want to go out and grab something?"

"I want to spend every minute we have wearing as little as possible until I have to leave."

"That might be hard." I stepped from the frame. "But not impossible."

"That's my girl."

I went to my bedroom to put on sweatpants and a long-sleeve tee. I wrapped my sexed-up hair in a messy bun and practically skipped downstairs.

I lit the flame on the stove and laid out bread and cheese while the pan heated. As I was slicing tomatoes for grilled cheese sandwiches, I heard someone walk in the front door and froze. *Please, God, let it not be Charlie.* What the hell would he think?

Chapter 14

Damian walked into the kitchen as I caught my breath. Even worse than Charlie, I thought, was my husband seeing me here with Cole.

"What are you doing here?" I prayed Cole stayed upstairs until he left.

"I thought I'd stop by and drop this off." He laid the water bill with a check on the counter, his eyes on the pan.

"Who's here? There's a car outside."

"Cole," I said, bracing for impact.

"Is Charlie home?"

"He's still at Kate's."

"So, why is his roommate here?"

I took a deep breath, and my hand shook as I turned off the flame. "We're having a passionate affair."

Damian started to laugh, but then paused and tilted his head as if studying me. I held my breath. Finally, he shook his head and sorted through the rest of my mail. "Passionate? You?" He snorted a humorless laugh. "I doubt the kid is into cold fish."

Tears sprang to my eyes as feelings of neglect and anger resurfaced. I turned and wiped them with the back of my hand. "Can you please leave?"

"Mr. Harrison, I didn't hear you come in," Cole said, and I swallowed a gasp. How long had he been downstairs? He wore faded jeans and a tee-shirt, his hair neatly combed.

"Cole." Damian shook his hand. "What brings you here?"

"I stopped by to see Mrs. Harrison."

Damian glanced from Cole to me. I couldn't read his expression. "How long are you staying?"

"Not long," Cole said. "How long will you be staying, Mr. Harrison?"

"This is my house, son," he said to Cole, though his eyes were still on me.

"Oh. I wasn't aware since you live somewhere else. How is Genna, by the way? Please send her my regards."

I stared at the sliced tomatoes, wishing I could just sink right into the floor and disappear.

"Right. She's well. I'll tell her. Heather, walk me to the door." Damian turned and left the kitchen.

I avoided Cole's face as I followed Damian to the foyer. With his hand on the knob, he spun around to me. "What the fuck is going on?"

My head whipped back as if his words physically pushed me. I felt ashamed at that moment, but also very angry. Angry that this man, who broke my heart, could still make me feel these emotions. Or, did I feel them because I knew what I was doing was so wrong?

I needed to keep this from my son. So, I did what I thought was best. I lied. "He came over to thank me for having him on Thanksgiving. He's visiting a friend he met here."

Damian stared at me, probably trying to decide whether to believe me. I was always truthful when we were married. Lying was his forte.

Just leave. Please leave, I thought to myself.

"Have Charlie call me when he gets home," he said.

I nodded and locked the door behind him. My head rested against the wood as the tension left my body. What if he would have walked in an hour earlier? Or yesterday? I thought of Cole and me in the den. It would have been a disaster. I'd been completely reckless this week.

Back in the kitchen, I turned on the stove.

"He walks into your house at will?" Cole spoke through gritted teeth. I was surprised at the rage I saw on his face. I was surrounded by anger today. What the hell happened?

"It's technically his house. His name is on the mortgage." I placed the bread onto the sizzling butter in the pan.

Cole grabbed my arm and turned me to him. "Heather, he can't do that."

"He can, and he does."

"That's bullshit."

"I don't want to talk about it, and it's not your business." I went back to the stove and finished the sandwiches in silence.

At the table, Cole stared at me. "He left you. He has no right."

"He has every right. It's his house. He still pays most of the bills," I said.

We ate while I tried to temper my emotions. Of course, I was frustrated by Damian's behavior. Did I feel beholden to him because, for years, he's reminded me that he paid for almost everything I touch? Yes. I hated my predicament, but until now, I had little cause to care if he walked in uninvited. I didn't have anything to lose aside from self-respect. And, in the back of my mind, there was the tiny possibility he'd come back to me. Until this week, it was a possibility I would have accepted.

Cole reached his hand to mine and held it. My eyes filled. I was exhausted from lack of sleep, and feeling emotional after Damian intruded into my perfect, very wrong week.

"Thank you for the sandwich," he said.

I nodded and said nothing while he cleared the table, washed the dishes, and put them away. He put the hot pan into the sink and filled it with water. While the faucet ran, he turned around. "I have to do something today."

"What are you going to do?" I said. Did my disappointment show? What happened to him wanting to stay in bed?

"I'm going to fix this problem."

"Please tell me you're not going to find him." I thought of his scars. Was this how they happened?

Cole turned back around, washed the pan, and dried it before laying it clean back on the stove. He walked to me and leaned over, resting one hand on the table and one on the back of my chair.

"As much as I'd like to, no, I'm not going to find him. I am going out for a little while. You'll be okay?"

"Of course. Would you like me to go with you?"

He leaned over to kiss me; his face still taut with anger. "No. You need rest. I won't be long."

"Wait. Take my cell number. Just in case you need to reach me. You don't know the area."

He pulled his cell from his pocket and typed in my number. Then he kissed me again. "I have GPS, but I'm glad to have your number anyway," he whispered.

He left me wondering what he was doing. I didn't ask because I wasn't sure I wanted to know. I crawled onto the couch and stared at the ceiling, trying to figure my way out of this. But when I thought about sending Cole home and saying goodbye, something in my chest hurt. No matter how many rules I must've been breaking, I'd never felt so damn good.

As exhausted as I was, I took the box Carl sent me from the dining room credenza and read more letters. I held onto Cole's letter, re-reading it and tearing up. What would I do? How the hell could this possibly end well?

I must have fallen asleep because I woke up sometime later when Cole dropped beside me on the couch and pushed my hair from my face. He kissed me gently on my eyes, over my nose, to my cheeks and nibbled on my chin. I grabbed him, still groggy from sleep, and pulled him close. When I finally let him go, he rested over me playing with my hair, propped on the pillow.

"I see you got my letter," he said.

I nodded. "I'm not sure how to answer it."

He smiled. "You already did."

"What time is it?"

"Three o'clock."

"You were gone a long time."

He ran his finger down my face to my neck. He touched some part of me always, connecting us, and it calmed me. He was so physical and adoring. It was intoxicating.

"I've been back for an hour." He reached into his pocket and pulled out a key imprinted with flowers. "This is your new house key. It fits in your new locks on the front and back doors."

I took the offered key. "You replaced the locks in my doors?"

He nodded. "You sleep like a rock."

"Where did you find the tools to do it?" I said.

"I bought them. They're in your garage."

"You're handy, and you can dance. You'll be married in no time."

He stared at me.

"Thank you," I said.

He nodded.

"I need to get a key for Charlie and Dottie."

"Dottie?"

"We have each other's keys in case we lock ourselves out."

"Ah, well," he reached into his pocket again and pulled out two more non-descript keys, "you probably want these, too."

I placed the three keys on the coffee table and raised my arms in a stretch. Cole reached up and held my wrists over my head. He tightened his grip, and I couldn't move. I didn't try too hard, either. He kept me in place with one hand while lifting my shirt with the other. In moments, all troubles from this morning evaporated.

I lost track of time, ignoring all responsibilities and not minding a bit. Trisha called me on Tuesday, Cole's fifth day at my house. I chatted with my sister, allowing her to rant about all that was wrong with her in-laws. Toward the end of our conversation, she told me I sounded different.

"Different how?" I said.

"I don't know. You sound relaxed, zen-like. Are you drunk?"

"No, Trish. It's noon on Tuesday."

"So? Who's there to tell you you can't? Are you high?"

I would have laughed, but I knew she wasn't joking. "Call me when you get home."

"Fine. But it sounds like you're having a better week than I am," she said.

You have no idea, sister.

Charlie called me Wednesday afternoon. Cole had just returned from a hike, and I put my finger over my lips when he walked into the kitchen, holding a bag in his hand. He nodded, seeing me on the phone, took out a pot, filled it with water, put it on the stove, and went upstairs.

"How is your visit with Kate going?" I paced the den and living room, retracing steps, back and forth.

"It's going okay," he said. "Her parents are pretty cool. She has a younger brother who's a little annoying, but I'm dealing."

I laughed. "You're not used to a sibling."

"Kind of glad I don't have one."

I paused. No, you would have liked it, I thought. "I can't wait to see you. When will you be home?"

"Friday. The train leaves here at eleven. I'll be in Penn Station by four and let you know what time to come get me."

"Great."

"Did Cole reach out to you?" Charlie said.

I froze in my tracks. "Why?"

"He's on Long Island. Remember that shop-girl he met when he was down with us last? He's visiting her. He mentioned he would stop over to say hi to you."

I squeezed my eyes shut. Damian saw him here. He'd tell Charlie. "He did stop by, come to think of it. The same day your father stopped over."

"Okay. Cool. I texted him earlier, but he hasn't gotten back to me. I told him if he's still on Long Island when I get home, I have to meet her."

I'd covered the entire lower level of the house three times and was ready to talk about something else.

"Tell me more about Kate. You must be serious about her to be at her house."

"Maybe."

Cole walked downstairs, his hair wet from the shower, and combed back. Seeing me still on the phone, he went to the fridge and pulled out the bag he put in a few minutes ago.

"I'll talk to you when I get home," Charlie said. "Lots of ears here, if you know what I mean."

"You're referring to the annoying brother, I assume."

"Bingo."

I laughed again. "Okay, baby. See you on Friday. Can't wait. I love you."

I disconnected the call and turned to find Cole at the kitchen door, leaning on the frame like he does, his hand loosely in his pocket.

"What?" I said.

"It sounds nice. Hearing you say I love you. You make it sound…" He shrugged and bit his lower lip.

Love? Oh no.

"What's in the bag?" I said, diverting the focus from a subject I refused to touch.

"Chicken."

"What are we making?"

"I'm making you Chicken Pad Thai."

"You're kidding."

"I'm not." His eyes shone. "I found rice noodles in the store."

He'd already had water boiling on the stove. He dropped the rice noodles into the water, and I watched while he mixed brown sugar, soy sauce, chicken stock, chili, tamarind sauce, and ground white pepper in a bowl. Putting that aside, he strained the noodles. Then he cut the chicken breasts into small pieces and coated them in corn starch and soy sauce while waiting for my frying pan to get hot. He fried up the chicken pieces in vegetable oil, garlic, and red chilies, adding chicken stock after a few minutes.

He appeared content and wore a half-smile as he put this together. I stared at the tendons in his arms as he manipulated the pan to move the chicken, the thick curl of hair on his neck while he leaned over the stove. Forget the food – he was a feast for my senses, this man.

Finally, he put the noodles into the pan with the chicken and tossed the whole thing for less than a minute. I could have watched him all day.

"I couldn't find bean sprouts, or this would have tasted authentic," he said.

Standing next to him at the stove, I inhaled the delectable aroma. "Smells delicious."

"It does, doesn't it? Let's eat."

I took out two bowls, and he filled them. We sat at the kitchen table. I took a bite and sat back. "This is amazing. Where'd you learn how to make this?"

He smiled as he speared a piece of chicken. "I lived with a family for a while in Thailand. The woman of the house taught me to cook. She was patient and didn't speak English. It was interesting."

"How did you come to live with a family? Did your parents set it up?"

"No, I didn't even expect to be in Thailand. I just ended up there."

"So, you had no plan when you left home to travel?"

"Nope." He put a large forkful into his mouth.

"That's crazy," I said. "Or brave."

He shrugged and chewed.

"How long did you live with this family?"

He paused while he swallowed his food. "A month or so."

"Why?" I said. I couldn't fathom showing up at someone's door and staying there.

"It was an accident. I was walking through an open farmer's market and saw a couple of guys harassing a girl. She needed help, so I got involved."

"What do you mean involved?"

"Let's just say they left her pretty quickly when I grabbed one of them by the neck until he turned colors. She was crying and shaken up, so I offered to walk her home."

"How old was she?"

"Couldn't have been more than fourteen. She carried this huge basket on her back. It was impressive. Anyway, when we got to her house, more like a hut, she told her mother what happened. The next thing I knew, I was sitting at their table, eating dinner with them. I ended up fixing a part of her roof, and well," he shrugged again as if this would make sense to me. "I stayed overnight because it was dark when I finished, and kept staying over, kept fixing stuff."

I was mesmerized. "Where was the woman's husband?"

"Working in China. I never saw him."

"He didn't come home the entire time you were there?"

Cole shook his head, focused on the food, while I focused on him.

"You had an affair with the woman."

He took a breath and stood. I thought I upset him until I realized he was getting two bottles of beer from the refrigerator.

"I didn't have an affair with anyone while I was there," he said.

"Then, I don't understand."

He sighed. "I liked it there. I helped these women with tasks that were difficult for them, and in exchange, they let me stay, taught me how to cook and run a farm, things I had not experienced. We took long walks around her property after dinner. She grew rice. It was interesting."

"How did you understand her if neither of you spoke each other's language?"

"Words are only one way to communicate." He paused. "I told her about my life."

"What did you tell her?" I said.

He looked at me. "Everything."

I held his eyes and felt pangs of envy that the woman spent this solitary time with him.

"What was her name?" I said.

"Malee."

I brought my hand to his neck and slid my fingers down the thin rope to the stone against his chest. "Did Malee give you this?" I whispered.

He covered my hand with his and nodded. "It's a bloodstone. Her daughter translated the meaning for me. It has calming properties, especially in challenging situations. I wear it as a reminder of my time there."

There's so much I wanted to know about the man sitting at my table. Somehow, I suspected I wasn't going to get much from him. Still, I said, "What situations have you faced?" As the words left my lips, I knew. He told Malee about his sister, Brynn. But there was more.

He put the stone back under his shirt and leaned over to kiss me. "It's a rock. Don't overthink it. Please eat."

He lifted his bottle. I did the same. "To a week I will hold in my heart forever," he said.

"As will I," I whispered.

We got tipsy and finished every morsel of food he'd prepared. While cleaning up, Cole asked how Charlie was doing at Kate's.

"I think he's looking to get out of there. Kate has a little brother. He's not used to siblings. He said he texted you, but you didn't respond."

Cole nodded. "Okay, I'll answer him. He asked about my new interest. I call you Sondra."

"When you went to the mall last month, was it your plan to tell Charlie you met someone?"

"It just worked out that way." He grinned. "My sister loved the sweatshirt."

"What will you tell him?" I said.

"Who?"

"What will you tell Charlie about your new interest?"

He put down his towel. "The truth. That I'm crazy about her."

I shut the faucet and stared down the sink. "Be careful."

"Why? It's how I feel."

I shook my head. "Lust is not love, Cole. Don't confuse them."

"I know the difference."

He turned me to him and, with his fingers, lifted my chin to see his eyes as I'd done to him when he knelt before me on the guest room floor what seemed like so long ago. He leaned down and kissed me tenderly.

I grabbed him around his neck and burrowed my face in his shoulder, hiding my worry. This can only end badly, I thought.

"We have a day and a half left," he said, resting his chin on my head. "Let's spend it in bed and get to know each other."

"I don't think there's anything we don't know about each other at this point."

"That's where you're wrong. We've only glimpsed the tip of the iceberg."

We spent the next thirty-six hours in bed, getting out only for bathroom visits, the occasional shower, and nourishment. I never tired of Cole reaching for me and at points, held him so tightly, I'd hoped we'd fuse into each other. We talked for hours, sharing about ourselves.

"Tell me more about what it was like growing up," he said.

"My parents were unhappy. My father screamed a lot, often without warning. Something that didn't bother him yesterday would put him over the edge today. We didn't know how to behave or what to say. We walked on eggshells around him. Trisha was brave. More so than me. She stood up for herself."

He ran his fingers through my hair as he listened. "Did it help?"

"I think it helped her feel stronger. Even when he went at her. She took it. I envied her. I learned to become very agreeable and never talked back. I thought if I became invisible, he wouldn't notice me. It helped. My sister took the brunt of his anger."

"She was tough," he said.

"She was protecting me. It's why I deal with her outbursts. She needs to do it sometimes. Charlie doesn't get it. But then, he doesn't know much about that part of my life. I don't like to relive it. It's painful to talk about."

"You're talking about it to me."

"I know. I'm not sure why. Something about you makes me feel…protected. Unjudged."

I closed my eyes, feeling soothed by his fingers in my hair and on my skin. The scenes that came to mind while talking about my childhood still hurt.

"So…college," Cole said, making me open my eyes and continue.

"I met Damian at the end of my freshman year. He was my escape. We became a couple, and I never looked back. He didn't yell or have an addiction problem. That was my criteria in a mate. Sad, right?"

"You were young," Cole said.

"Yeah, well. It turned out I should have been more careful. We were happy for a few years. He started to go out with friends on the weekends. At twenty-three, he was a father, and the social life, or lack of, didn't sit well with him. We didn't communicate. He went out. I stayed home. Sometimes, I'd be so angry and hurt I wouldn't talk to him for days, but I'd never expressed my feelings because if he left, I'd have nowhere else to go but back to my parents. And no way was that happening. So, I kept my mouth shut, cooked, cleaned, and agreed with whatever he said. No matter what I thought. That's not the basis of a marriage. That's just me escaping one type of hell for another."

Cole's forehead wrinkled with concern. He brought me to his chest, and I rested my cheek on his skin, felt his pulse, and listened to the noises coming from his stomach, sounds that brought me solace.

"It wasn't Damian's fault. He did the best he could under the circumstances. He was young, too. He stayed with me for Charlie, I think, though we do have a few nice memories."

"What about Trisha?"

"She has a good marriage. Or she did. Adam loves her, with all her loud brashness. She's colorful and interesting."

"So are you," Cole said, tapping my shoulder.

I ignored him. I knew the truth.

In our warm, bubbled cocoon, I would have happily stayed with Cole forever. After making love at dawn, the sky a pale pink through the window, we both felt the end near. Charlie would be home in a few hours, and reality would replace this brief, inexplicable gift we'd discovered in each other. Both facing the window, Cole held me in his arms and hummed softly in my ear, a tune for only us, he said, until I fell back to sleep.

Friday afternoon arrived quickly. Charlie called at four pm, asking me to pick him up from the station in town at six. Cole and I showered one last time and dried each other without words. We dressed and went downstairs. Standing at the door, facing each other, he put his hand against my cheek and smiled.

"Thank you," he said.

"No. Thank you. You brought me to life."

He kissed me lightly on my lips and hugged me tight. I breathed him in deeply and then gently pushed him away. "Go. Be safe," I said.

I watched him walk down the driveway, his small duffel over his broad shoulder. At his car, he turned to me. "I left you something in the den." Then he smiled again, his beautiful face lighting me up inside.

It would have been the perfect ending to a perfect week if my ex-husband hadn't driven past us as Cole was getting into his car.

I walked through the house to make sure there was no lingering remnant of proof that he'd been here. In the den, I looked at the knitting chair and saw a small, wrapped package on the seat. I sat on the chair, with a private, wanting smile and opened the gift. It was a small padlock and key.

I went upstairs to change the bedding in the guest room, holding the sheets to my nose, breathing in our mixed scents before reluctantly putting them into the washing machine. As I drove to pick up my son, I hadn't even thought to worry about what Damian would think. And for the moment, I couldn't care less.

Charlie talked at length about Kate on the drive home from the train, glowing as he did. I felt a stab of worry that he was getting too involved with someone so early. I hoped this girl wouldn't distract him from his schoolwork.

I voiced my concern when he finally stopped talking about her.

"I'm eighteen, Mom! At some point, you'll have to trust that I know what I'm doing. God!" He turned away in a huff.

"You're right. But eighteen or eighty, I'm still your mother, and I'll always worry."

"Great." He sighed and rolled his eyes. I'd put a damper on his high with my parental nagging. How quickly we fell back into our regular routine.

We ate dinner, and then he called Damian to tell him he was home, and they made plans to see each other on Sunday. Charlie went out with some friends as I climbed into bed. I gave him his new key, and he didn't flinch, didn't ask why I changed the locks, just took it, dumped the old one, and slid it onto his keychain.

Alone, I replayed the entire week I'd spent with Cole, relishing every moment, and wondering if I would ever see him again, make love to him, or share private conversations. I shared so much of myself, of my life, my past. More than I've ever shared with anyone but Damian. And even Damian didn't know the details of what makes me, me. Cole listened without judgment and held me when I stopped talking. I felt lighter, somehow. He was my own private, sexy therapist. My heart was full as I fell asleep.

Chapter 15

I received a text from Cole. *How's my knitting chair? xo*

He called me on my cell phone at dawn on Christmas morning. I held my phone close under the covers. The gray sky outside my window had me nestle even further under my down comforter, warding off the chilly air in the room.

"Merry Christmas," he said softly in my ear.

"Merry Christmas," I whispered back.

"Mmm. I love that sexy morning voice. I wish I were right next to you."

I smiled into my pillow. "Stop. I need to focus on cooking for a houseful of people today. I can't be thinking of you."

He sighed. "I have to figure out how I can see you again. I'm in agony here. All I can think about is the week we spent alone."

"You can't come back here." I hated being so logical. "That was a dangerous stunt we played. And I won't be responsible for you not doing well."

"Heather, I can see you *and* go to school. I sit in the library for most of my free time. There is nothing for me here. This is not my concern."

I closed my eyes and pinched the bridge of my nose. Cole should have everything he needs there and I shouldn't be a part of his world. "What do you have planned for today?"

"My parents are entertaining a group of people they can hardly stand. I'm taking my sister ice skating before dinner. She starts school in a week, and she has every day planned for me."

I smiled, thinking of the thirteen-year-old girl, enamored with her older brother, monopolizing his time. I could hardly blame her. If I could, I'd do the same thing.

"Has Damian given you any trouble about the locks?" Cole asked.

"No. He won't do that while Charlie is home."

"Good. Let me know if he does. I promise I'll make it so he doesn't upset you again."

I squeezed my eyes shut. I don't want Cole feeling like he needs to protect me.

"Heather."

"Okay. I'm sure there'll be no problem. Have a nice Christmas, Cole," I said quietly, not wanting Charlie to hear me talking.

"You, too."

I went to Dottie's a few days after Christmas, after her children left. She loved the pink cowboy boots I bought for her and made me promise to go line dancing with her on Friday.

So, three days later, she drove us to a western bar a few towns over, a place I never knew existed. Dottie wore her boots (they looked great with dark jeans), and I wore the navy blouse she'd given me, which offset my faded jeans.

I sat out the first several dances, so I could have a few cocktails and see what line dancing was all about. Dottie appeared comfortable out there, moving in time with the group. With her thumbs hooked into her belt loops, her face flushed with contentment. I thought about the year her husband passed away. I'd spent a lot of time with her in the months after he died, keeping her company while Charlie was at school, reluctantly leaving to meet his bus. She and George had a healthy marriage, and she was despondent naturally. I remember thinking while I sat with her, how I hoped I'd never be alone, preferring my loveless marriage over my own company. Now, six years later, my friend was in the center of a dance floor, having a wonderful time.

Dottie lost patience by the fourth or fifth song and pulled me onto the dance floor.

"Watch me. It's easy," she yelled in my ear. She was perspiring, and her eyes twinkled, making me laugh.

It took me a few tries, but I eventually learned the steps to the dance around me, and I stayed on the floor for two more songs before escaping back to the bar. I downed a glass of water and watched the group on the floor move as one, my friend right there in it. A middle-aged man in full western gear and cowboy hat approached me.

"You're new here," he said. He held a bottle of beer.

"My girlfriend made me come." I kept my eye on Dottie.

"Are you having fun?"

I looked at him. "I am," I said, realizing it was true. "I don't know what I'm doing, but it's a good time."

He smiled, and his long mustache rose. "You don't have to know what you're doing to have a good time, honey."

Ain't that the truth.

Dottie walked off the floor and to me. "Hey, Don," she said. "This is Heather."

"This your friend, Dot? It's nice to meet you, Heather. You make sure you come back now." He sauntered off, leaving Dottie and I alone.

"He's a regular." She raised her hand to catch the bartender's attention.

"Looks like you are, too."

The bartender placed an ice water in front of her.

"I like it here. I get to put my lessons to good use. What do you think? Want to go home?"

"Let's stay a little longer," I said.

She smiled wide. "Well, okay."

The third week in January, a week before his vacation ended, I drove Charlie back to school. I didn't want to, but he wanted to see Kate and introduce us. I was leaving in a few days for a writing conference in Seattle, so I agreed to take him back early. Wrapped in coats and scarves, I navigated the car through light snow until we got to campus on Wednesday evening. We had dinner alone, and Charlie stayed at the hotel with me even though the university was open. Kate arrived the next afternoon and called Charlie from her dorm. We picked her up, and I treated them to dinner at an Italian restaurant in town.

Kate was a pretty girl, brown hair and eyes, and a sprinkle of light brown freckles across her nose that scrunched every time she laughed, which was often. My son couldn't take his eyes off her.

They held hands almost the entire meal. I chalked off their uncontrollable need to touch each other to the fact that they'd been apart for three weeks. As I ate, I tried not to compare my behavior the week I was with Cole to these two teens. Did I behave the same adolescent way? What I couldn't get my head around was the idea of Charlie having sex with this girl. With any girl. I still saw the little boy with skinned knees who cried for me on the first day of kindergarten.

Over dessert, Kate began to relax, now that she survived dinner. "Kate, your parents don't mind that you're here a little early from break?" I asked.

"Not really. They like, really love Charlie. I mean, they're cool with me hanging out with him."

Take out the stilted conversation and the lack of experience or profound thoughts and she was lovely. Her depth would form through life. I hoped.

I stayed at the hotel one more night, knowing my son and his girlfriend preferred to spend time alone before the rigors of classes began for the second semester. They met me for breakfast at the small diner next to the hotel, the one where Cole had his breakfast date when I was up on parents' weekend. Afterward, Charlie walked me to my car. I put my hands on his widening shoulders. He was taller than me by a few inches. "Stay focused. Please."

He smiled, a happy boy in new love. "Of course. Thanks, Mom. I'll call you Sunday."

"Call my cell. I'll be in Seattle through Wednesday for the writing conference."

"Right. I forgot. Have a good trip."

He allowed me a more prolonged hug than usual, and I tried to commit it to memory, not knowing when I'd get one again. My boy. My man-boy.

I drove through town and back toward 91. I didn't ask about Cole. Didn't ask when he was returning to school, was he already back, or did he stay home. The last time we spoke, New Year's Eve, was seventeen days ago. When we hung up, I thought perhaps it would be the last I heard from him. I prayed he'd leave me alone so I could be free from worry and guilt and desire. He'd find someone perfect for him. It was just a matter of time.

Driving along the highway, my thoughts continued to return to him. I wondered what he was doing, who he was spending time with, if he thought of our time together as often as I did. I sighed and tightened my grip on the steering wheel. I'm as childish as Kate, acting like a schoolgirl with a crush.

I pulled into my driveway, my mind whirring with thoughts. No more. No more with Cole. Move on, Heather. But the wanting...I couldn't stop it.

I checked into the hotel in Seattle on Sunday evening. I decided to do some work, grateful for the upcoming busy days. An hour later, I re-read my presentation, satisfied with its message, and shut my computer down. Tomorrow, I would spend the day listening in on other seminars and seeing the writer friends I'd missed during my last conference. The only one I had spent time with was my mentor and friend, John.

I turned on the television but couldn't find anything of interest, so half an hour later, I turned it off. I was on New York time and should have felt tired, but I was restless from sitting most of the day and not ready for sleep. Still dressed in jeans and blouse, I went downstairs to the hotel bar, sat at an available stool, and ordered a Cosmo. I played with my phone so I wouldn't look lonely and was startled to hear my name.

I looked up to see John walking toward me.

"I thought it was you," he said and grinned.

"John." I stood and gave him a quick hug before returning to my seat. I patted the stool beside me, and he took it. "I was hoping to see you here."

"I never miss one," he said. "I missed you in Cleveland."

"Charlie came home for the holiday, and I wanted to spend time with him."

"Ah, yes, of course. He's doing well, I hope."

"He loves it. I just brought him back. How's your daughter, Sarah?" I asked.

"Enjoying married life. No pregnancy news yet, much to my wife's dismay."

"Baby? Don't rush her. Let her be married and have fun before starting a family." I sipped my drink.

"That's what I tell Joann, but she won't listen. She's ready to be a grandmother." He shook his head. "Not me. No one should be a grandparent before sixty."

"Get a dog," I said.

He looked at me. "We have two."

We shared a laugh, and John ordered a beer for himself. He

pointed at my near-empty glass, and I nodded that I'd take another. I had a free day tomorrow so I could sleep in.

"Something's different about you," he said.

"How do you mean?"

"The last time we saw each other in September, you looked sad."

"I did?"

He nodded. "You had a lot going on between Charlie's departure to school and your recent separation." He turned fully to me. "You're glowing. You've met someone."

I leaned back, surprised.

"What? I'm attuned to women. I'm surrounded by them at home," John said.

I sipped my new drink. It went down like water. Delish.

"So, you did meet someone."

"Yes."

"That's wonderful, Heather." He looked genuinely pleased. "Is it serious? Already?"

I chuckled. "Hell, no. In fact, it was a quick, torrid affair. And it's over."

He appeared confused. "I don't get it. Is he married?"

"I would never do that. Don't you know me at all?" I said.

"I see you a handful of times a year. I'm sure there's a lot I don't know."

I finished the Cosmo, feeling a warmth run through me as I thought of Cole. "No. Not a married man. I don't want to say anymore."

He swiveled back to face the bar. "Fine. For the record, whatever it was looks really good on you." He raised his hand to signal the bartender for another. "When do you speak?"

"Tuesday. You?" I said.

"Tomorrow. Two o'clock in the Willow Room."

"Perfect." I accepted a third drink and finished it while John talked about his work and his kids. When I slid off the bar chair, I felt the effects of the alcohol. That third glass was so not necessary. "I'll see you tomorrow at two," I said. Was I slurring?

"Are you okay?" John put his hand out to steady me.

"I'm good. I need a bed." I waved as I stepped away. "Good to see you. Sweet dreams."

"You too, Heather."

I focused on the elevators, aiming for the center doors when my phone chimed a text. I stopped where I was to try to read it. It was from Cole. I smiled and looked around the near-empty lounge and back at my phone.

I hear you're in Seattle. Take a picture of yourself on the Space Needle for me.

He really was so sweet, I thought. I texted him back. *If you want a picture, come take it yourself.*

I dropped my phone in my pocket and giggled as I stepped onto the elevator.

The next thing I knew, the winter sun peeked through my exposed window. I rolled over in the bed and smacked my lips. My mouth tasted of dirty socks. My head pounded as I peed and brushed my teeth. I don't recall stripping out of my clothes and into pajamas, but here I was, in my pj's. Impressive, Heather. With one eye closed to manage the pain in my head, I put on sweats, threw my hair in a loose ponytail, and went down to the lobby to get a cup of coffee from the complimentary breakfast lounge.

I rested my head against the elevator wall on the ride down. How does Trisha do this?

Thankfully, it was early enough that the speakers and guests for the conference hadn't yet assembled for the day. Not long from now, this lobby would be jam-packed with people. I filled a large paper cup with coffee and went to sneak back to my room. I passed some familiar faces at the front desk, checking in to the hotel. In no mood to chat, I kept my head down and waited alone for the elevator, stepping in carefully when the doors opened. As they closed, an arm pushed in and re-opened them.

At first, I thought I was still drunk. I blinked and again saw him. Standing in front of the elevator was Cole, in all his glorious self. He was wearing worn jeans and a sage sweater that somehow made his eyes look more green than blue. Over his arm was a thick canvas coat.

"Going up?" he said.

I nodded, too stunned to speak. He stepped in, and the doors closed. We rode the elevator in silence to my floor, each staring ahead. His musky scent filled the small space. I struggled with an internal dilemma of wanting to touch him and wanting to push him out of this car onto another floor, away from me. The doors opened, and he followed me into the hall and to my room.

My hand shook as I tried to fit the card in the slot over the doorknob. He put his hand over mine from behind, and we slid it in together. We stepped into the room. He closed the door, and I turned to him. "Why are you here?"

His smile faltered for a fraction of a second and then recovered. "I'm here to take a picture of you on the Space Needle."

"What are you talking about?" Why did that sound familiar?

He frowned. "Last night, you texted me back. I took it as an invitation."

"To come here?" My headache strengthened.

He took out his phone and showed me our exchange. I felt woozy. Cole gently led me to the bed. "Are you okay? You look a bit green."

I nodded and then shook my head before I ran to the bathroom, where I threw up the vodka, cranberry juice, and bile. I don't know how long I sat on the tile floor with my head hanging over the toilet, but when I finally could stand and brushed my teeth, I felt a bit better.

The room was empty when I stepped from the bathroom. I slumped into the bed, upset with myself. He came all the way across the country to surprise me, and I made him feel unwanted.

I rolled over, my coffee forgotten, and sunk into the pillow. I could hardly blame him for leaving. I'm a hot mess. Housekeeping walked in, which annoyed me because they really should give people a chance to get up and have their morning ritual.

"Do not disturb," I croaked from beneath the sheets.

"Okay, I won't," Cole said.

I opened my eyes and turned over to see him standing by the bed, still in that sage sweater, dammit, holding a glass of ginger ale and two aspirin.

I took the glass and sipped. Then I took the aspirin and sipped some more. He took the glass from me and placed it on the nightstand. Then he pulled the sheets back to my shoulders and tucked me in.

"I thought you left," I said. My voice still sounded ragged from vomiting.

He sat on the desk chair next to the bed. "Why would I do that?"

I closed my eyes and swallowed. "I didn't exactly give you a warm welcome after you flew all the way out here. Who does that, by the way?"

Cole crossed his ankle onto his other leg. "I have a lot of miles racked up. I can pretty much fly free anywhere in the continental U.S. I went standby."

"That's not what I meant. I mean, who flies across the country for someone you just met and hardly know?"

He uncrossed his leg and leaned over. I stared at the thin leather rope that hung around his neck, the bloodstone dangling in front of his sweater. My heart fluttered, remembering our time together last month.

"I know you enough to know you're worth the trip," he said. "I like you, Heather."

"I like you, too."

He smiled. "Well, all right."

He sat vigil in that chair while I slept. When I awoke two hours later, there was a cup of broth waiting for me on the nightstand with more ginger ale. I ate the soup and felt almost like myself.

"I can't believe this is how I respond to three drinks. That never happens."

"Sometimes, it doesn't take much to upset your stomach. You just flew in yesterday, probably over-tired from the time change, and did you eat dinner?"

I shook my head. I didn't remember eating after the plane.

"There you go," he said. "You do look better. You have color again."

I put my hand over my face. "I'm embarrassed. Thank you for this."

"My pleasure."

I got out of bed, still in full sweats. My ponytail was barely holding on. On my way to the bathroom, I turned. "I look a mess. I'm sorry you have to see this."

Cole stood but stayed where he was. "Don't ever apologize for how you look. You're the most beautiful woman I've ever seen."

I turned away before he could see my eyes tearing. Stop being so good, I wanted to say. I don't know how to handle it. In the shower,

I stood beneath the steaming water, letting it massage my aching body.

My skin was blotchy when I pulled the curtain back to reach for a towel. When I did, Cole was leaning against the sink, holding one for me. Without a word, I stepped to him and let him wrap the terrycloth around me. He hugged me and gently kissed my cheek. Then he stood back and went to leave me to finish drying, but I took his hand. "Stay," I whispered.

He took my hand and kissed each knuckle, a light tickle of his lips. I put my palm on his cheek, and our eyes locked. I leaned in to kiss him, and he responded, kissing me deeply until the towel fell to the floor. He lifted me under my legs and carried me to bed.

It was a full hour before our next words were spoken.

"I've never drunk texted before," I said.

"I didn't realize you were, or I wouldn't have come."

I lay curled beside him. He scratched my back, trailing shivers over my skin in a lazy meander. "I'm happy you did," I whispered.

He leaned over and kissed my back. "I'm happy I did, too."

"When do your classes start?" I said.

"Wednesday afternoon. I'm flying out on the redeye Wednesday. I want to see my favorite speaker first."

"You're crazy."

"I just might be. I'm crazy about you."

I closed my eyes. "I thought you met someone."

He leaned back to look at me. "I did meet someone."

"You're so open with your feelings," I said.

"Is that a bad thing?"

"No. It's refreshing."

"If you feel something, act on it. If you want something, go get it," he said.

I laughed. "It's not that easy."

He brushed my hair from my forehead and ran his fingers gently over my eyebrows. "It is that easy. I met a woman who floored me. I did something about it."

"And how did she take it?" I started to giggle. Cole tickled me beneath my arms, and I shrieked in tortured delight until finally, he took mercy on me and stopped.

I still had the remnants of laughter in me. "You're going to make someone very happy."

"I'd like to make you happy."

I put my finger on his lips to quiet him and shook my head.

He rolled on top of me. "Let's play a game."

"No."

"Come on. Close your eyes."

I exhaled and closed my eyes.

"Pretend today is a free day to do anything you want." He nibbled my ear, and I shivered. "If we could strike it from the calendar tomorrow, what do you want to be doing right at this moment?"

I smiled, my eyes still closed and whispered, "This."

He gave me that low rumbling chuckle that warmed the pit of my belly and kissed his way slowly down my body. When I opened my eyes, he paused and put his fingers over his lips, telling me not to speak, not to deny what he believed to be true. That I was desirable. That I was a woman to be loved.

Cole got dressed while I showered again. When I stepped back into the room wearing a robe, I saw he had brought up lunch. While we ate, we discussed our plans for the rest of the day. I told him I was going to sit in on a few speakers and say hello to old friends.

He frowned. "That's it?"

"Well, I came for the convention."

"Have you ever seen the view from the Needle?"

I shook my head.

"How about Kerry Park?"

Again, I said no.

"Is this your first time in Seattle?" he said.

"It's my eighth."

He stood. "You've been in this great city eight times, and you've never seen it?"

"That's right."

"No. That's wrong. Look at what's around you. Don't stay contained in this hotel. Go see stuff."

"See stuff. Cole, this is my work. I'm not here to sightsee."

"You can do both." He put his hand up, preventing me from arguing. "What's the importance of today? You'd like to see some friends. Fine. Do that, and I'll be back here. Meet in the lobby at five?" He waited for me to nod and continued. "I'm going to show you the city."

"Okay," I said, growing excited at the prospect of doing something different after so many years.

He left after a quick shower to spend the day touring the streets of Seattle while I went down to the conference rooms to listen in on some presentations. By two o'clock, I grew restless, unable to focus on anything but seeing Cole again and spending the afternoon with him. I texted his phone, something I'd been avoiding so as not to be seen by the wrong eyes. I felt confident we were safe here from judgment. *I can't wait until five. Where are you?*

He responded immediately. *At a café to the right of the hotel.*

B right there.

Bring a coat. It's cold.

As I reached the door leading out, I heard my name. I turned to see Rachel, an author and friend I met years ago, who usually traveled my circuit. "Skipping out? That's so unlike you." She was at the reception desk, checking in.

"I was wondering where you were," I said.

"I got held up. School function." She rolled her eyes. "Seriously, where are you going?"

"I thought I'd check out the city for a bit before tomorrow," I said.

She looked confused. "Okay. What time do you speak?"

I held up two fingers.

"Are you joining us for dinner tonight?" By "us," she referred to our usual annual dinner, including a dozen of the regular speakers, a good group, easy-going, lots of laughs.

"I have to miss it tonight. I'm meeting with a friend."

She pouted. "Okay. See you later. Have fun."

Outside, I stopped at the window of the café and saw Cole before he saw me. A young waitress stood at his small table, holding a carafe, talking with him, while an older gentleman at an adjacent table tried to get her attention. She didn't fill Cole's mug, nor was she delivering food or clearing his plate. They were just talking. My reflection in the window was an aged woman, compared to the youth on the other side of the glass. The scene was a completely normal one that made sense.

As she gesticulated a story with her hand, Cole looked under her arm and saw me through the window. His face lit up, and I felt a wave of gratitude wash over me. Her pensive face smiled when she saw me, and she said something to Cole, who shook his head and responded. She turned back to me with a look of surprise. Her expression read, *Really? Can't you find someone your own age to play with?* Perhaps it was my imagination, but I'm sure I wasn't far off. He dropped money on the table and walked through the café to the door as her eyes lingered on him.

He grabbed me on the sidewalk and planted a full kiss on my mouth before pulling me into a hug. Over his shoulder, I glimpsed her shake her head in disbelief. *I know,* I wanted to tell her, *I can't believe it, either.* One day he's going to wake up, realize what he's doing and disappear from my life. I'm waiting for it. I'm prepared for it.

Holding hands, he led me away, and I followed dutifully, glancing once over my shoulder to make sure no one from the conference saw us.

Wrapped in coats and scarves, we walked the streets of the city, pausing to gaze into windows, occasionally stepping into a boutique or chocolatier to warm up. We meandered for hours, stopping for food at *Mamnoon* for Middle Eastern cuisine. Cole ordered man'oushe, hummus, and lamb, and we ate at a small table, sitting close. Amid tastes of food, we talked, kissed, and I felt as if I were in another world, in another time, thousands of miles away from my life.

"I thought you were going to take me to Pike's Market, or to a museum," I said.

He shook his head. "Tourists. I wanted to see the city, feel it, as the locals do. Eat their food, walk their streets."

This unique, young man dazzled me.

"Of course, I do want to see Bruce Lee's grave, if we have time," Cole said.

"Jimi Hendrix is buried somewhere around here, too," I said.

"Who's Jimi Hendrix?"

I stared at him until he winked at me. "Give me some credit, Heather."

We held hands and then linked arms as we walked for miles through the streets until we came to the famous Space Needle.

"Are you afraid of heights?" he said.

"Yes."

"Don't be. I'm with you."

I tossed my angst aside and allowed him to take me to the observation deck, five hundred and twenty feet up. The lights of the city sparkled as darkness enclosed it. Our view was spectacular.

"This is my favorite time of day," I said. "When the sky turns from blue to indigo to ink. From up here, we get to watch this incredible palette change before our eyes."

"I planned it this way."

"No, you didn't," I said.

"I know."

I laughed out loud and flung my head back. He put his arm around me. "You're beautiful when you laugh. I see all your worries fly away when you do."

"My worries?"

"About us," he said.

I stared at the city, resplendent below.

"I've never felt this way about anyone," he said.

Me neither, I thought, but I refused to voice it. "What did the waitress say to you when she saw me?"

He appeared confused. "Waitress?"

"The one at the café, earlier today, when I met you outside the hotel."

It was as if she dropped from his mind the moment he walked away from her. He put his hands on either side of me, resting them on the safety bar, and we looked over the city together. "I don't remember," he said.

"I think you do. She asked if I was your mother, didn't she?"

He sighed in my ear.

"Older sister?" I said with a grin.

"Let it go." He leaned into me. "Be with me. Be. With. Me."

My insides heated with his words, the proximity of his body to mine. I turned to him and held him. "I'm with you right now, aren't I?"

He grabbed me tight and rocked me. I didn't look around us, didn't wonder or care what people thought of seeing us.

"You're only young once," I whispered. "Use it wisely."

We skipped dinner to return to the hotel, tearing at each other's clothes before we had shut the door to my room. I couldn't get enough of him and called out his name over and over.

Drunk on sex, we ordered an obscene amount of food to the room and ate while watching a movie on TV. We fell asleep wrapped in each other. I slept a dreamless sleep.

I woke up before Cole and rested my head on my hand, watching the morning light through the window play on his features. His hair fell back from his face, his eyes danced in dreams. Gently, I traced my finger over the fresh scar above his eyebrow, the back of his jaw, his chin, and then to the small smile that played around his lips while he slept. I touched the scar below his collarbone, a pale strip against his smooth skin, trying to imagine him fighting with someone, wondering what set him off. I envisioned Cole as a rambunctious, curious child who never stopped moving, who jumped into a situation without thought or caution. As an adult, he behaved the same.

His broad chest led to a concave stomach. I watched his chest rise and fall with his breath, timing my own with his, learning the music of his inhalations. As I retraced his face, he moaned so softly it sounded like he was purring. Eyes closed, he reached for me.

"Who was the man I saw you with outside of the diner on Main Street on parents' weekend?" I said.

Cole lay on his back, satisfied, and relaxed from our lovemaking. His eyes opened with my question. "What man?"

"You were near the hotel when I went to see Charlie at school in October. You were leaving the diner together, right before we ran into each other. You looked close like he's a good friend or an uncle?"

"Oh," he said. "That was Dave. He's a friend from home." He sat up and got out of bed. "What time is your thing?"

"Two. I'm going to head down a little earlier to firm up a few things: the projector, mic, et cetera."

He nodded. "Do you get nervous speaking before a group?"

"Yes. But not nearly as much as when I started. Speaking in public is not so bad. And my friend, John, helped me in the beginning. He's been doing it much longer."

On the bed, I stretched my arms. "I wouldn't do that," Cole said, crawling over me. "Not if you want to get out of this room today."

I kept my arms up, tempting him. "Don't you get tired?"

"Of what? Making love to you? Unh-unh."

He lay on top of my body, his elbows on either side of me. "You do know we're each in our prime. I'm surprised there aren't couples everywhere our ages. A woman reaches her prime at forty. I'm sure you know that."

He looked so satisfied with himself, I laughed. I did know that. By forty, most women had been living with the same man for years, so the sex was not as exciting as what I'd been experiencing. Maybe he was on to something.

"Maybe. I do enjoy it so much more now than when I was younger. But I think it's the partner, not my age," I said.

"It's both. It's the perfect storm."

When we finally left my room, my body felt like Jell-O in low heels. I usually looked forward to this conference, but now I just wanted it to be over and meet Cole back in the room. I glanced at him in the elevator. He winked at me and looked straight ahead, hands clasped in front of him.

The doors opened to a busy lobby of people congregating between sessions. We stepped out, and I walked him to the door. He wanted to explore more of the city while I worked.

"See you later," I said.

He kissed me on the cheek. "Knock 'em dead, baby."

John found me at the coffee station. After the past thirty-six hours, I needed all the caffeine I could ingest.

"Morning, Heather." He checked his watch. "I mean, afternoon."

"Hi, John. I got a late start today."

He walked with me down the corridor, holding a bottle of water. "I missed you yesterday."

I winced. I had forgotten about his seminar. "I'm sorry. I really am. I decided to play hooky and sightsee."

His face registered surprise. "You went sightseeing?"

I paused, and he stopped with me.

"I thought I needed a change," I said.

"Good for you. Change is good."

Yes, I thought. Yes, it is.

My session was full, thankfully, and I started my spiel on time. I discussed my gradual start in journalism and publication, leading to my taking over Dear Aunt Emma. I shared with the audience a few of the more remarkable letters I'd received over the years (The one where an inexperienced reader said her mother warned her to be careful of men with beards asked me if her mother was right. I told her yes, and to be cautious of those without beards, too. Always a crowd-pleaser).

The audience applauded, and I opened to questions.

"How long have you been Aunt Emma?"

"Fourteen years," I said.

"Do the questions you receive start to repeat themselves?"

"There are as many variations on a theme or problem as there are people. And then, there are some doozies." The audience chuckled.

"Why do you think advice columns are so popular?"

The question came from somewhere in the back of the room. I've often thought about it, the popularity of not only my small local column but of the well-known national syndicated and online columns. "I believe readers are hoping for a little nugget of wisdom in an answer, a new perspective that will help them view their own lives differently. I'm not an expert. I offer suggestions and advice based on my own experiences and mistakes, of which there were many." Audience laughter here. "People read the column to see what others are going through. If they can relate, maybe they won't feel so alone."

"How much longer do you think you'll stay as Aunt Emma?"

I stared out at the audience, stumped by the question. How long, I wonder? Carl's offer to take over the gardening column crept into my thoughts. How long do I keep doing the same thing? I cleared my throat and then spotted Cole in the back corner. He raised his eyebrows, and my heart fluttered. I returned to my audience.

"That's an excellent question, and one I can't answer. But for now, you're stuck with me."

The crowd erupted in applause. My session had come to an end.

John came to me as I gathered my notes at the lectern. "Well?" I held my breath, waiting for his approval, as usual.

"It was perfect. You're changed. Single looks good on you."

I hugged him. "Thank you."

"So, I'll see you at the reception later?"

I glanced at Cole, standing in the corner, ignoring curious glances his way.

"I'm sorry. I'm going to miss it. But I'll see you at breakfast," I said.

John nodded, unable to contain his disappointment. If I wasn't so totally consumed with my new plans, I would have felt worse, but I couldn't see past the man waiting for me. "See you tomorrow."

On my way out, I stopped to chat with colleagues and audience members. Cole watched from a safe distance. At the door, several minutes later, I turned, but he was gone, and I knew he'd gone up to the room ahead of me to avoid scrutiny.

"I can't believe you came to the session," I said when he opened the door for me.

"You were awesome. I thought you'd be good, but I didn't expect that."

"Really?"

"Yes, really." He kissed the tip of my nose. "I thought you might bring up the gardening article during the questions."

"That did come to mind," I said.

Cole smiled and put his hands on my shoulders. "That means you're going to do it."

I didn't respond. He seemed so sure of me. Why couldn't I feel it, too?

Cole pulled my jacket from my shoulders and slipped it on a hanger. "Was that your friend, John, who met you at the podium?"

I sat on the bed to slip off my shoes. "Yes."

Cole unbuttoned my blouse.

"We're just friends," I said. I don't know why I felt the need to add that.

He pulled my shirt down my arms and laid it on the desk chair. Then he faced me. "You don't have to explain your relationships. I'm not jealous."

"Okay. I don't get jealous, either. So, when you meet someone who rocks your world, go, and I'll be only happy for you."

"I already met her."

I put my hand on his. "For now. I don't mind. I'm having the time of my life. For as long as it lasts." It may even be worth a broken heart. Broken hearts mend.

He took my blouse from the desk chair and dropped it on the bed. Then he sat me down on the chair, kneeled before me, and put his hands on my thighs. I thought about the knitting chair, and my body immediately responded. But he didn't sit me down to seduce me. He looked somber.

"This is not a phase for me. You are not a conquest. I don't know how I can convince you. Tell me how."

I ran my fingers through his hair, and he closed his eyes. "You have so many wonderful things to experience: young love, babies…"

He squeezed my hands. "I don't want children. Ever. I had a sister. I lost her. It's the worst pain I'll allow myself to go through. I don't even need to be married. I want to find another soul who speaks to mine. A person who fills up my senses and makes me feel whole. Did I expect to find her now? No. Did I expect her to be older? No. I don't care. Now that I found you, I'm not walking away."

His eyes were full, though his voice never wavered.

"When I'm with you," I said, "I want nothing else. Everything seems right. But when we're apart, I see us as what we are. It's wrong."

"That's because when we're apart, you see us through the eyes of everyone who is not in this relationship."

A lump lodged in my throat. "You're right."

We went to dinner at a romantic bistro he found earlier and ate ceviche and drank sangria.

"When is your birthday?" I said.

"June."

So, for two months, we'll only be sixteen years apart.

We returned to the hotel and stayed in bed until the taxi came to pick him up at one- thirty am. At my door, we kissed and held each other. I held his face in my hands and looked him in the eyes. I opened my mouth to speak and closed it.

"What?"

I sighed. "Nothing. Go."

He left the hotel for the airport while I went back to bed, swallowing the words, please stay.

Chapter 16

The airport van pulled onto my street as snow started falling. Up ahead, I saw what looked like Damian's car speeding down the block away from my house. That couldn't be right. There was more than one black Lexus sedan that drove through this neighborhood.

The house was silent and cold. I dropped my bags and put up the thermostat, keeping my coat on a bit longer. Two messages were waiting for me: one from Trisha and the other from Bill, who wanted to take me to a movie. I deleted both and returned my sister's call, where she caught me up on what I missed over the four days I was gone, which was very little. Then I checked in with Carl, who had forwarded some snail mail that I should receive the next day. Finally, I called Charlie, who said it felt weird to get back to classes after such a long break and that Cole, who returned to the dorm yesterday, said hello.

Once the chill eased from the air, I shrugged off my coat and left a message for Dottie, to let her know I was home. After a hot shower, in my robe, I lit a fire in the living room, heated up a mug of milk, and added chocolate shavings, making a thick, soothing hot chocolate. I ignored my laptop in its case, along with my full suitcase in the foyer, to be dealt with later.

Tonight, I would treat myself to a quiet evening of reflection, of my life and where it headed, now that my identity as a wife and mother shifted. I accepted my role as a single woman. A single, dating woman. Maybe not dating exactly, but I was certainly getting my groove on.

I sipped my hot chocolate and stared into the roaring flames. What would I do about this new, exciting relationship? Was it even a relationship? An affair? That sounded so forbidden. Unacceptable. Yes. *I am having an affair with a younger man.* I dropped my head back and luxuriated in the memory of our unexpected couple of nights.

He's Charlie's roommate.

Charlie. My role as a mother was changing, too. The day-to-day demands of a needy, helpless child were well behind me. I'd always be his mother, but as he grew more independent, he'd require less from me. That would be the ultimate level of loneliness.

Someone rattled the knob of the front door, and I stood, startled. Putting down my mug, I tiptoed to the foyer and exhaled when I saw Damian through the side window. I opened the door. His face was beet red.

"What the fuck, Heather? My key doesn't work. You changed the lock? On *my* door?!"

The relaxing feelings from moments ago evaporated as I stood in front of my ex. Anger rose within me. "What do you want?"

"I want to come into my own house." He pushed past me and walked into the kitchen. "What's the deal? How can you lock me out?"

"Don't yell at me! This is not *your* house right now. You know it. I'm tired of you barging in on me. That stops now!" I followed him inside and halted when he suddenly turned around.

He growled at me. "Who says?"

"I say. Damian, what right do you have to treat me like this?" My body shook with frustration and rage as I finally saw my situation for what it was.

"I have every right. I bought this house. I paid for this house."

"Don't do that. I paid into this, too. And you gave up your right to intrude on me the minute you climbed into bed with Genna. You walked out on me. You broke us, Damian! Not me." I breathed and tried to compose myself. "If you want to sell the house, just say so."

He stood back, surprised.

I wasn't finished. "Was that you leaving the block when I got home two hours ago?"

He didn't answer me.

"Why do you keep coming back here?" I asked.

Damian sat at the table. "I just want to make sure..." He paused and shook his head.

"Make sure what? I'm taking care of the house: the landscapers, the oil. I can do it. I'd like to stay here at least until Charlie's out of school."

He crossed his arms and leaned back. "Does Charlie know his roommate spent five days here before he came home?"

I felt the blood drain from my face, and he sneered at my reaction. I wanted to correct him, to tell him Cole stayed for six days but swallowed the words.

"That's what I thought," he said.

"Have you been stalking me?"

"What are you doing, Heather?"

"What do you think I'm doing?" I stood frozen, my mind racing with the ways this could backfire. Do I back down? What was he capable of?

We stared at each other in a showdown of anger and distrust. No, I thought. I'm done with this behavior.

"Like you said, 'who could be interested in cold fish?'" I said. Tears stung my eyes.

Damian took a breath, trying to see the truth behind my hurt expression. "I'll just call Charlie tomorrow."

"You do that," I said.

He stood, very slowly, and I trailed him to the front door.

"Does Genna know how often you come to see me? Where does she think you are?"

He paused, holding the doorknob. "Watch yourself, Heather. This could be bad for you."

I shut the door behind him with all the force I could muster and wiped tears of frustration from my eyes as I returned to my mug in the den. The hot chocolate had gone cold. I tossed the remaining drink onto the flames.

I was still reeling from our argument the following morning. I tried to focus on my work, peeking at the clock every hour, waiting for an accusatory call from Charlie that never came. The son-of-a-bitch never followed through on his threat. An empty monster. That's what Damian was.

I shut my computer at two, giving up on any sort of productive day and called Trisha. I needed to talk to her. I needed to tell her what was going on in my life.

She heard the angst in my voice and agreed to come over for dinner, insisting she'd bring in Chinese food. Over sesame chicken, I told her everything: the first time I knocked on Charlie's dorm-room door when Cole answered in his towel, oozing confidence, to subsequent visits and his surprise arrival at my house. I talked about our undeniable attraction that I managed to deny for only three days before I gave in to my need, to our impromptu liaison in Seattle, and ending with Damian's supposition and threat to tell Charlie.

We went through a bottle of wine and a plate of chicken and rice. When I stopped talking, Trisha whistled and sat back to digest what she'd heard. It felt good to share with her. I hadn't realized how much I needed to talk to someone. I knew she would give me her unfiltered thoughts, as much as it would hurt to hear them.

I held my breath while I waited for her to say something.

"Well, I didn't see that coming. I thought you were going to tell me you and Damian were getting back together."

My jaw hung open. "Why on God's green earth would I do that?"

She shrugged and looked away. Because I'd done it before. But she didn't say it.

"You think I can't be alone. Is that why you tried so hard to set me up?" I said.

"I'm worried about you. You're not exactly worldly," she said.

"And you are?"

"I'm trying to protect you."

I dropped my head. "I realized how miserable I've been these past years now that I'm alone."

Trisha stared at me.

"I never enjoyed sex or intimacy this way. I'd been with only one person, and he was selfish. I see that now." I took a breath to calm myself. "Trisha, I never knew it could be this good." I took her hands. "I feel alive. You've been protecting me my entire life, and I'm grateful. I need you to be my sister and my friend. You don't have to take care of me anymore. It's time I take care of myself."

Trisha pulled me to her and put her arms around me. For a moment, I felt my mother's presence.

We abandoned the leftover food and dishes and went into the living room. I lit a fire, and we let the flames hypnotize us.

"You know, your new fling only works if you're Cher or Madonna," Trish said.

"So, I have to be filthy rich and gorgeous?"

"That. Or," my sister said, "you have to be known by one name."

We giggled and then fell silent. The flames flickered and popped in the fireplace.

"You know you can't be with this guy," she said.

"I'm trying to convince myself of that."

Several more minutes passed. "So, tell me about it."

"What?" I said.

She sighed. "The sex. With the kid."

I thought about how to temper my response and decided to preserve the integrity of what Cole and I shared.

"It's not about the sex. Though I've had more of it in the few times we've been together than I've had in twenty years." I smiled, but she didn't. "It's how he makes me feel."

Trisha turned to me, eyebrows knit in question.

"He makes me want to leave what I know and open myself up to every possibility. It's exhilarating and terrifying, and I like the person he sees when he looks at me. I'm beautiful and interesting, and when we're together, I feel like I'm twenty-years-old again, but this time, I'm not afraid of everything," I said.

She held my eyes before turning away.

My confession to Trisha did little to alleviate my distress. I threw myself back into my routine: waking up alone, working all day alone, dining alone - save for the occasional visits to Dottie.

During one visit, she and I talked about my new status as a single, empty-nester.

"Actually," she said. "Are you considered single? What is your status exactly?"

"We're separated."

She frowned. "For how long? When will you divorce?"

"I don't know. When Damian left last March, I couldn't conceive of being another statistic. I thought if I waited it out, maybe my situation would fix itself like it did the last time he walked out. But now...now, I know I can stand on my own and, I truly believe, be happy."

I kept my sexual encounter to myself. Decided I didn't need to hear from someone else what I shouldn't be doing.

"You'll get used to it," Dottie told me, referring to being single, speaking from experience. "You'll gradually develop a new social circle unique to your own needs."

Her calendar looked like a color wheel, marked up with plans in nearly all the boxes, yet somehow, she always had time for me.

"I'm not as social as you are. I won't fare as well as you," I said.

"Nonsense. Don't compare yourself with anyone else. You are your own unique you. Follow your heart."

I wanted to tell my friend that if I followed my heart, I'd be with a certain college freshman every waking moment.

I went into the office twice in a week, signed on to a computer to work, and accepted an invitation to lunch both times.

Charlie called me on Sunday. I was apprehensive at first to speak to him but quickly realized Damian never said anything about Cole staying at the house and enjoyed hearing him talk about his classes, the food, and Kate. He casually mentioned they might go to Clearwater for spring break with a small group, but glossed over it as if it were just a thought. I knew he was feeling me out for a reaction. Spring break was six weeks away. Of course, I was disappointed, but I tried not to let on how I felt.

Cole texted me messages daily, little romantic quips and thoughts that made my heart yearn for more. I deleted every message after committing them to a small treasured spot in my mind. I knew in time his interest would wane and I prepared for it. So, I decided to return Bill's call, and we set a date to go out.

February was frigid and dry, keeping me indoors. Damian showed up only once, uninvited, of course, using the excuse he wanted to make sure the oil burner was working. I left him to it, knowing it was working just fine but trying to keep some semblance of peace. He didn't mention our previous argument or acknowledge his empty threat. It was clear I wasn't entertaining. I almost told him about my recent date with Bill, a pleasant evening watching a simple, predictable rom-com followed by eggs at the diner and an unthreatening peck at the door, but decided the less Damian knew, the better.

I gratefully accepted a speaking engagement in North Carolina for the first week in March. They had a speaker who canceled and needed to fill the spot. Two weeks later, I was packed and on my way to the airport. The trip only required me to stay one night, but I reserved my room for three, needing to escape the quiet house and poor weather.

I texted Charlie to let him know where I was and remind him to call my cell if he needed me. He wouldn't, but I couldn't let that reality take over yet. It felt good to let someone know my whereabouts.

I checked into the hotel and found my way to the conference registration area, where I confirmed the room I'd have the following day. I ordered room service, watched three hours of mind-eroding reality television, and drifted to sleep.

The following afternoon, I stood at the small podium, assembled my notes in order, futzed around with the microphone attached to the lapel of my jacket, and greeted attendees as they entered. The space held sixty chairs, an optimistic amount, considering the size of this conference, which I figured to be about a quarter the size of those I usually attended in Seattle, Philly, and New York. Still, it was a paid gig.

At three o'clock, I decided to start my presentation, staring at more empty chairs than occupied. I cued an intern to lower the lights and focused on my projected PowerPoint notes for the duration of my talk, falling into my practiced manner until an hour had passed, and I was ready for questions. The lights went up, and I was happy to note more seats had filled while I spoke. I liked to leave fifteen to twenty minutes for comments and questions and had just announced I would take one more when a woman's hand shot up. I smiled, looked in her direction, and froze.

Seated next to this woman was Cole, wearing a Henley shirt unbuttoned below the collarbone, hair finger-swept back, and a beautiful, warming gaze. I'm not sure what the woman asked or how I responded. All I remember was how I felt the moment I saw him and how I needed to get out of this room. The applause was generous. I operated on autopilot, shaking hands and thanking attendees for coming until I finally reached the door.

He stood just outside. We looked at each other, and neither spoke as we walked to the elevator, rode up four flights, passed eleven doors to reach the last one right before the window at the end of the hall. As I swiped the key over the lock, I thought if I jumped out that window, the beating of my heart would propel me along the air.

Inside the room, I stepped ahead and turned to him as he shut and locked the door. I remained several safe feet from him, and we locked eyes. His chest rose and fell as if he'd run up the four flights to get here. His hands tightened and loosened in fists by his sides, his desire palpable and filling the air around me. I looked at the thin rope around his neck hidden beneath his shirt, knowing the exact spot where the bloodstone fell on his chest, knowing how it felt against me when we pressed together. My entire body tingled with desire.

I took a small step back, so I could look at him, wanting me for an extra breath.

"Let's play a game," he whispered. "Close your eyes."

Unable to stay away any longer, I crashed into him, grabbing his hair in my fists, pressing my whole body against his so he had to hold himself steady. Cole tasted of everything I'd been denied for so long: youth, sexuality, salt, and sweat, and I wrapped my legs around his waist tightly as he carried me to the bed.

Perspiring and panting, we lay on our sides facing each other, reckless, almost violent lovemaking in our wake. I was so satiated and calmed, I could only weep. Wordlessly, he wiped my tears until I stopped and then pulled me to lie on top of him, touching me so tenderly I thought I'd never in my life feel this wonderful, this wanted, sexy and beautiful again. This boy was a gift, a prize for all I had been through until now.

We finally drifted to sleep, entangled. Not one more thought passed through my mind before I fell off.

I awoke to see a full breakfast beside the bed. Cole wore a robe, already showered, and sat on the chair watching me.

"There she is," he whispered, his eyes soft, stubble along his jaw, his hair falling over his forehead.

Our first words since seeing each other yesterday. I held my hand out. "Hi, I'm Heather. And you are?"

He let out a low growl and moved toward me on the bed.

"Are you reading Charlie's texts?" I said.

He shook his head, feigning innocence. "I simply asked how you were, and he volunteered that you were away. Getting the rest was easy." He kissed my bent knee, exposed from the sheets. "You don't answer my texts. I wasn't sure I'd be welcome."

"You're not." My voice was scratchy, and he smiled.

"I can hardly wait to see how I'm received when I am."

I covered my head with a sheet to hide my embarrassment. He pulled it down.

"Don't play bashful now. That's not you."

"I don't even know who I am when I'm with you," I said.

He leaned over me, his face inches from mine. "Yes. You do." He kissed my lips, the barest of a whisper, a promise, and then pulled back. "You need to eat. Your stomach is making funky sounds."

He dried me from my shower, rubbing the towel over my back, hugging me from behind.

"How can you afford to jump on a plane at a moment's notice and come down here?" I said to his reflection in the bathroom mirror.

He opened the towel, and I turned, naked, to him. He gently wrapped it around me. "I told you, I have miles."

He rubbed the towel over me.

"I think I'm dry," I said.

He bit his lip in thought. "Let me look, just to be sure." With a wicked smile, he lowered to his knees, pulled the towel away, moved my feet apart, and proved me wrong.

The next twenty-four hours found us within inches of each other, indulging in touches, whispers, the most intimate behavior I'd ever experienced. I was hungry for everything Cole gave me, taking, taking, until I was no longer heady with desire. We talked for hours, and the exchange filled me as much as the lovemaking.

"You've awakened something within me," I told him. It worried me. How do I return to my mundane existence when we part?

I managed to convince him to leave on Tuesday, to return to classes, to his peers, to leave me be, so I could come down from whatever higher plane I teetered on. I needed to be by myself, I said, which secured his decision. He wanted to make me happy.

I walked him to the lobby and embraced him.

"This is a big step for you," he said when he reluctantly parted from me. With his duffel slung across his back, he held out his hands. "This public display." His dimpled cheek seared at the forefront of my mind as I returned upstairs.

I stretched out in the bath, running my hands down my body, feeling what he felt, trying to understand what kept bringing him to me. If it were possible, my legs felt smoother, tighter, suppler – the medicine of his caresses my personal fountain of youth.

Chapter 17

Dear Aunt Emma,

I'm separated from my husband of six years. We have a young daughter, Molly, and she's been shuffled between our homes for the past six months. It's hard on her. I think it's primarily because we can't even get through the pass-off (of this child), without having an argument. Usually, our arguments start off with one of us showing up too late or too early to pick her up or drop her off. Then they escalate to everything else. How is it possible that just six years ago, I was so helplessly in love with this man? We were so happy at first. How can two people come to this? I really want us to get along, for Molly's sake, but whenever I am near him, a different person comes out. Help!

~Don't want to fight anymore

Dear Don't,

I'm sorry about your split, even more so for your daughter, who must listen to her parents bickering whenever they're together. The fact that you don't want to fight is a big step in the right direction. Think about Molly. Her happiness right now should be your only goal. For both of you. I suggest you arrive to pick her up or drop her off at the agreed time. No earlier and no later. And if he happens to be late, hold your tongue and forgive him for it. Forgiveness tastes sweeter than anger. From there, perhaps you can find common ground and see eye to eye. Just like marriage is work, so is divorce.

Good luck.

~Aunt Emma

Trisha invited me to dinner. I accepted her invitation only after she promised me - on her children - that there would be no single, available man at her table. The girls monopolized conversation at dinner, relieving me of having to field an interrogation on my life of late.

After the dishes were done and the kitchen cleaned, the girls disappeared, Adam left for a boys' night out, and Trisha led me into the den. She opened a bottle of wine and poured two glasses.

"Adam was quiet tonight," I said.

She said nothing.

"How often does he go out during the week?"

Trish dropped onto the loveseat and crossed her legs. She took a mouthful of wine before answering. "This is the second time this week."

"It's only Tuesday," I said.

She stared into her glass.

"Trisha, do you drink every time he goes out?"

"Can we stop talking about me?"

"No. I'm worried about you," I said.

"I'm not the one sleeping with a child."

I glanced over my shoulder to check for nosy ears. "Please! Don't say that. And he's not a child. He's a grown man."

My sister finished her glass. "Have you seen him since we last talked?"

"No," I lied.

She watched me. I didn't blink. Then she rested her head back against the cushion. "You know, it's not that it's so wrong for you, but don't you wonder if he gets too serious, he'll miss out on all of the opportunities he'll have?"

"What opportunities? I wouldn't hold him back from anything."

She cracked a smile. "Do you want to have more kids?"

"No."

She raised her eyes, making her point. We listened to the girls' voices inside, discussing something incoherent.

"Do you remember how badly I wanted another baby after Charlie?" I said.

Trisha nodded.

"Did you know when I told Damian I was pregnant the second time, he wasn't happy? He said he wasn't sure he wanted another child. I couldn't understand. We were married and had Charlie. Why not give him a sibling?"

She sipped her wine.

"He asked me to get an abortion."

She coughed, and wine sprayed on her shirt. "You didn't tell me."

"I was embarrassed. I refused. We never fought so hard before or since." Trish wiped herself down with a napkin while I stared into my glass, as the memory of that time still pained me. "I cried myself to sleep every night for weeks, wondering if I should do it. Why wouldn't he want this baby?" I sighed. "It was my first realization that he wasn't happy with me. He left shortly after that episode." I swirled the wine, watched it rise, and leave legs against the glass. "When I miscarried, as much as I mourned, part of me was...relieved." I forced myself to look at Trisha. "I've never admitted that before."

"There are a lot of nice men out there, Heather. Men your age you can relate to."

"What if I said Cole doesn't want to get married or have children?"

"I'd say he's lying to sleep with you."

"And that's a problem?" I smiled.

Trisha pulled herself up and refilled her glass. "It's not a problem unless one of you falls in love. If it's you, then you got what you deserve and had a good time doing it." She looked down at me. "If it's him, you're taking his life away. Or at least, you're taking his best years away."

We sat in silence while I considered what she said. Of course, I'd thought about all this already, but hearing the words spoken was much harder to face.

"Just imagine a scene," Trisha said, breaking into my thoughts. "Picture the day he brings you home to meet his parents."

I inhaled.

"That's what I'm saying," she said.

"Cary Grant married Dyan Cannon, 33 years his junior. Jackie Kennedy married Onassis, a 23-year age gap." I waved a flippant hand in the air. "It happens all the time. Why isn't it alright for me?"

"Because they were rich men with young wives who could still have children," she said.

"Jackie didn't have more children."

Trisha stared at me. "Listen, have your fun, get your fill, but cut it short. Find someone else. You are not an island. Neither is he. Don't be selfish."

My sister said this because she loved me and didn't want to see me hurt. That's what I repeated in my mind on the way home. I left my almost full wine glass on the coffee table, knowing she'd be drinking it before my car left her driveway.

I let myself into the dark, empty house and prepared for bed. Lying with my thoughts, I knew that whatever drove her to say it, Trisha was right, as usual. But I didn't care.

The day after dinner at Trisha's, I found a bumpy, manila envelope in my mailbox among bills and junk mail. My address was handwritten in penmanship I didn't recognize, mellifluous scrolls and fluid lines. Tossing the rest of the letters aside, I ripped the envelope open to find a tiny packet, a small bag of dirt, and a note.

"Plant this seed in the soil provided, in a small cup. Give it a little water and wait. I promise you can do this. I won't tell you what will grow. You'll have to wait and see. Love, Cole."

I picked up the phone to call him but put it down before I dialed the full number. I can't start calling him. Instead, I pulled a small glass cup from the cupboard, poured the soil in, pushed the seed down into the center, added water, put it on the kitchen table by the windows, and went back upstairs to work.

Charlie called me two weeks before spring break, which started the first of April, to broach the subject again of going to Florida with his friends. I bit back my desire to tell him no, that I wanted to see him, that I missed him more with every week he was away, but I heard the longing in his request. I never went home during my college breaks. I managed to get myself invited to friends' houses, or made Damian stay with me off-campus until classes started again – anything to avoid going home. I could never afford to go away and experience a fun, carefree trip with my friends. I didn't want to hold Charlie back.

"I still have money saved from when I worked last summer, and on Christmas break, so you don't have to pay," he said.

"It's okay. I'll pay for your flight. Maybe your dad can help, too." If Charlie hadn't made dean's list, I might have said no, but he made me so proud. I knew Cole was instrumental in helping Charlie get his grades, but I knew my son worked hard. I wanted him to have fun.

"Dad thinks I should come home and stay with you. He insisted, in fact. I'm not sure why, but I figured if you said it's okay, then he should, too."

I paced the floor. Why would Damian say that? Does he want Charlie watching over me? No, I thought. I'm paranoid. "Charlie, I'm sure he just wants to see you."

"I don't know. He was asking a lot of questions."

"Like?"

"Like who is going with me," he said.

"He's a parent. Understand, he worries about you."

"Maybe. He didn't mind so much about Kate coming. But he kept asking if Cole was going. I guess he thinks Cole would be a good influence. I don't know. He must have asked three times."

I held my breath, knowing why he asked. This was not good.

"Mom, if you want me to come home, I will."

"Go have fun with your friends - within reason, please. And don't worry about your father."

He exhaled relieved. "Of course. I'll be careful. Thanks, Mom. Love you."

I wanted to mimic Damian's questions about who would be going, but now, I felt it would diminish the trust I had for Charlie in his eyes. Would Cole be joining them? I picked up my cell to text him and stopped, deciding against it. What would I say?

Dottie suggested I took a trip when I told her Charlie wasn't coming home until the semester was over.

"You should go away," she said.

"I was just away last month."

"No, I don't mean work. Go somewhere tropical. Get your face in the sun and dig your toes in the sand. Read a book, drink a daiquiri. You deserve it."

"I don't know."

"You just mentioned the Dominican Republic not too long ago. Someone at your work just went, right?"

I nodded. Carl took his wife to an all-inclusive and raved about it. "Trisha wanted to go there," I said.

Dottie hesitated before saying, "I think you can use a break from her, too."

"Do you want to come with me?"

She frowned. "Cheryl's visiting with the baby for a few days while her husband is out of town. I'm sorry."

I thought about what Dottie said. The last vacation I'd been on had been seven years ago. Charlie was eleven, and we decided to take him to New Hampshire. We spent a week in a cabin on a lake. Charlie and Damian woke up early every morning to fish, the lake a sheet of glass, undisturbed but for their lines in the water. We barbequed at dusk, tired from sun and swimming, and played board games until Charlie could no longer keep his eyes open. Then Damian and I would have a beer on the screened-in porch and listen to the tree-frogs sing, watching the lake glistening in the moonlight.

Time softens the jagged edges of memory until it is called upon with only fondness. I'm sure there must have been moments of distress, a fight, or two even though I could no longer recall over what or when. I reveled in the memory of Charlie happy with both of us together for more than a few minutes. It was our last trip as a family.

I'd tried to plan another getaway a few years later, my last quest to pull us together before we disintegrated, but Damian was always somewhere else and not with me, and Charlie, who was in puberty and mostly disinterested, refused.

I'd reached for Damian over and over, and he pulled farther away, emotionally and physically. He wouldn't touch me, and I sank into a private, shallow abyss of depression, somehow keeping myself from plunging too far that I'd be irretrievable. Charlie needed me, and I held onto him through the final years of my marriage.

Damian called the next morning. "Can I come over? I'd like to discuss something with you."

I held the phone, surprised. I didn't want to speak to him, knowing why he wanted to talk. Could I keep lying? Did I have to?

"Heather, please," he said. "I'm calling and asking you to see me. That has to account for something."

I sighed. "Fine. I'll be free later, after four."

"I'll come over at six."

I tried to brace myself for the onslaught of threats and denounce-ment of my lifestyle and had worked myself up to a mini-frenzy that had me dreading his visit by the time Damian rang the doorbell at six o'clock. I opened the door to find him still in his suit from work, standing with a calm, perhaps humble expression. Confused, I let him in and led him to the den.

I sat on the club chair, and he took a seat on the couch. He looked around the room. "That chair is still hideous."

I stared at the knitting chair, as I gripped the arms of the couch, ready to defend myself. If he only knew how much I enjoyed that chair...

"Why are you here?" I said.

He rubbed his hands up and down his thighs. "I want to come home."

I dropped my shoulders, and my face went slack. "You're kid-ding."

"I'm not kidding."

"What happened with Genna?"

"I'm not happy. I want to come back and try to make a go of our marriage."

I had no words. I thought when Damian first left that he might come back, that history would repeat itself. But I wasn't the same person I had been a year ago.

He picked at the sole of his shoe, resting on his knee. "Are you seeing someone?"

I stood. "It doesn't matter. This is about me. You hurt me." Again.

His face wore a pained expression. "I know. I'm sorry. I want to try again. For Charlie."

I walked into the kitchen, and he followed me. I reeled around, and he flinched. A fleeting feeling of satisfaction filled me by his discomfort.

"You're a piece of work. For Charlie? When were you thinking of Charlie when you broke my heart? Was he on your mind as you screwed other women while I was here, *with Charlie*? When I tried to keep us together, and you worked so damn hard not to make that happen? I don't know who you think you are. Or who you think I am." My voice choked on the words. "You never loved me the way I needed to be loved, and it's screwed me up. I don't even know what I'm doing."

He stood in the center of the kitchen, stunned.

"I think it's time we hammer the last nail in the coffin of this marriage. I'll speak to a lawyer and start our divorce." I shook my head when he didn't answer. "How could you, Damian? How could you torment me all year, walking into this house, making me feel small and damaged while I knew Genna was waiting for you? And you think I would let you back in? Don't you know me at all?"

He put his hand on the back of his neck. "I thought I did."

We stood in awkward silence. I swiped my eyes roughly and blew out a breath.

"What happened to you?" he said.

"I woke up from a very long sleep."

He smiled sadly, and for a moment, I glimpsed the man I fell in love with in a warm bar on a cold night a lifetime ago.

"I'll go." He appeared lost, turning but not moving.

Something softened inside of me. I had taken him back before. He expected me to do it again.

"Do you want a cup of coffee?" I said. "I have more to say."

"Do you have wine?"

I grabbed a bottle of red from the dining room credenza and returned to the kitchen.

"What's this?" he said, nodding to the glass of dirt on the table.

"It's a flower."

"It is?"

I felt him studying the budding green behind my back as I uncorked the bottle, but didn't offer more. I'd been checking the glass daily and felt a small thrill when the first piece of green poked through the dirt just a couple of days ago.

"You should put it on the window ledge," Damian said. "It will get more sun."

I placed our glasses on the table and sat down. "Good idea. Thank you."

We talked for the first time in months. I told him I wanted to take over the utility bills if he would continue to pay the mortgage. He agreed, and then we talked about Charlie, about our conversations with him this year, his adjustment to school, our change to him not being home.

"We talk every week, but I miss him," Damian said. "I miss not being able to see him whenever I want."

"Me, too. Those days are gone, I'm afraid."

The real reason he wanted to leave Genna came out without warning. "She wants to have a baby," he said.

I stared at my ex, trying to formulate a response. This was why the age gap was so damn significant. Damian was proving Trisha right.

"You don't want one with her?" I said.

He shook his head.

I played with my placemat. "Just tell Genna no, like you told me," I said softly.

He pressed his lips together, and our eyes met. "I'm sorry for what I've done to you."

I felt myself well with emotion. I needed to hear that. "Okay," I said.

When he left an hour later, we both felt better, though I stood my ground and confirmed that I'd speak to a lawyer. He went home to decide what to do about his relationship with Genna.

I went upstairs to my bedroom and took my empty passport from my top drawer. Feeling tougher and a bit reckless, I texted Cole and asked him to call when he was available and alone. My phone rang within a minute, and I answered with butterflies in my gut.

"Hello, beautiful," he said.

I decided to get to the point of the call before I lost my nerve. "What do you have planned for spring break?"

He paused, and I held my breath. "I was planning on taking a trip to Long Island," he whispered, and I squeezed my eyes.

"I have a better idea. How would you like to go to Punta Cana?"

Another pause. I waited for him to say no, fully expecting to go alone. I would go anyway. I needed a vacation, but the thought of spending a week with Cole outside of the watchful eye of my sister and ex-husband filled me with such a pang of want, I found myself mouthing 'yes' over and over until he spoke.

"Should I pick you up for the airport?" he said.

I stopped pacing my house and dropped onto the couch. "I'll book the flights and hotel and send you the details. How about we meet at Newark?"

"Hold on. Let me check something."

I waited, listening to his breath through the line.

"No, fly out of JFK. It's closer to you. I'll fly out of Logan and meet you at the airport in the DR or whatever hotel you choose," he said.

We agreed on a date of departure, and I set about making plans and spent the next two weeks ignoring the voice in my head telling me I was crazy, that this would somehow backfire.

Chapter 18

Dear Aunt Emma,

I've been married for twenty-five years to the same man. Our sex life went from fulfilling and exciting to predictable and boring. I know every move he'll make before he makes it. I found some soft porn on cable recently that I'd like to watch with him, but I'm too embarrassed to suggest it. How can I put the spark back into our bedroom?

~Bored in bed

Dear Bored,

I'll bet my mortgage that your husband will embrace your suggestion. Speak your mind and get what you want. You're together this long, you shouldn't feel embarrassed by your womanly needs. Trust me. Suggest the cable, and you may find your love life resembles the days of old.

~Aunt Emma

On my way to the airport, Charlie called to tell me he'd landed in Florida. He then texted me the details of his hotel and his return flight to Boston the following Sunday. I felt deceitful, not letting him know of my plans. Still, once on the plane, thoughts about the upcoming six days, lying on a white beach under a southern sun, overlooking the ocean with one hand around a cold piña colada and the other holding Cole's, drowned my guilt in incredible anticipation.

As the plane descended through the clouds and the Dominican Republic coast came into view, my heart thumped in my chest. I was deliberately meeting a young man here. In another country. For six days. I inhaled deeply and held my breath, trying to calm myself down. *What am I doing?*

The plane landed and taxied down the runway, stopping a few hundred feet from the airport building, which was covered in thatched straw, looking like an enormous cabana, a far cry from the airport I left four hours ago. I stood on the tarmac surrounded by heat so dense I felt I could reach out and touch it with my hand. My jeans and thin sweater clung to me. Clutching my carry-on bag, I waited for the rest of the passengers to disembark the plane and board the buses for the terminal. As we pulled up to the main building, I whispered to myself to remain calm.

My flight had been delayed due to storms in New York, and I didn't know if Cole had the same problem out of Boston. A part of me was convinced he changed his mind and wouldn't come, and I'd be at an all-inclusive resort alone. It wouldn't matter. It would be for the best. I am here to relax and do something for me. I'll make a new, clean start. Erase my recent mistakes, my adolescent behavior.

The Arrivals screen showed the incoming flight from Logan landed forty minutes earlier. There was a waiting area where I figured he would be until I arrived. I scanned the seats and the crowd around me but didn't see him. So, I went to the bathroom to freshen up, pulled one of my new sundresses I'd bought last week from my rolling suitcase, and put it on, followed by flip flops I'd stored in the front pocket. Shoving my warm clothes and sneakers in, I zipped the case and returned to the waiting area, not sure what to do. When it started to empty, I swallowed the idea that he didn't come, that he changed his mind and went to Clearwater with Charlie. Or stayed home with his sister.

Passing the baggage belt, I pulled my carry-on behind me toward the customs line while I pushed my growing disappointment down.

I followed the designated trail, the taped arrows along the floor, stepping in sync with the rest of the passengers. The woman in front of me stopped short, and I glanced up to see the immigration sign ahead. My heart stopped as I saw Cole in cargo shorts and polo smiling at me beneath the sign. I dropped my bag at our feet and held him.

We took a shuttle to our resort, holding hands and pointing at the scenery through the window, the empty fields, and small, run-down buildings dotting the landscape.

"You look great," he said. His hand let go of mine, and he placed it on my bare thigh showing below my sundress.

I grinned and leaned my head toward his shoulder, feeling happy. He kissed the top of my head.

The bus entered the resort area of the island and pulled up to a spectacular, open reception lobby that boasted the most incredible view I'd ever seen. Through the marble pillars of the lobby was the enormous pool and just beyond it, a darker shade of blue, the Atlantic.

I looked at Cole and squeezed his hand. Ours for the next week. After check-in, we were escorted to our room, getting a detailed tour along the way. I had booked us the adult-only package, and as we passed families frolicking in the large pool, I felt a twinge of regret.

Our guide pointed to the left. "There is your pool. The buffet is served here from six to eleven and then noon to four. There are nine restaurants in the resort. I highly recommend making reservations."

We followed her along a walkway lined with palms and overgrown hyacinths, through a cluster of stucco buildings three stories high. She led us to the fourth building, up the outdoor stairs, and to a door.

"Here we are. Your suite." She led us into a large room with a king-sized bed and an open bathtub/Jacuzzi beside it. "Enjoy your stay." With a smile, she left.

It took no time before we were undressed and finding each other after five weeks of being apart. He kissed, nibbled, licked every inch of me, and I writhed and groaned, laughed, and cried out his name.

"I could lie here holding you for the week with no regret," he said after when we finally caught our breath. "But the view is spectacular from the beach, and I'm starving."

I sighed and rolled off the bed. "I'm hungry too." He stayed on his back, watching me. "This is my first time out of the country," I said.

"I know."

I pulled the sundress over my head. "You do?"

"You told me in your kitchen over Thanksgiving break."

"You remember?"

He nodded. "My question is, how did you have a passport if you've never traveled out of the country? Or..." He smiled. "Did you foresee this happening months ago and order it?"

I laughed. "I definitely did not see this happening even last month."

Cole climbed off the bed and pulled linen pants over his beautiful, tight body.

"I was supposed to go to London with Damian three years ago, but he told me a week before we were to leave that the business trip wasn't a spousal event, and he'd just found out."

Cole stood shirtless, looking at me. He knew Damian took someone else. And my passport sat empty and neglected in my drawer. He stepped close to me. "Let's fill that book."

We grabbed cheese and fruit from the buffet and found two chairs on the beach where we stayed for the rest of the afternoon. I felt peaceful and content. I turned to Cole. "Thank you for coming with me."

He lifted his Ray-Bans, exposing those blues. "I'll go anywhere you are."

"You didn't want to go to Clearwater?"

Cole shook his head. "Not for a minute."

"But they'll go to bars and clubs. You could hang on the beach with your friends. That's not fun for you?"

He stood, reached his hands for mine, and pulled me up to stand. "No. That's not fun for me. I'll show you what I'd like to do."

He led me to the water, and we waded into the warm surf toward the pier where there were no swimmers until we were in up to our chests. He lifted me, so I straddled him and moved the bottom of my bikini over. Our faces were close together while his fingers touched me. "Have you ever made love in the ocean, Heather?"

"No." I kissed him. "Have you?"

He looked at me for a long time and slid himself into me. I closed my eyes, and my head fell back. "No," he said. And I believed him.

We shared a bottle of wine at dinner and afterward, meandered with our pinkies clasped through the large rotunda filled with white chairs and couches. Very tipsy, I pushed Trisha's words from my mind, *You're selfish* and convinced myself this was okay.

We stopped at an outdoor bar and ordered two margaritas. He never finished a drink, and I realized I drank most of the bottle of wine we ordered at dinner. He asked me more about my past, before I was married, before I was a mother, trying, he said, to get to know me as a young girl.

"I wish we were at the same point in our lives," I told him.

"We are," he said. "We're together." He took my face in his hands like he often did. "We're exactly where we should be."

I nodded in agreement. Then I smiled and felt my cheeks struggle against his palms. He laughed softly and kissed me.

On the walk back to our room under the stars, next to the gentle lapping waves against the shore, the sand was cool beneath my feet, and the texture so fine, I wanted to stay longer. The music from the outdoor bar accompanied us. Cole stopped walking.

"Dance with me," he said. He held out his hands. I dropped my flip flops and fit myself to him. We danced on the shore to the music in the air. He hummed in my ear, and I thought, I can be this happy. When we were finished, I fell to the sand. He sat beside me, and together we watched the moon's light lay a sparkling trail over the ocean.

"Puts everything into perspective, doesn't it?" he said.

I nodded, understanding.

"We're here for a blip of time and gone, and this ocean will remain a living, breathing thing for millions of years," he said.

"You're not supposed to think like that. Not yet, anyway."

Cole gazed out at the horizon.

"You okay?" I said.

Lost in his thoughts, he didn't appear to have heard me. I laid my head on his shoulder, and he rested his on mine. I took a deep breath feeling invigorated, from the sun, from the sex, and from our talks. I was happier than I've ever been. I wasn't too old for this. I closed my eyes, imagined a future – Christmases and traveling, working and falling into bed tired from a long day – next to Cole. I looked up at his face, tanned and relaxed, and saw a future loving him, a man who believed in me, complimented me, inspired me to want to do more.

He looked at me in question, and I must have been wearing my thoughts because his expression relaxed into a knowing smile. He leaned over and gently kissed the tip of my nose.

The following morning, I found two chairs under a cabana and spread our towels down. Cole had gone exploring after breakfast. I was in my book, hiding from the sun when he leaned under the awning.

"Okay," he said. "Get up."

I stood. "Where are we going?"

He pointed to the sky over the water. "Up there."

I shook my head. "No way. I'm scared of heights."

Yet twenty minutes later, I stood by the surf while the parasail operator was strapping me in next to Cole. "I can't believe you got me to do this."

"The best twenty minutes of convincing I ever did," he said.

My body shook, and my stomach turned as the Spanish-speaking man left us, and the boat's engine roared to life.

"Don't be afraid. I'm here. You're going to love it," he said.

The boat sped up, distancing itself from us, and the rope connecting us pulled taut. "Ready? Start running, Heather." We took steps along the sand and quickly lifted into the sky. I screamed a compulsive outburst as my feet lost touch with the ground, and he grabbed my hand.

A full minute passed. "Open your eyes."

I took a breath, opened my eyes, and gasped. We rose high into the air, with the beach well below us. There was no sound. It felt as if we were removed from the world, able to watch from above. The water ebbed and flowed, so clear, it allowed us to see what she was hiding below her surface. I gazed along the beach and to Cole. "It's so peaceful up here," I said.

"I know."

We spoke little for the entire ride, craning our necks to see the expanse of the shore. I breathed deeply and swung my legs, feeling free and alive. I laughed out loud, my wide, smiling cheeks massaged by the soft wind.

Cole looked at me. "I love you."

The words ran over me like a warm rain. Silently, I took his hand and gazed ahead at the clouds.

We relaxed on the beach until dinner. I kept bringing up the parasail ride, and Cole enjoyed my enthusiasm. The next day he took me off the compound to a thick forest. I embraced my first zip-line experience, screaming my head off the entire time. On the ride back to the hotel, we passed a sign that read Monkey Exhibit. I looked at him and said, "Should we?"

He laughed out loud. "Look who's adventurous." He shook his head. "I have a better idea."

We drove to a large field with a modest wooden shed in the center. Inside we met Eduardo, a small man in leathery skin and a quiet demeanor who grew coconuts and made his own coconut milk. He explained he also sells his crop to a local manufacturer who makes coconut oil. Then he presented me with a bottle of freshly made oil, refusing the money we offered. On our way back, clutching the bottle of oil, I said, "I feel bad he wouldn't take money. He has so little."

Cole maneuvered the Jeep along the bumpy road. "He has what he needs. None of us need all the crap we have. That's the problem. We're never happy with enough." He changed course, and the road became smoother. "We never have enough."

"It's easy to say that when you have as much money as you do," I said.

He kept his eyes forward. "My father worked long hours. He spent his life building his company. Successfully." He bit his bottom lip. "Now, he's semi-retired with a fat bank account and a wife he hardly knows or appreciates." He looked at me. "There's got to be a better way."

We rode in silence for a while before he spoke again. "I did leave Eduardo money," he said.

I looked at him in surprise.

"I put it on his workbench while he was walking you out," he said.

"How much did you give him?"

He shrugged but didn't answer.

"Cole, how do you know where to go? What to do?"

"Just takes a little effort."

"I had no intention of leaving the hotel grounds. Hell, I thought maybe we'd never leave the room," I said.

"If that were the case, we should have met at a motel in New Jersey. But you wanted to come here. And I want to do more with you than make love." He glanced at me and back to the road. "Though it is my favorite thing to do in the world."

"Drive faster."

"Yes, ma'am."

On our third day in Paradise, we lounged by the pool and swam beneath the water, stealing kisses under the bridge like forbidden lovers.

"You don't talk about Charlie at all," I said.

"You don't ask."

I swam, and he caught up to me. "I don't want you to think of Charlie when you're with me. I don't want you to feel about me the same way," he said.

He twirled me around the pool. I felt intoxicated by the aroma of coconut lotion and chlorine, summer's fragrance.

"I couldn't possibly think of you in the same way," I said.

We languished in the water cheek to cheek.

"Is there anything I need to know about him?"

Cole put his palm on my back. "No. He's a good guy, Heather. You don't have to worry."

"Thank you."

After dinner, we walked to the open patio in the center of the resort to find a market where treasures were sold at various tables. Cole bought me a necklace, a sphere of deep brown coral with a Larimar stone, indigent to the Dominican Republic, so I'd remember our time together here. As if I'd ever forget. We took no pictures, no recording of memories, but for the indelible mark he made on my heart.

In bed that night, I spoke in the dark. "What are your dreams?"

His breathing was steady, and I thought he might be sleeping.

"I want to be happy. I want to live in love," he said.

I hadn't expected his answer. I'd expected him to say he wanted a prosperous career, to travel the world (again), and yes, to find love, but as part of the equation and not the whole. Then I thought of what he said while we parasailed, I love you. We'd crossed that safety line, and I was losing sight of it.

"You don't want a career? A comfortable living?" I said.

"I have a trust. And a position in my father's company, if I like."

"Then why do you work so hard at school? Your father has laid out your future for you."

Cole rolled over and pulled me to him. "First, I love to learn, and I enjoy the challenging classes. It beats sitting home watching the hours pass. Second, I haven't decided yet what I'll do. I have some ideas."

"Like what?"

"I met with my lawyer in January to work out an annual allocation of money to Shriner's Hospital for Children."

I let that sink in. "You're giving money every year to the hospital?"

"As of now. I may change that when I have access to more. My trust allotments change as it matures. It led me to think about starting an organization completely dedicated to funding children's hospitals."

"That's wonderful. Is that the hospital where they brought your sister?"

He swallowed and paused. "Yes."

I traced the scar on his collarbone, once again trying to imagine him fighting someone, and couldn't. "You're fortunate. Your whole life is in front of you. You can do whatever you want," I said.

"You can do whatever you want, too." He brushed my hair from my face with his fingers. "I try to live in the moment and not look too far into the future," he said.

I nestled further into him.

"What are your dreams?" he whispered.

"I don't have any. I'm not sure I ever did."

The silence lasted a long time.

"What do you have if you don't dream?"

"Memories," I said. "Some of them good."

He rolled on top of me. "Let's make more."

After we made love, as we drifted into satisfied slumber, he whispered, "It's never too late to dream."

A tear slid down my cheek as I let myself go, holding onto my last thought. *Isn't it?*

We dined outside at the buffet for lunch the next day, having slept in and missing breakfast. Though he ate salad and fish as I did, Cole filled his plate three times while I kept to one so I could stay in my modest bikini a few years longer.

"If I were you, I'd be loading up with pizza and fried calamari. You're in great shape, and your metabolism is still on your side." I gestured to his dish. "Instead, you eat like me."

"I have to stay healthy. I have to make sure I have the energy to keep you satisfied."

I loved how he spoke his mind, regardless of how much it embarrassed me.

I forgot my book in our room and told Cole to go to the beach while I went back to get it, relishing the meandering path to our building, drinking in the aroma of fragrant flowers. I felt exhilarated by being outside, under the healing sun's rays after being cooped up indoors all winter. I went parasailing and zip-lining. Who the hell *am* I? I giggled to myself, feeling joyful and light.

I paused on the walkway to touch a flower of deep pink. Its petals felt like the barest of silk against my skin, and the intense fragrance tickled my senses. I fingered the surrounding flowers and plants, ignorant of what they were called and wanted to carry the feeling they brought me home. My house was flanked with simple bushes and shrubs planted with little thought when Damian and I moved in fifteen years ago; no flowers, no vibrant colors or aromas like this.

"Beautiful, aren't they?" The voice startled me, and I spun around. A man holding hands with two young children, a boy and girl both of a similar age. He had a deep tan, shown off by a tank top over his bathing suit and brown hair with hints of silver. "I didn't mean to startle you," he said. "If my kids would let me, I'd stand here and enjoy them too." He pointed one finger, lifting his son's hand with his in the process, to the deep pink flower. "That's a corallilo. They're all over the DR this time of year. It's a great flower, isn't it?"

The children stood, mute, wearing bathing suits, and smelling of chlorine. They must be twins, but the boy more closely resembled his father than the little girl.

"I have no idea. I just know they're gorgeous, and I want to take them home," I said.

"Unfortunately, they thrive here, in this climate. I'm assuming you're from the States?"

I nodded. "New York."

He shook his head. "They definitely wouldn't enjoy that weather. We're from Jersey. Same climate."

I laughed.

"It's one of the many reasons I keep coming back here. This is my favorite place. I bring these guys now when it's my turn to get them," he said.

I nodded and moved back to the path. "It's my first time here."

"Welcome to Paradise. I'm Joe, by the way."

"Hi, Joe. Heather." I looked at the children, who were now both leaning against their father's legs. To the boy, I said, "I have a boy too. But he's big. He's in college."

Joe's eyes widened. "You have a college-aged kid? You look too young."

I flushed with the unexpected compliment. "I was twelve when I had him."

Joe laughed. His daughter looked at him in question. He squeezed her hand and shook his head down to her, to let her know I was joking.

"Are you traveling with friends?" he said.

Without thought, I shook my head. "No, I'm with…" What do I call Cole? My boyfriend? My lover? Joe waited for me to answer.

"I'm here with someone," I said, finally.

"Ah. Well, I promised ice cream, so I don't want to hold these guys up any longer. The nanny will be wondering what's taking so long. It was nice to meet you, Heather."

"You, too." I let Joe and the children walk ahead before I continued to my building and room. If Joe were around forty, he could have had his children in his mid-thirties. If I tried to date someone my own age, there was a good chance I'd also be dealing with younger children. Did I want to do that?

In the room, I grabbed my book and glimpsed myself in the full-length mirror next to the door. My loosely-knit cover-up fell mid-thigh showing my tanned legs. Some sunspots were dotting my shins, but my tan helped to cover them. My hair looked windswept and wild, falling haphazardly around my head to my shoulder blades and my face, well, it glowed. I didn't think I'd looked this healthy or happy in years. Is that what made Joe stop to talk to me?

I swung my book with a spring in my step on my way back to the beach. The sun and relaxation were working wonders for me. I took a few more steps and smiled inwardly. *Yeah, right, Heather. The sun has nothing to do with your glow.*

I stepped onto the sand and saw a young woman at our cabana, talking to Cole, who rested back on the lounge chair. He said something, and she laughed, tossing her thick dark mane behind her while her belly-button ring moved in and out. She was flawless in her tiny, turquoise bikini. Her legs were long and bronze, vein-free, hairless, freckle-less. Two perfect limbs that met at wide hips and a flat stomach. Her breasts were round and still defied gravity. I never looked that good. Not at twenty and certainly not now. As fit as I was, there was no denying this body had seen its share of life. The age spots on my shins would only worsen with time. Not far from now, my skin will lose its elasticity, and the difference between us will be even more substantial to a viewer. To him. To me.

But that's not what stopped me in my tracks. The woman held a little girl's hand, no older than two. Cole leaned forward toward the toddler and said something to her. She held her small hand out to him, and he lifted something from her palm and inspected it.

The woman said something that made Cole laugh, a deep, throaty sound that had become my favorite song, but his focus was on the small child. He pointed to the item in question, and the child leaned in, so their heads nearly touched as they both looked down.

Right then, I saw what I had been avoiding since I allowed myself my fantasy. This. This was waiting for him. He'd make an amazing husband and devoted father. Oh, Trisha, why didn't I listen to you?

I swallowed the bitter pangs of jealousy and regret. I held back, not wishing to interrupt them, spun around and walked back to the suite. Cole returned to the room half an hour later.

"Heather? What's wrong? I was waiting for you at the beach." His face held genuine concern.

"I'm sorry. I checked in with my editor to make sure he was publishing the correct letters. Time got away from me," I lied. I had shut down my cell service before the plane landed, so I wouldn't get hit with roaming charges. I figured Charlie was away as well and wouldn't need me, and I wanted to cut myself off from the rest of the world.

He furrowed his brows. "No. We have two days left. No work today, okay?"

I exhaled and picked up the book that had shined a cruel light on everything I was doing.

"Forget it," he said, taking the book from me. "Leave that here. Let's go."

His face was open, not a care in the world. If I hadn't seen it, I'd never know by his actions that he'd just spent the last half hour with a beautiful young woman and a captivating little girl.

But I had seen it.

He woke me early in the morning of our last day in Punta Cana. His hands roamed up and down my body, coaxing me from sleep until I was awake and wrapped around him.

"It's our last day," he said from behind me after we'd made love. His hands were around me, locked at my stomach.

My eyes opened and stared at the window. Our last day.

"Let's live here." He pulled me tighter. "I'd drop everything now for this."

Me too, I thought, if only the world didn't exist.

"We can live on sun and coconut oil," he whispered in my ear. "Maybe Eduardo will give us a job."

We drifted to sleep as the sun came up, bringing light into the room. I woke up hours later and listened to his calming breath. The sun felt strong through the window. I didn't want to move, didn't want to disturb the peaceful feeling that covered me like a shroud.

When he finally woke, we laid in bed watching each other.

"What are your plans this summer?"

"I'm getting a place in Boston," he said. "I have a couple of prospective jobs lined up. And of course, my father's company is an option, as well. I may travel a bit."

I closed my eyes and listened to him breathe.

"Where do you want to go?" he said. "Tell me, and I'll take you." He traced the outline of my face with the barest whisper of a touch. "Wait," he said. "Paris. You want to go to Paris."

I smiled with my eyes still closed. He remembered. Knowing

he listened to what I said was as satisfying as the idea of going away again with him. But it would never happen. After seeing him with the baby girl, I knew it was time to end this.

We spent the day back and forth to our room, reluctant to let each other go. Maybe I could hold on a little longer, enjoy this respite from life until we pulled away naturally. It would hurt less. We dressed for dinner as a dark cloud seemed to form over us. Or perhaps I felt it alone.

At the table, Cole took my hand. "Heather, what's wrong? You've been quiet these last two days. Did I say something to hurt you?"

"No." I squeezed his hand. "I'm just sad it's over."

"Me too." He smiled that glorious smile. "It's okay. We'll plan something else."

I didn't respond. I wasn't talking about the trip, but I wasn't ready yet to say what I had to say.

On the morning of our flight home, I stopped at the reservation desk to check us out while Cole showered. I gave the woman behind the counter my name and room number and waited for the bill. She checked the reservation screen.

"You're all set," she said.

"What do you mean? I haven't seen the charges yet."

"Your bill was paid last night by Mr. Prue. In full. You're good to go. We hope you enjoyed your stay and come back soon."

The scene at the airport was the hardest we shared yet. Cole looked as distraught as I felt to be leaving.

"I say goodbye to you far too much. I'm coming undone," he said.

"Cole, don't contact me for the rest of the semester, okay?" I tried to maintain a light, breezy attitude, but I could see his thoughts as plain as that damn dimple on his cheek.

"Don't," he said softly. "I'm going to need to talk to you. To see you."

Not here, I thought. Don't do this here. I said nothing as my eyes filled.

"We'll be together, Heather. I promise." He put a hand to my cheek. "Hey, I never asked...did you plant the seed I sent?"

I blinked and quickly wiped my eyes. "I did. The day I got it. To my surprise and awe, it started to grow," I said.

"You see? You can grow something."

He held me until the last passenger to Boston boarded. The flight attendant called his name.

"Please go." I led him to the ticket agent. He kissed me and stood behind the doors of the jetway as she closed them. With a last, small wave, he turned and disappeared.

I watched his plane take off, while silently repeating his last words whispered in my ear before he walked away. *I love you. I love you. I love you.*

I waited for my flight and watched travelers cross my blurry line of vision. My eyes rested on a young couple with two children, near ages two and four. The father, not much older than Cole, held his son on his shoulders. The boy was the spitting image of him and held onto his Dad's head as they walked down the corridor toward the main terminal. The mother pushed a stroller, on which sat a baby girl who sucked her thumb and kicked her chubby leg out. The woman said something to her husband, and they laughed.

I swallowed and wiped my face, my resolution growing fiercer as the signs around me cemented my decision. Sure, Cole will be upset, but in a year or even sooner, he'll forget this and start on the right path. I'd already experienced it, the early years of marriage and parenting, the joy of raising a child, of learning through trial and error, growing old together. I'd had it. Some of it. I'd be growing old alone. Even with Cole, I'd be growing old alone. I refused to drag him with me.

A middle-aged woman sat beside me. She took out her reading glasses, opened her book, and started to read. I guessed her age to be around mid-fifties, like Dottie. Where would I be in a decade? Gray. Through menopause. I wanted to disturb this woman, ask her if it was true that sex was harder after her changes. Did we dry up without our hormones, like Dottie said?

Cole will be thirty-four in ten years. Still young. Still vibrant, sexual. Wanting. Ten years will hardly make a difference to him. It will be a world of difference for me. There was no denying it. I could only keep my state of mind for so long. Nature takes over, whether we want it to or not. Whether we allow it or not. Good decision, Heather. Good decision.

I boarded my flight two hours after Cole left me. I could still feel his skin on mine, his breath in my ear, his profession of love, as I strapped myself into my seat. As the plane rose into the sky, I watched Punta Cana, our six days of paradise, get smaller and smaller until all I could see were thick clouds through my window.

I pulled the screen down, keeping the outside world out.

Chapter 19

"You're a busy lady, Mrs. Harrison," the driver said into the rearview mirror. He pulled the town car out of the airport and onto Grand Central Parkway. "This is the third time I'm driving you home this year. It's only April." He smiled at me. Carl insisted I use the newspaper's car service for this trip. He was so happy I was getting away. I think he wanted to make sure I got to and from the airport.

I stared out the window at the passing scenery, missing the heat and view of the Dominican Republic. Back to reality.

"This trip was for pleasure," I told him.

"Ah, good. You have a dark tan. It's nice to take a break. Treat yourself."

Yes, it is. I dozed in the car, having slept so little our last night at the hotel. I couldn't wait to get home and go to bed.

The driver woke me in my driveway. "We're here, Mrs. Harrison. No traffic because it's Sunday."

I let myself into the house, bone-tired. My cell was dead, so I plugged it into the kitchen outlet, checked my sprouted flower on the window ledge, expecting it to have withered and succumbed to death from neglect the past week. I was pleasantly surprised to see it still there. In fact, it was a wee bit taller. I gave it some water and dragged myself up to bed, leaving my bag sitting in the foyer. Though only seven-thirty, I was drifting into sleep, the television on low, when the house phone rang on the nightstand beside me. It was Damian. I let the call go to the machine. The last person I wanted to talk to after a most memorable vacation was him.

"Heather, it's me again. I don't know if you're home yet, but Charlie is on his way to the house. He's pretty upset." My eyes opened, and I sat up. As he left the message, I heard the front door open, and I ran downstairs to find Charlie in the foyer, sunburned, and looking despondent.

"What are you doing here? I thought you were flying directly back to school from Florida."

He shook his head, which sunk down below his shoulders. "I came home Thursday and went to Dad's. I've been waiting for you to get home."

"Thursday? Babe, what happened?"

He started to cry. I put my arms around him and held him. When he composed himself, he pulled from me and walked into the den. I followed and sat beside him on the couch. Charlie hadn't cried in several years, and it pained me to see him so upset.

"Kate and I fought on the trip. She went to stay in Brendan's room. I walked in on them. Mom, they were…" He leaned over, putting his face in his hands. "She told me she doesn't want to see me anymore. I just called her again from Dad's, and she hung up on me." He let go, starting to sob, and I put my arm around him, wanting to cry, too.

The first heartbreak is monumental. And he had to wait four days to tell me.

"I needed to get out of there. I jumped on a plane to JFK and couldn't reach you. So, Dad picked me up, and I stayed with him."

I'd turned my cell off for the week, never once considering my son might need me. A deep stab of guilt cut through me.

"I'm sorry. I'm so sorry, babe. I'm here now."

He calmed down and sniffed deeply. "I can't believe how much it hurts." He leaned into me, and I kissed his head.

"What did you argue about? Before she went to Brendan?"

"She was bitchy all day for no reason. I called her out on it, and she lost it. She told me to back off. I was suffocating her."

I held him. There were no words that could soften a heartbreak. As his mother, I felt helpless.

"What the hell am I gonna do?" he said into my shoulder.

"You're going to go back to school. You'll have the summer to figure it out. That's all you can do."

He kept his eyes closed for a long time, leaning against me, breathing in shaky breaths of despair. "Where did you go?"

"Dominican, for a little getaway."

"With who?"

I squeezed my eyes. "I went by myself."

He looked up at me with red-rimmed eyes. "That's sad. I'm sorry. I would have gone with you if you'd asked."

I smiled. "I had a nice time. I met some nice people and did a lot of reading. It was relaxing." The lies fell from my lips without thought. I was a horrible person. But to tell my son who I spent the last week with would surely have sent him off the deep end.

"I'm hungry," he said.

I jumped up, eager to solve one problem for him, even if it was a basic need. "What would you like?" I checked the fridge, not sure what was still in there, and not spoiled.

"I don't care. Whatever you got is good. All Genna has is Nutella and crepes."

I found eggs, English muffins, and a few slices of cheddar cheese. I scrambled the eggs and added the cheese while the muffins toasted, trying not to think of chocolate crepes, which I would have loved myself. Charlie sat at the table, staring ahead. He ate, though, and I felt better. When he finished, he put his fork down and sighed.

"I know you don't want to hear this right now, but it will get easier," I said. "There is someone who wants you exactly for you."

He rubbed his eyes.

"I'm sorry I wasn't here for you," I said.

"It's okay. I hung with Dad." He finally looked at me, as if seeing me for the first time since he walked in. "You're really tan."

"I used sunscreen."

"It looks good. You look good." He lifted his burnt arms and dropped them. "These hurt bad the first day. I laid out as soon as we landed and didn't put anything on." He rested his head in his hands and sighed again. "What's with the glass?"

I lifted my baby plant from the window ledge and brought it close to him. "Check it out. There's life in there."

He lifted his head to see the thin green stem. "What are you trying to grow?"

"I'm not sure."

His eyes moved to me. "Seriously?"

"Yes. It will be a surprise."

"That's weird."

I put the glass back.

"Oh, I get it," he said.

"What?"

"You're doing that gardening column, aren't you? Did Carl send you that?"

"No, I'm not doing the column. I just thought I'd grow something."

Charlie lost interest and was on his phone. Small blessings.

"Are you staying here tonight or going back to Dad's?" I asked.

"I'll stay here. I have my bag in the car." He pulled himself up from the table. "I'll get it."

He was in his room by the time I finished washing the dishes. I had been so tired earlier and now felt the despair for my son on top of my exhaustion. I looked in on him.

"I'm going to bed," I said from his doorway. "Are you okay?"

"Can I hang with you for a while?"

We sprawled across my bed, watching a movie I could barely concentrate on. I was so caught up in a mixture of gratitude to be able to sit with my son and exhaustion from a week of complete physical and emotional fulfillment.

I woke up to shots ringing and realized the movie had ended and another began. Charlie was not in the room. My bleary eyes managed to make out the dim clock on the dresser. Eleven o'clock. I felt like I'd slept five minutes and not the two hours that had passed. I straightened myself onto my pillow, slipped beneath the sheets, and listened to Charlie opening drawers in the kitchen while I waited to fall back to sleep.

As if a shot of adrenaline ran through me, I bolted upright on my bed. My phone! It was plugged in on the kitchen counter. If Charlie saw a text from Cole, there would be no way to explain it. I ran downstairs and straight to the phone, exhaling only when I saw my son on the couch, holding a bowl of cereal. He gave me a sad smile. He hadn't looked.

"Hey. I can't sleep. Did I wake you?" he said.

"No. I just wanted to get my phone." I unplugged it and glimpsed three texts from Cole, asking if I got back safely, asking me to let him know, telling me he loved me.

"You're getting worse than me with your phone," Charlie said. He put in earphones and started to scroll his own phone.

I tapped his shoulder. "Anything from Kate?"

He shook his head, and tears welled up again.

"Sorry."

He returned to the screen.

Back upstairs, I texted Cole a quick note to tell him I'd made it home and then turned it off so I couldn't receive any more from him tonight. If I must hide a relationship from my kid, I shouldn't be in it. I knew what I had to do. I knew it all along. I'm ready now. Game over, Heather.

My niece called the house at midnight, distraught. Her father was out with friends, and she didn't know who else to call. She was trying to reach her mother, who hadn't been answering her texts. Again, I pulled myself from the bed, threw jeans and a sweatshirt on, and drove down to the pub near my sister's house where I knew she liked to go. I parked next to her car and found her inside, sitting at the corner of the long bar.

I slid onto a seat beside Trisha.

The bartender placed a napkin in front of me.

"Just a Coke, please," I said.

"Sure thing." He filled a glass and placed it on the napkin.

Trisha sat, less than poised, eyeing me warily. "Why are you here?"

Because your thirteen-year-old daughter is worried about you. "I'm here to take you home."

She pushed her empty martini glass away. "I don't need you here. I have my car."

"Right. I'd like your keys." I held out my hand, but she shook her head.

"Go home, Heather. I don't need you." She felt her pockets and then looked in her purse. No keys. "What did I do with them?" She half-stood, half-fell from her stool, and bent down to check the floor. Standing, she banged her head under the bar. "Shit." She rubbed her head, and her eyes welled.

I held her arm gently. "Let's go outside. Let's talk."

She yanked her arm from my grip and leaned on the bar. "I don't want to talk to you. Mike!"

The bartender glanced our way, and I shook my head behind her. He placed another glass of Coke on the bar in front of Trisha and returned to putting glasses away at the other end.

Trisha shoved the glass away from her, and soda spilled down the sides.

"Bullshit," she mumbled.

"Let's go."

She turned to me with anger spitting from her eyes. "No." Then she grabbed her purse and loped toward the door. I passed the bartender, Mike, seconds after her and stopped.

"Does this happen often?" I said.

He frowned. "More so the past few months. Adam's been picking her up. She hasn't made a scene yet, but she's on her way. Here." He handed me her keys.

"Thanks."

Trisha was in the parking lot, puking by the driver's door of her car. She pulled herself up, wiped her mouth, and yanked on the handle.

"It's locked. We're taking my car."

She turned to me. Her eye makeup had melted, and black pools puddled below her lower lashes. Even through the mess, she was a pretty woman. Like our mother.

"How are you gonna help me?" She was slurring, but her words stung. A drunk person speaks the truth. Sober, we keep what we feel inside. That's how it's been for us. She's been looking out for me my whole life. I couldn't tell her that as much as she tried to protect me, the damage had been done. She'd be more resentful than she is now.

"Just get in the car," I said. Now was not the time to talk. My words would be lost to vodka. And I had no idea what to say. What did I know about a healthy marriage?

She looked around the parking lot, swayed a bit, decided there were no other options and walked to my passenger door.

In the car, we both stared ahead.

"He doesn't touch me," she said.

The aroma of vomit mixed with perfume sickened me. Or perhaps Trisha's words made me queasy. I'd uttered the same thing to myself before Damian finally left.

How did we both get to this same place? Genetics? Example? I held the wheel and squeezed it tight. I knew we shouldn't blame our parents for our mistakes. We were adults now. But I did blame them. I blamed my mother for teaching us to hide from the truth, to accept the decisions we made, and not to change them. She stayed in a loveless marriage, hid in alcohol like Trisha was doing now. For a long time, I was also too weak to stand on my own.

"I don't think he's with another woman," I said. "I think he might be getting tired of picking up after you."

Trisha sniffed. "Whatever."

"Trisha, think of your girls. Stop this."

She stared out the window. "Just drive."

I pulled up to the house to see Adam waiting at the door. I looked up at him as we made our way toward the stoop. My sister, wearing two-inch wedges, stared at the ground as she carefully climbed the three steps to the front door.

"Are the girls sleeping?" I said.

"It's not something they haven't seen," he said, sounding exhausted.

I stared at him.

"Yes. They're sleeping." He stepped down and guided his wife through the door.

"I'll wait out here. We'll get your car," I said.

He followed her inside and came out ten minutes later. On the way back to the pub, he ran his fingers over his chin. "I can't control her. The girls are getting upset."

I pulled into the parking lot, next to Trisha's car and put it in Park.

"Adam, are you cheating on her?"

He turned to me, despondent. "No."

"She feels neglected."

"So, this is my fault?"

"No. But you're not helping by leaving every night."

He exhaled. "You know, it started innocently enough. Drinks on the weekends, wine on Sundays. Then Sunday rolled into Monday, and now it's every night. She's a different person. I don't want to be around it."

I bit my bottom lip. For years growing up, Trisha hid the truth of our family from me, finding my mother passed out on the small couch in the basement, covering for her when our father asked where she was. As I grew older and understood what was happening, I helped her. Usually, we cleaned up Mom's mess and left her there, under a blanket. She was too heavy to move upstairs. Told Dad she'd fallen asleep again watching television, and listened to his rants about her laziness. On those nights, Trisha and I would stare at each other, knowing without speaking that she was hiding from him, from his temper and disappointment. I'd busied myself in the kitchen making him dinner to appease him, while Trish sat with Mom.

I looked at Adam. "I'm not making excuses for her behavior. I don't know how much she shared with you. Maybe if you understood more about what it was like…" I shrugged. "I don't know. I don't know the answer."

"I love her. I always have. But it's tough to live with."

"Don't give up on her. She feels like you don't want her." I took a deep breath. "Take it from me, feeling unworthy is a great motivator to self-destruct."

"It didn't hurt you."

I stiffened. "Not everyone shows their pain. Some of us hide it better."

"That was out of line," Adam said. "I'm sorry."

An awkward silence settled over us.

"My sister is an open book. Anyone can see that. If your marriage is worth saving, then fight for it. She needs help, and she needs your support."

I climbed into my bed at two-thirty, bone-tired, and emotionally spent. Relationships can be so hard.

Chapter 20

I called Damian the following morning and offered to drive Charlie back to school. Then I put our son on the phone and tried not to listen to their conversation before he handed it back to me. "Dad wants to talk to you again."

"Yes?"

"Heather, do you think he needs to stay home another day or so? He still sounds a mess."

I waited as Charlie went upstairs to pack his bag before answering. "I don't think it'll help. He needs to get back to school. He only has a few weeks left before finals."

Damian sighed on the other end. "Okay. I trust your judgment."

I nearly dropped the phone. Was that a compliment? Was Damian sick? "Thanks," I said and quickly hung up the phone before he could add something derogatory or condescending and ruin the moment for me.

Charlie was despondent most of the ride up to school. We spoke when he needed to talk and rode silently when he couldn't. My heart hurt for him. I hoped his pain would pass quickly.

I pulled onto the campus at four o'clock in the afternoon. Charlie dragged himself out of the car as if he were going to the electric chair.

"Are you coming?" he said.

I thought of Cole in the dorm, wondering if he could masquerade his reaction to seeing me, how my next move with him would be my last, and I wasn't ready to face him or that conversation, certainly not within earshot of my son. I shook my head.

"No. I'll hang at the hotel and leave in the morning," I said.

He shut the door and started toward his building. I gave a quick honk and rolled down the passenger window. "Babe? If you want to have dinner later or just need to talk, text me. I'll be here."

He smiled, and my throat closed. "Kay. Thanks," he said.

I read through my emails in the hotel café since I was losing two days of work with this unexpected trip to Massachusetts. It took me three hours, one panini sandwich, and a cup of tea to finish my responses for Aunt Emma. I texted Charlie, and he responded he was okay. His hall-mates were going to watch the Red Sox pre-season game in the lounge and had convinced him to join them. Feeling better, I gathered my laptop, notes, pens, purse, and left the café to go back to my room.

Cole was standing by the reception desk. The sight of him, as always, took my breath away. His bronze skin accentuated those eyes. Eyes that saw only me right now. God, he was something. I wanted to grab him and run away from everything and everyone. But life wasn't that simple.

His smile fell when he saw my reaction. I couldn't contain my frown. I hadn't expected to see him so soon and wasn't prepared for a confrontation.

"I didn't know you were coming up," he said.

"Me neither. Have you seen Charlie?"

"Yes. He'll be okay."

"I know. But he's my kid. I kind of hate the girl right now," I said.

He watched me, and I turned away. I didn't want to do this. I was hoping to avoid having to tell him in person what I'd decided.

"Can I escort you to your room?" Cole said.

"No. Let me put my stuff back, and we'll take a walk."

I started for the elevator when he said my name. I turned to see him, confused. How was I going to do this in public?

"Come up," I said.

The elevator ride had a different vibe than when we were last together just a few days ago. The electric anticipatory sexual air had been replaced by a tense, knowing dread today.

In my room, I held my arm out, keeping him a safe distance from me.

He knew. I didn't have to say a word.

"You were acting strange on the last days of the trip." He took a shaky breath. "Don't do this." He stepped to me, and I backed up. His face crumbled for a fraction of a second before he regained his composure.

"We have to talk."

"No talking after the week we just had," he said.

I sighed. "The week we spent was amazing. I'll hold onto what we shared forever. But I figured something out on that trip. Something I'd been trying to ignore since we met." I paused and tried to formulate my words carefully. "We don't belong together. Life can't be secret nights spent in hotels or a week in paradise. Life is not as pretty as that. It's the everyday grind. It's work and bills and family and all that goes with it."

He nodded his head as I spoke. "I'm ready for that."

"Perhaps you are. But not with me. You're ready to go through all of that with someone who hasn't done it yet." I stepped toward him, and immediately his body reached for me, causing me to back up again.

"Cole, I won't take that away from you."

"I don't want it with anyone else."

"For now, maybe. You'll change your mind," I said.

His nostrils flared. "Stop telling me what I want!"

"You're too young to make these decisions!" My voice rose with his. After the deer incident, we had never yelled at each other.

"Enough about age! Goddammit, Heather! You don't know what you're talking about. I'll decide what I want and when!"

I'd never seen him this angry. Never heard this muted rage in his voice. I put my hands up to calm him.

He breathed and circled the small room, running his hands through his hair. My fingers tingled, knowing exactly how it felt to do that, already missing him. I wasn't afraid of his anger. I knew he was hurting. He wore his pain like a cloak over his entire body, evident in his rising chest, fisted hands, the grimace on that beautiful face. All I wanted to do was to hold him, peel away his clothes, and feel him on top of me, inside of me, making me feel better than I'd ever felt. Trisha's voice in my head came back to me. "Selfish." I told myself to stay strong. I was doing the right thing. But the hurt. I almost couldn't bear it.

He sat on the bed. "We're perfect together. I want to be with you. I'm in love with you."

I knelt by his feet and put my hands on his thighs. He covered them with his. "I love being with you. I do. We can continue what we're doing and let it take its course, but it will only hurt more when it ends, and we'd have lost years in the process."

"It won't end."

I closed my eyes and took a deep breath. "Everything ends." I looked back up at him. "I don't want you to lose wonderful opportunities. Let's take this for what it was. Amazing. For me, life-affirming. You gave me a gift, Cole."

Tears fell down my cheeks. His eyes filled.

"Think of Charlie and how he would feel if he knew I was with you," I said.

"Tell me you're not pushing me away to please someone else. Even Charlie. We could get past that."

"I'm not sure we could. He would feel betrayed."

"Betrayed how? This has nothing to do with him."

"He's my son."

"He's a man who'll have his own thing going on. Then what will you have?"

There was no right answer. "Cole, I'm asking you to respect my wishes and go."

He squeezed my hands. "I know you love me."

"Sometimes love isn't enough." My chin quivered.

His jaw clenched. He stood, and so did I.

"Let's play a game," he said.

"No more."

"There are no tomorrows, Heather. There is only today."

"Not for me. I live my life for tomorrow."

"Don't say that." His eyes were glassy, and his voice shook.

I folded my arms across my chest and stared at my feet.

"Don't give up on me," he said softly.

I didn't answer.

"I told you I'm a fighter. I'm not giving up on us."

"You have to move on." I brought my eyes to meet his.

"I just want to make you happy," he said.

My arms dropped. "You do. But I won't make you happy. Maybe you think I do now, but what about years from now? What then? I can't take your life away from you. That will make me sadder than I've ever been."

"That's not true."

"Yes, Cole. It is."

"You can't know that."

"I can. I have a lifetime of experience."

"There's so much you don't know about me."

"Then tell me. What do I need to know?"

He stared down at the floor. I waited to hear what he had to tell me. He opened his mouth to speak and decided against it. "Just trust me. Don't leave me," he whispered.

I took his hand in mine and kissed it. "You are more than anything I've ever hoped for. But it's not right, and I can't live with myself if I let this go on any longer. I shouldn't have allowed myself to get this involved."

"We can't control who we fall in love with."

"No. But as adults, we can control what we do about it. You're going to have a great life."

He grabbed me, wrapped his arms around me, and again, I felt safe and loved, and questioned what I was doing. How was I going to walk away from this? I wanted to be the person he saw, more than I'd ever believed myself to be.

I lifted my face to his, this wonderful man who walked into my life when I needed him most and lifted me to a place I'd never been. Maybe we're meant to pass each other on our journey through time, share moments that shape us, and then move on. I don't know what the future holds, but I want Cole's to be filled with everything he deserves. He deserves more than me.

I put my hands on his cheeks and leaned up to kiss him. Our tears mixed together and tasted of longing, sadness, and regret. Finally, I pushed him away.

"Go," I said and turned away to the window.

I waited while he pulled himself together. At the door, he paused. "Life doesn't have to be the way you described. It's all what you make it, Heather."

I couldn't respond. I kept my back to him.

"You'll change your mind," he whispered. "I'll wait for you."

The door closed behind him. I stared out the window, but I couldn't see a thing.

I woke up early the next morning from a fitful sleep. My head felt as if it were cracking in two. I stumbled to the bathroom, popped two extra-strength aspirin I found at the bottom of my makeup bag, and looked at myself in the mirror. The face I saw aged overnight. My eyes were dark and puffy and not my own. I didn't recognize the sad woman staring back at me. I'd been so euphoric just days ago.

I showered, dressed, and checked out of the hotel. Trisha had texted me during the morning. I wasn't ready to speak to her yet.

From the car, I texted Charlie that I was leaving and I'd call him later and then I hit the road.

The four-hour drive passed in a blur. The radio was on low, but I didn't hear it. I went over and over our last conversation in my mind, trying to figure out if there was anything Cole could have said to change my mind and came up with nothing. I made the right decision based on logic, reason, and statistics. It made total sense.

Why, then, did it feel so wrong?

Damian was sitting on the front porch when I pulled up to my house at lunchtime. He wore a dark suit and looked as handsome as ever, sitting on the rocking chair.

He stood as I got out of the car. "How did he do?"

"He's okay, I think. He was pretty upset when I dropped him, but his friends will pull him out of it."

Damian tilted his head. "Are you okay? You look…sad."

Maybe it was the kindness in his voice or the fact that he showed concern for me, but his question unclogged an emotional dam I'd had in place. I let go of all that I'd been holding in for the past months. I started to sob, as gut-wrenching wells of grief washed over me. My knees weakened, and Damian caught me in his arms.

He held me as I cried.

When I pulled myself together, I let him in the house and brewed a pot of coffee. He sat at the kitchen table.

"What just happened out there?"

Still hiccupping from the outburst, I put my hand up. "Please."

I poured mugs and made his coffee the way he liked it before placing it on the table and joining him. He sipped, eyeing me warily, as if afraid I might lose my mind again.

"I think I'm finally allowing myself to feel everything that has happened to me since last year. I haven't mourned us yet, and with Charlie gone and the changes in our lives, I feel sort of over-whelmed."

Damian put his mug down and leaned back. "Have you given any more thought to what we spoke about last month? Of me coming home?"

I was suddenly so tired. "Why the change of heart?"

"There's something different about you lately. Something…" He bit his lip in thought. "A fire within you. It's appealing."

"I feel different. Better, if you can look past that outburst outside." I tried to smile. "I didn't like who I was when we were married, and I don't want to go back there. I allowed myself to become this person who shrunk in the face of anything that wasn't safe. It's done. You know it, too. I don't want to fight with you anymore or have you showing up at the house uninvited. I need to finally begin my life."

His head dropped in defeat. "We had some good years, though, didn't we? I mean, it wasn't a total shamble," he said.

I thought about it. "No. Some of it was great. It wasn't entirely your fault. We were kids when we got together. And we didn't really know each other. I was trying to escape my house and latched onto you. I should have spent time on my own and figured out who I was. That was no way to start a marriage."

When he left, Damian hugged me goodbye. It was the first time in a long time.

Cole called me at midnight, and I let the call go to voice mail. *Heather.* His voice sounded soft, and my heartbeat quickened. *Call me. We need to talk.*

I deleted the message.

I called Charlie the following morning as he was walking to class, and he sounded much better, which relieved me. The next time I would see him would be when he came home for the summer. I couldn't wait.

For the next several weeks, I answered my letters and ran five miles every morning to clear my mind and exhaust myself, so I could sleep at night. Sometimes it didn't work, and I'd run again in the evening, the early spring air still cool to my skin, racing the crickets in the dark, always losing but always trying. Dottie called a few times and asked me if I wanted to join her line dancing, or go to a movie or lunch with her girlfriends. Each time I begged off. I needed to be by myself.

Cole left messages and texts daily. All went unanswered. The sooner he disconnected from me, the better it would be for him. I was sure I did the right thing, but I still felt the loss of something so beautiful.

I woke up on a Friday in late April, made a cup of coffee, checked my growing flower in the kitchen, as usual. It rose six inches from the soil, a slight, proud stem. What would it be? I decided to sit in the backyard on a lounge chair to enjoy the solace of the early morning. There was no sound but for the soft calling of the birds in the trees above me. Over my mug, I watched a chipmunk scatter across the corner of the pool cover. The lounge next to me was empty, but I could see Cole beside me and remember every word of our conversations, the ones that changed my perception of myself.

In tee shirt and sweats, the early morning chill left me as the coffee, and the rising sun permeated my pores. I watched the shade and shadows play along the perimeter of the yard. The east corner remained covered, blocked by the dense branches of an old oak. By eleven a.m., the west sat in full light. I stood, propelled by an idea and walked to the corner, my head toward the sky, and felt the morning warmth upon me.

You should grow a garden. I think this area gets ample sun in the summer.

How would you know this?

Well, there are no trees over it, for one.

I smiled at the memory of our conversation last Thanksgiving weekend. Five months ago, we stood right here when he suggested the garden. It felt like a lifetime.

I placed my mug on the grass and took ten steps forward, slipping a sandal off and leaving it there. Another ten steps south, the other sandal was abandoned and finally, ten steps back north, opposite the mug. The imagined square was fully exposed to the sun, more so than any other area of the lawn. Barefoot, I returned to the house, grabbed a roll of string, and on the walk back to the corner square, picked up four thin branches from the ground. Ten minutes later, I surveyed the cordoned area, sandals reclaimed, mug in hand, and went into the house.

I took a break from work at one, checked the patch of grass, heating under the full sun, and went back inside. I did this again at three and at six, mentally noting the hours of exposure before falling under shadows of sunset.

It took me all of Saturday and Sunday to cut out the one hundred square feet of grass. At dusk Sunday, I limped into the house, resting my heavy shovel in the garage and sat under the hot shower spray until the brown water running down the drain was clear, and my aching muscles were soothed. Two aspirin and a cup of hot tea, and I was blissfully down for the count.

I went to the newspaper office for a few hours on Monday morning, skipping my run due to complaining muscle fatigue. At lunch, I packed up my laptop and papers and went to a nursery I've passed countless times in my years of living here. It was larger than it appeared from the road, extending back several acres. I stood just inside the entrance, intimidated.

"Can I help you?" came a voice through a plant. I caught a portion of his face through a spray of bright pink pansies. He stepped aside and wiped his hands on a dirty towel.

"I hope so. Can you point me in the direction of your vegetables?"

He pointed a thick, calloused finger straight. I meandered down and up aisles of pre-planted vegetables, herbs, spices, and garden plants, my brain woozy with choices.

Before deciding on what to include in my modest garden, I walked through the entire nursery, reading names as foreign to me as another language, their instructions for care and growth. I felt leaves, pressed my nose to petals, growing drunk on intoxicating fragrances, before returning to my task at hand.

Two hours later, I drove home with six cherry, four Beefsteak and two Roma tomatoes, three bell pepper, four basil, two cilantro, one parsley, one thyme, three hot pepper, three cucumber, and two zucchini plants. Since I missed the window to start at seed planting, I bought pre-planted versions, each a few inches tall, like the one in the house, and carried them directly from the car to the empty garden.

The nursery owner, Anthony, the same calloused-handed man, explained the importance of fertile, prepared soil, the need for six or more hours of sunlight, and a soaking bath each week as I paid for the crops. I listened politely on the off-chance I might pick up some small tidbit of which I was unaware. To my pleasant surprise, I was rewarded.

"Lay an inch of mulch along the soil to deter some pests and to help maintain even moisture levels. If you have a pest problem, come back. I have a natural deterrent that might help. Don't want to put all those chemicals on your plants. Not if you plan on eating them."

Back home, I stood over the patch of dirt, which I'd turned and aerated before I left, and wondered if I would be able to harvest a piece of food at season's end.

At six o'clock, dirt under my fingernails and smeared along my cotton pants, I preened over my first garden ever. A sprinkle with the hose and I returned to the house with my first sense of satisfaction in weeks. I longed to share my new venture with someone. In the shower, an idea sprouted. Before I was thoroughly dried, I threw on my robe and went to my desk, with thoughts pouring out of me. I typed until the screen became blurry from exhaustion and then passed out before I could think any more.

My routine remained the same, with one new difference. After my morning run and before work, I visited my infant crops, cleared the impending weeds before they had a chance to interfere, and watched, waiting for change.

Chapter 21

I called Carl the following week and scheduled a meeting with him. Two days later, I sat in his office, holding a folder, waiting as he finished a phone call. He hung up, sat back, and smiled.

"Whadya got for me?"

I opened the folder and pulled out a few sheets of printed paper. "I didn't want to email this because I wanted to talk about it first. I have an idea."

"For Aunt Emma?"

"No. I decided to take Pete's spot in the paper. The gardening column."

His bushy eyebrows rose. "Oh."

"This is what I propose. I know next to nothing about gardening. What if I wrote an article about my experiences planting a garden for the first time? Maybe those readers who are like me will be enticed to start one, too?"

Carl rubbed his chin and leaned his chair back so far, it groaned in protest. I waited.

"So," he said, finally, relieving the chair and returning to an upright position. "You're going to lead the inept to an herb and flower mecca?"

"Vegetables."

He nodded. "Vegetables. It's the blind leading the blind."

"Well, when you put it that way – "

"No. I love it." He pulled himself up with his hands and stepped around his desk to me. "It's brilliant. What changed your mind?"

I looked down at my pages, a record of initial experiences so far, and back to Carl. "I'm tired of being afraid to try things. If it fails, then I'll think of something else."

He beamed and patted my shoulder. "I'm proud of you, kid."

Words I rarely heard from my father enveloped me like a warm blanket coming from my boss. I had walked in here, expecting he wouldn't embrace my proposal. Part of me thought it was a ludicrous venture. Blog about planting a garden? But as I dwelled on it the past few days, and visited my modest patch of dirt, I thought, if someone had written this first, I would have read it.

I handed him the first pages. When I reached the door, he stopped me. "Pete's last article is next month. I'll put this initial post after. It's a nice segue to yours."

Dottie showed up at my house the following Saturday evening with two copper cups and a kind smile that I needed badly.

"Moscow mules," she said when I opened the door. "Let's sit out here."

Holding the cups, she sat on a rocker and waited for me to sit on the other one before handing me my cocktail. The warm air, budding leaves, and birdsong made the perfect evening for sitting on the porch.

"I haven't heard from you in weeks," she said. "I see you running away from something every morning, your face in a determined grimace that concerns me. I figure, let me come by and see if I can't help in some way." She sipped her drink. "We've known each other for many years. Whatever it is going on, you can share it with me. If you need to. My guess is, it's more than Damian and Charlie. There's a change in you."

"You're right. I've been wanting to tell you what's going on, but I don't want you to think less of me."

"Less of you?" She put her hand to her chest. "Have you taken a life?"

"God, Dottie, no." I laughed at the absurdity of what she suggested.

"Then whatever you say could not make me think less of you. We're friends. How could you doubt me or my loyalty to you? This is why we have each other. To share what's going on. To get things off our chests. To feel better." She leaned toward me. "A woman needs another woman."

I told Dottie the whole story of Cole and me from the beginning, finishing long after our drinks were gone. When I finally stopped talking, she stared into her cup.

"I think we need more of this."

We walked to her house, and she showed me how to make a Moscow mule, my new favorite drink: vodka, ginger beer, simple sugar, and lime juice. Heaven in a cup, she said, and I agreed.

We returned to my porch.

"So, you've made your decision," she said, referring to my ending ties with Cole.

"I have."

We sipped our drinks.

"How would I have explained to Charlie what I was doing? He would have been devastated," I said.

"Our children are so important, aren't they? We spend much of our adult lives raising them, devoting everything we are to their well-being. Then they grow up and leave. They begin their own lives, separate from ours."

"Where are you going with this?" I said.

"In the end, it's you and only you." Dottie put her hand on my chair. "You're a wonderful mother. Charlie is a good person. You've done your job. Now, do for you. Whatever it is that may be."

"You think it's okay to be with a man almost half my age?"

"It's not important what I think," she said.

"I'm asking. As a friend."

She looked out over the front lawn, her hand around her cup. "Okay for you, maybe, not so much for Cole."

I nodded. "That's why I pushed him away."

Dottie lifted her eyes in thought. "You may have done the right thing. Only you know that. What I know is I've never seen you as happy as you've been the past few months. And now you're distraught. "

I sighed, defeated. "I know."

"This, too, shall pass."

"I hate that saying."

Dottie smiled. "You'll find happiness."

"How can you be so sure?"

"When you showed up at my door last March, the day Damian moved out, you sat at my table, feeling a failure, to quote your own words. You believed your only chance at happiness walked out the door."

I barely recalled the day, my vision for mine and Charlie's future so fogged with doubt I sought refuge at Dottie's while Charlie was at school.

"I never thought you were that happy anyway. Do you remember what I told you?" she said.

I shook my head.

"I said you would have many more chances and that you would find the peace you sought."

"Have *you*?" I said. "Have you found peace since George died?"

She scanned the lawn and the trees and sighed at the sky. "I have."

"I envy you."

"Don't. You've already proved to yourself you can connect with someone else. Someone who made you happy. Now you know it's out there. You have plenty of time left. You're young."

We rocked and sipped and listened to the leaves rustle in the gentle wind.

"Let's face it," she said, eyes closed, head resting back against the rocker. "What woman doesn't fantasize about having a younger man? You lived the dream for a little while."

I looked at her, shocked. With eyes still closed, she smiled.

Cole continued to text me daily. I savored each message and then deleted it.

Charlie checked in on Sunday and told me he started seeing a girl from his business class. His voice no longer held that twinge of sadness that kept me thinking of him for hours after our conversations.

A letter arrived by FedEx on May 10th. I signed for it and opened the envelope to find a round trip ticket to Paris scheduled for June 1st to return June 16th, with a note included.

Meet me at the skybox at Kennedy. The City of Lights waits for us.

I waited until Charlie was in class and called Cole.

He answered before the first ring echoed. "Heather."

I swallowed. "I can't accept this ticket. Please get your money back. Or offer it to someone else."

There was an uncomfortable silence. I chewed on my thumbnail, waiting, and almost disconnected the call when I heard his voice. "Please don't do this. You can't be okay with the way things are now. Not after what we shared."

I squeezed my eyes shut. Cole's voice brought my heart to my throat, and I wanted to say, Yes, I would be there to meet him. I wanted so bad to go - not to see the city - but to be anywhere with him. Instead, I said, "I need you to move on. Take a friend with you. Show her the world."

"Stop it."

I gripped the phone. "Please, Cole. I can't. Please stop texting. I promise you will see this for what it was."

"And what was it for you, Heather?" he whispered, not bothering to hide his anguish. I felt tears burn my eyes for the pain I was inflicting and feeling. I berated myself for allowing it to get this far. If only my ex would have fought this hard for me.

"A brief, wonderful exploration of what could never be. Let's hold on to the jewel it was. And let go. I have."

I hung up before the sound of his voice could weaken my resolve. He texted me immediately.

There are things I need to tell you. I'll be at the airport on June 1ˢᵗ, waiting for you.

I considered calling him back, just to hear what he could tell me that would change my mind. I decided there was nothing that would work. With a swipe of my finger, the message disappeared. I walked through my living room, past the knitting chair and outside.

Trisha showed up at my door unexpectedly at noon the following day. She wore sweats, dark glasses, her hair back in a ponytail. "I need to talk to you."

"Let's sit out here." I motioned to the chairs on the porch, needing a break from work and fresh air in my lungs.

We sat and rocked. This porch was getting a lot of use.

"How long are you going to stay mad at me?" she said.

"I don't know."

She kept her glasses on, though we were protected from the sun under the overhang.

"I've been doing a lot of thinking." Her lower lip quivered, and she took a deep breath. "I don't want to be like Mom. I need your help."

My anger dissipated, and I looked to my sister. "Of course."

She nodded and sniffed. "There's a group that meets at the lodge near my house. I can't go there alone."

"What about Adam?"

She wiped her nose on her sleeve. "I want you with me. He doesn't know what it was like."

"Have you told him? You've been married for twenty years."

"It's not the same as living through it. I need you there. I won't have the courage to go if I have to do it alone."

"You won't be alone. I'll be with you."

She exhaled and rested her head back. "Adam said he'd go to couples counseling, but I need to fix myself first."

"He loves you, you know."

We rocked in silence.

"She was wonderful in so many ways, too," I said.

Trisha knew I was referring to our mother and nodded. "She was. The other day, I told the girls how Mom used to sneak into our room at dawn on our birthdays to be the first person to say Happy Birthday."

Tears instantly filled my eyes. "I remember. She'd crawl into my bed and hug me and whisper the song until I woke up." I pressed my fingers against my eyes. "I haven't thought of that in years."

Trisha nodded. "We should talk about the good things more."

"Yes."

I took a speaking engagement for the following week and told no one where I was going. Charlie was taking his finals and needed to be picked up a few days after I returned, so even he had no idea of my whereabouts, and I felt safe from any surprise visits.

I spent two days in Philadelphia and was happy to see my friend John, who was speaking at the same time slot I was. After our seminars, I caught him walking back to his room as I was returning from mine. I'd changed into jeans and kept my blouse and blazer on.

"John?" He stopped.

"Hey!" he said. Always ready with a smile, I realized how nice it was to see him. The last few events we worked together, I'd brushed him off in favor of being with Cole.

"Would you like to go out with me today and see the town?" My voice cracked.

"Are you okay? Heather, are you crying?"

I shook my head and wiped my eyes. "I'm fine. Really. Don't mind me. It's my new hobby. I cry a lot now."

John stared at me until I forced a smile on my face.

"I've been in Philly a handful of times and have only allowed myself to venture to a three-block perimeter of the hotel. I need to see the world around me and stop closing myself in," I said.

He squinted his eyes, considering what I said. "That's a switch."

I waited and swallowed the grief that threatened to overtake me. These were Cole's words I was saying. And he had been right.

"Sure," John said finally. "I'll just go put my laptop away. I'll meet you in the lobby in five minutes." He jogged off, and I went to the front doors to wait for him.

We spent an afternoon walking through the city. It really is a wonderful town, filled with rich history and delectable cuisine, and I'd missed it all these years. While we waited on line for the famous steak sandwiches, we talked about work and family, plans for the summer. I explained that Charlie would be studying in Spain beginning in August, and we'd need to get him a passport, along with a list of other necessities for the trip. John mentioned he was writing a novel, and it was going slowly. Sandwiches in hand, we found seats along the sidewalk with the other patrons and ate.

"What's the book about?" I said.

"A married couple."

"Ah, a thriller, you mean."

We laughed.

"I don't really want to talk about it while in the early stages," he said finally.

We threw our garbage away, and under the warm sun, John led me through unfamiliar streets lined with pretty brownstones with colorful doors. He took my hand and put it in the crook of his arm. A fatherly gesture that made me feel young.

"So, what's changed in your life?"

"What do you mean?" I said.

"Well, you're here with me, for one."

I laughed. "I missed not spending time with you at the last few conferences."

"You're a terrible liar."

I leaned my head toward his shoulder. "I promise, that is the truest thing I've said to you."

We arrived at Reading Terminal Market, and at once, I was taken with the rows and rows of merchants selling cheeses, chocolate, meats, and seafood, an odiferous orchestra that teased my senses. I wanted everything. In the end, I settled on a half-pound of aromatic homemade chocolate, and John bought Whoopie pies. Joann wouldn't let him in the house without them.

Cole texted me as John and I left the market two hours later. *Pack a light sweater. Paris nights may be chilly in early June.*

I stared at the message. My finger hovered over the Delete button.

"You okay?"

I deleted the text and forced a smile. "I'm good."

I returned home the following night and felt better than I had in days. As I made myself a salad, I received a text from Charlie confirming I should pick him up Friday.

I answered immediately. *Of course. See you then.*

I wondered if Cole would be there, but decided that I would face him if I had to. I'd be strong and decisive, and he'd see finally that it was over.

Damian called. "Charlie told me you're bringing him home."

"Yes."

He paused. "You're okay to do that?"

"Damian, it's what's keeping me going. I can't wait to see him."

"Do you want company?"

I paced the first floor of the house. "No. He'll call you when we get home."

When the morning came that I was to leave for Amherst, my stomach was in knots, and my palms were moist for the entire trip up. I'd convinced myself I'd be strong, but if Cole was there, I might crack, and he'd see it. I longed to talk to him, to hear his voice but refused to break down. I was doing what was best for him.

I arrived at Appleton Hall at noon to find Charlie sitting in his room among packed bags and boxes. Cole's side was bare as if he'd never existed at all, and sadness held me briefly before letting go.

I stood at his open door. "Can you believe it's over already?"

Charlie looked around and nodded. "No."

We laughed, and he picked up a box.

"I'm parked right out front," I said as he passed me.

It took an hour to pack up the car, do a quick sweep of the room, and leave the dorm for the last time.

"Is there anyone you want to say goodbye to?"

Charlie shook his head. "I said my goodbyes yesterday."

I drove through the campus, past cars with students and parents performing the same end-of-year ritual, a less chaotic scene from the one where we arrived. Final exams were scattered throughout the last two weeks. Some students left up to a week earlier.

I merged onto 91. "So, good year?"

Charlie, who'd been looking out his window, turned to me. "Overall, yeah."

"Good."

My son didn't want to make small talk. He looked tired, and I was excited to get him home. We stopped for dinner at a rest stop. Over hamburgers, he spoke. "Missy lives on Long Island."

"Missy?"

"The girl from my Economics class. We might see each other over the summer."

"Okay. Have you resolved the issues with Kate or just let it go?"

He shrugged, obviously still hurt. "She turned out to be such a bitch. Cole was helpful. He talked to me a lot about it. He said he had experience with heartbreak and that it would get easier."

The last of my burger sat in my throat. I forced it down. "When did Cole go home?"

"He left on Monday. He skipped his last final."

"Why?"

"I don't know. He's been down the past month or so, but he wouldn't say why. I thought I was bad with Kate, but he was worse. He wouldn't talk about it, didn't eat much or sleep, and looked pretty bad. His counselor, Dave, came to see him a few times, but it didn't seem to help."

"Counselor?" I said.

Charlie stood, threw out his garbage, and stretched. "Come on, I want to leave."

In the car, I couldn't let the conversation go. "What does he need a counselor for?"

Charlie leaned his head back and closed his eyes. "I don't really know. He had some issues in high school, and he told me Dave helped him out a lot. They're friends."

This must have been the man I saw him with outside the diner in town when I visited last October, before we…

Charlie's head rolled to the side, and he slept the rest of the ride home.

I thought about reaching out to Cole to see if he was okay, but knew my actions would mislead him so, just as quickly, decided against it.

Why did he need a counselor? I thought about the times we were together, how he didn't drink, and on the rare occasions he did, he had very little. But a recovering alcoholic must abstain completely. It didn't make sense. Did he have a drug problem? Could that be why he took a few years off before college? To get clean? Oh God, would I be responsible for him having a relapse? A few miles passed while my brain whirred. Finally, I took a deep breath. *Heather, you're not responsible. Stop beating yourself up.*

We pulled into the driveway as the sky turned navy and left the car full, both of us too tired to do anything but go to sleep.

In the morning, I dragged Charlie to the backyard and proudly showed him my garden. The tomato plants had grown several inches already, and I had placed protective cans around them, as suggested by Anthony at the nursery, so they would keep contained and not fall over under the weight of the heavy fruit I hoped to grow. And just last week, I placed a small white picket fence with a mesh screen tied to it every ten inches. I noticed small rodents darting between my plants and found this obstacle kept most of them out. Charlie was sufficiently shocked and circled the perimeter in silence.

"I know what you're thinking, but I really think I can do this," I said.

He pursed his lips. "This would be a new one for you. What's this one?" He pointed to a stalk that was taller than the tomato plants. It grew just outside the small garden fence.

"Remember that little sprout in the glass in the kitchen? Well, I finally moved her here. She'll oversee the garden, whatever she is."

"Why do you call her a she?"

I leaned over and lifted a lower leaf. "Nothing there," I said, holding back a smile.

"You're losing it, Mom."

"Maybe I am. But I'm having fun. Here." I pulled off an immature basil leaf and handed it to him. "Smell this."

He put the leaf to his nose and sniffed deeply.

"I know, right? I want to bottle it and dab it behind my ears."
I laughed. "They're still small, but when they grow, I'm planning to
make pesto."

He rubbed his thumb over the leaf. "Good job. It's very nice."

He stared at the ground, and I stared at him. He'd matured this
year. I could see his face thinned even more. Gone was my baby.

"What's that?" He pointed to a small plant at the base of one of
my Roma tomatoes.

"I don't know. I haven't seen it. Is it a weed?" I bent over and
pulled it out of the ground, bringing it to my nose. "It's mint."

"Cool. You're growing mint, too."

"No. I'm not." I looked through the rest of my garden and saw
another mint plant near the border, on the other side of the mini
fence. "How did that get there?"

Charlie shrugged, losing interest in my new hobby. He left me
pondering this development and went to unpack the car.

Chapter 22

Dear Aunt Emma,

I met a wonderful man at work. We hit it off immediately and started dating. It hasn't been that long, but I am falling in love. I think he is too. He showers me with gifts and notes and just asked me to take the next step and spend the weekend with him at his cabin upstate. I really want to go, but the problem is, I am hiding something from him, and I'm afraid once he finds out my secret, he won't want to see me anymore. I had a single mastectomy last year and have not had reconstruction due to personal reasons. Instead, I've been wearing a mastectomy bra, which hides my asymmetrical breasts under clothes.

What should I do? Do I come clean or just tell him I can't go away?

~ Uniboob

Dear Uniboob,

If this man truly likes you or loves you, then he will accept you exactly as you are. Be honest from the beginning. All secrets come out eventually, and the sooner you treat him with the respect you want in return, the sooner you can get to that cabin for some fun.

And if he doesn't want just one boob, then you don't want him, either. I have a feeling you'll be fine.

~ Aunt Emma

The week Charlie came home, he spent an inordinate amount of time catching up with his high school friends, and life for me hadn't changed from the months he'd been away. He saw Damian twice for dinner, and I worked on my letters, tended to my garden and ran or hiked, trying to keep myself from missing the man who occupied my thoughts. Sometimes, it worked, and sometimes I let go, allowing myself a good cry to ease the searing in my heart.

Cole's daily texts somehow kept me connected to him, and I felt a sense of solace reading them before hitting delete. I should have wanted him to stop and get on with his life, and my silence certainly reflected that thought. But in my heart, I wanted to hear from him and know that the happiness we felt while we were together was mutual.

I was at my computer one evening when a text came through. I'd expected to see another simple note confessing his devotion. When I read the words, my hand flew to my chest.

Will you be at the airport?

My heart sank to my feet as I opened my desk drawer and pulled out the plane ticket. Tomorrow was June 1st. He wanted to take me to Paris.

Charlie walked into the house and called out to me from the kitchen.

"I'm home! I brought dinner."

My hands shook as I stared at the ticket. What would happen if I just got up and left for two weeks? Charlie would be fine. In fact, he'd hardly bat an eye, continuing his socializing and working. I closed my eyes. I'd rather be doing more than anything…

"Mom? Are you home?"

I swallowed my desire and opened my eyes. Fool. You're not going anywhere. With a resigned sigh, I responded to Cole's text. *No.*

I went downstairs to my son, the ticket torn up in the trash beneath my desk.

"Hey," Charlie said when I walked into the kitchen. "My boss gave me these." He pointed to two eggplant heroes on the table.

"Thanks."

"What's wrong? You look upset."

"I do?" I smiled, though it was a struggle. "I'm fine. I'm hungry. Let's eat."

He pulled a sandwich toward him and unwrapped it.

"Tomorrow, Missy and I are going to Fire Island, so I won't be home. Do you mind?"

"Don't worry about me. I'm taking Aunt Trish to her meeting, so I'll probably eat dinner with her." I picked at the food in front of me.

"How's it going with that?" Charlie said.

"It's a daily fight. But it's a good group of people. She has good support."

He looked at me. "She sure does."

I smiled, grateful for the boy.

Eventually, Charlie and I settled into a routine that worked for both of us. He slept late in the mornings while I quietly worked. We had lunch together (this consisted of lunch for me, breakfast for him) and Charlie left for work at the Pizza Depot or out with friends. He started spending more time with Melissa, who lived in Nassau County, about thirty minutes away.

I didn't hear from Cole the day we were to leave for Paris nor the days following, and I struggled to accept that he'd finally given up. He must have moved on as Charlie did after his breakup with Kate. I saw firsthand how quickly a teen could recover from a broken heart.

The thing is, Cole was no longer a teen, and he was nothing like Charlie.

I stepped into my garden, gingerly moving among my growing plants, pinching dead leaves, and withered branches. I touched the growing fruit, squatting among the leaves, and breathing in the life around me. The basil was thriving, its rich aroma wafting up my nose. The Roma and cherry tomatoes started to sprout. Yesterday, I counted thirty flowers, and there were many more waiting to bloom. I didn't think it was possible. But here it was. Proof I didn't kill everything. I stood and stretched the kinks from my legs. You knew it before I did, I said to Cole in my mind. I missed talking to him so damn much. He'd love this. His flower stood proudly outside the garden fence. Her sturdy stalk, growing faster than the vegetables, already stood six feet tall. I smiled as I took in her gorgeous face. I had grown my very first sunflower. She was magnificent: strong, yet elegant, opening her face unabashedly to the sun.

I stepped out of my magic square, as I'd come to call it, to find more mint had spread along the cement wall of the house. "How the hell are you getting here now?" I asked the pesky invader. I yanked hard and tore the root from the ground. Bringing the leaves to my nose, I breathed in the aromatic scent. It smelled appealing, but I had little use for it. I didn't plan for this and remembered Anthony from the nursery told me that anything I don't want is considered a weed. I don't want this here.

Before leaving to pick up Trisha for her group support meeting, I stopped at Dottie's. She let me in and asked me to wait while she went upstairs to show me something. She came back into the kitchen, holding a passport.

"What do you have there?"

She smiled. "My first one."

"You've never been outside the country either?"

Dottie shook her head. "George hated to fly."

I laughed. "Where are you going?"

She placed the passport gingerly on the counter and leaned over it on crossed arms. "I am taking the kids to Italy. I decided I want to see the world, and I want them with me."

"How much does that cost?"

"A lot. George hated spending money. He worked so hard, saving for the future and died before his future got here. I recently met with my accountant, and I have more than I'll need. I want to spend some of it. I want to experience new things, and I don't have a partner to do that with, so I figured I'd take the next best thing. My love's children. I want to get out of this house and see something."

She had a spark in her eye and a glow on her cheeks.

I put my hand on hers. "It's a year of firsts," I said.

The meeting tonight was particularly tough for my sister. It was her turn to share the experience that ultimately brought her to seek help. She held my hand tightly while we faced the circle, and she admitted her recent behavior and how she felt viewing her actions from her family's perspective. We both cried as she talked. When I dropped her at her house, I asked her to join me the following day to spend at the pool with her girls. Charlie was hardly home, so I liked it when the girls were over, splashing around and enjoying themselves. She needed the company. We both did.

"Do you feel better?" I asked. We lounged under the warm sun while the girls swam and talked. Trisha knew I was referring to the meeting. We didn't discuss it on our way home last night.

"I do. As painful as it was to admit peeing my pants in front of my daughters, I feel like something has lifted." She shielded her eyes with her hand and turned to me. "Don't get me wrong. I still want to bury myself under a rock, but hearing other peoples' issues makes me sort of feel not so alone."

I nodded. Some of the stories we heard over the last weeks were tough to digest. My sister's situation, as rough as it's been for her and her family, wasn't nearly as devastating as a few in her group. People lost everything: their jobs, marriage, children. Trisha was heading down that highway, and I felt grateful every day that she decided to get help when she did.

"Heather," she said, breaking into my thoughts. "Without you, I don't know what would have happened to me."

I put my hand on her arm. "Adam wouldn't have let you get too far."

She shook her head. "He would have. He doesn't know what it can do. You do. Thank you, sister."

I couldn't answer. This was a big step for Trish. And for me. I squeezed her arm in response and let it go.

"Charlie's working?" she said.

"Yes. He's out a lot. Between work, his friends, and his girlfriend, I rarely see him. Sometimes, I walk around the house and think it's too big for me."

"It is, but you can't sell it, can you? And besides, where would you go?"

"I don't know. We have rooms that are barely used."

Trisha rubbed more lotion on her arms. "Damian wouldn't be happy if you sold."

"Why not? He would have his money, and I would have no more need to speak to him."

"Exactly."

"What are you saying?" I said.

Trisha pulled her sunglasses down to show me her eyes. They were clear, and I felt optimistic. "Does he still come over?"

"Not as often. He stopped by a few weeks earlier to see Charlie. He knocks on the door now, and we've reached a civil agreement when we're together. I don't ask about Genna, and he doesn't ask about my social activity, of which there is none."

"He wants to come back," Trisha said, slathering more sunscreen on her chest. "Why do you think he wants the bills to still come here? Damian won't send money. He wants to hand it to you. Who the hell does that?"

"He did ask to come back."

Trish sat up and whirled her legs over the lounge. "What?"

I rested my head back and closed my eyes. "Before Charlie came home. He said things weren't going well with Genna, and he wanted to try again."

I heard nothing and opened my eyes to see my sister, speechless.

"I told him no. Obviously," I said.

Silence.

"Trish, you're making me nervous. Relax. Lie down."

She did. But not before she let out a whistle. "Who are you, and what have you done with my sister?"

I took a deep breath, feeling tougher, and closed my eyes again. "We did have a nice visit. We came to a truce. For Charlie's sake, at least."

We listened to the girls play Marco Polo in the pool.

"When's the last time you spoke to the roommate?" Trisha said.

It took me a few breaths before I could answer. "May 10th." One-thirty pm.

Trisha put her finger to her lips in thought. "So, nine weeks."

Ten. Cole had texted me every single day for fifty-two days. The last text I received was on June 1st, forty-five days ago. The day we were to leave for Paris. *Don't give up on me.* The last words I have of his to hold onto. My phone has been dead silent since, and I find myself still checking it. This was the one text I kept. And I couldn't help but feel the cruel irony of his message – for after weeks and weeks of unanswered pleas, he finally gave up, and I'm mourning the loss all over again.

I felt her eyes on me for several beats before she rested her head back down against the lounge.

"He's moved on," I said.

"How do you know?"

I shrugged, grateful to be wearing sunglasses. "It was a matter of time before he came to his senses."

"I'm sorry."

Amanda called her mother from across the pool. "Is there anything to eat?"

"Go in the kitchen and get out the sandwiches I made," I yelled over to her.

Wrapped in towels, the girls left us. Trisha and I sat in complete silence.

"I'm going to the next meeting by myself."

I turned my head to my sister. "Are you sure?" She nodded. I reached my hand to hers and held it. "Okay."

"Adam said Bill asked about you the other day."

I thought about the afternoon I sat on this chair, surrounded by dark leaves and an autumn sky.

"Maybe I'll call him," I said, surprising Trisha.

"That's what I wanted to hear."

Bill and I sat in a half-empty theater, sharing a tub of popcorn while we waited for the movie to begin. He was telling me about his recent visit with his grandson when a couple passed us. The woman, hearing Bill's voice, turned, and recognition swept over her face. Bill was oblivious, and I interrupted his story to point to the person waiting to speak to him. Her husband stood next to her.

"Bill. I thought that was you!" He stood to greet the couple with a kiss and a handshake. Then he turned to me.

"Heather, this is Matt and Charlene. This is Heather."

She wore a halter shirt, gathered at the neck, and as we shook hands, I couldn't help but stare at her. Amid the smattering of freckles along her chest sat a scar just below her collarbone. It was the same size, at the same spot as Cole's. It was uncanny.

The couple spoke briefly with Bill, friends from the past, said goodbye, and found seats up front. Bill resumed his seat and reached into the bucket. "She was close to Elaina," he said.

I held a piece of popcorn in my hand. "A friend of mine has a scar just like hers. The one near her collarbone."

Bill popped a handful into his mouth. "Too many do, I'm afraid."

"I don't understand."

He lowered his voice to barely a whisper. "Charlene is a survivor. The scar is what's left when they take the port out."

"The port?"

Bill frowned at me. "You don't know what a port is? Haven't you known someone with cancer?"

I shook my head, and the blood drained from my face as he explained to me that the port is the way chemo is administered.

It was a fight, Cole had told me.

"You're lucky," Bill continued, unaware he'd lost me. "Too many go through it." He sighed and reached for another handful of popcorn. I handed him the bucket. I'd lost my appetite.

The lights dimmed, the screen came alive, and I spent the next two hours in disbelief, asking the same question. Did Cole have cancer?

Chapter 23

Dear Aunt Emma,

I have a problem and need your advice. My girlfriend and I recently broken up over a stupid misunderstanding. I walked away angry, and now I regret it. I've been trying to reach her to tell her that I am being deployed, but she won't answer my texts or calls. I need to tell her what she means to me before I leave, in case I don't return. What can I do?

~ Out of ideas

Dear Ideas,

Write her a letter. Keep nothing back. The written word holds power and is something she can save. You might find true feelings emerge while you're gone. For both of you.

Trust me. You have a better shot of her responding to that.

Thank you for your service. Be safe.

~Aunt Emma

Charlie was in his room, listening to music on his bed when I walked in from being out with Bill. I stopped at his door. "Where's Melissa tonight?"

He pulled his earphones from his ears. "She's visiting her grandmother."

"Oh." I tried not to ask, but couldn't help it. "Have you spoken to Cole lately?"

"Not lately. We texted a bit, but I haven't talked to him."

"Maybe you should call him," I said.

Charlie nodded, and I started to walk to my room when he called me back. "How was your date?"

I leaned against his door. "It wasn't really a date. We're just friends." On paper, Bill was a good fit for me: he had grown children, more my generation, though a bit older, with a decent personality, but he didn't push my heart into overdrive just by looking at me the way Cole had done. Bill had been receptive when I told him I'd like to keep our relationship platonic. And anyway, it was nice to have another friend to go out with.

"You're not into him?" Charlie said. He propped himself up on an elbow.

"Not in a romantic way, no."

"Yeah, I noticed you're not enthusiastic when you talk about him."

He checked his phone. If my relationships with Damien and Cole had taught me anything, it was that I shouldn't settle for status quo. Charlie seemed to think so, too.

"Babe?" I said.

He looked up.

"You're okay with me dating someone romantically, right?"

"Sure. It's your life, Mom." He looked back at his phone and texted someone.

I pressed my lips together and decided to take it a step further. "What if I got involved with someone younger?"

He put the phone down and pulled himself up to sit. "How do you mean? Like Dad and Genna?"

"Kind of."

Charlie frowned. "The whole idea of you with *any* guy is disturbing." He shrugged. "But that's because you're my mother."

I laughed. "Okay. I'll stop here then." I stepped back. "Goodnight."

I went to my room, slipped on my pajamas, and got into bed. Charlie walked in.

"Is there something wrong?" I said, immediately thinking of Cole and wondering if maybe Charlie did know something.

He shook his head and sat on the end of my bed. "I gave my notice at work."

"I still can't believe you're going to Spain for a whole semester. And so soon. It feels like I just picked you up." When he applied to study abroad at Christmas, I was happy for him. Now, with only a week to go before he leaves, part of me wished he were just going back up to Massachusetts.

"Summers always pass too quickly," he said, looking down.

"Maybe I'll visit you in Seville."

"You're kidding."

I gritted my teeth and widened my eyes, making him laugh.

"Wow, I wouldn't have expected that, Mom. That would be great."

I'd never been farther than The Dominican Republic my whole life. Stayed within the confines of the States, and for the most part, the confines of my house. An adventurous streak was not a gene I acquired. My son's reaction was proof of that. Though the idea of going across the ocean terrified me, I'd do it for him.

"I'll be home at Christmas, so don't worry if you can't," Charlie said as if reading my mind. He started back to his room and then stopped and turned around. "Are you sad that Dad is with someone, and you're not?"

"No. Not anymore. It was hard at first, but now I see it's for the best." He stood by my door as if waiting for me to say more. "Charlie, are you okay with everything? I know it's been a tough year."

He paused as if thinking about the question. "Not as bad as I thought it would be. I mean, you both seem happier apart than together." He looked at his feet. "It's just...Nevermind."

"What? Tell me."

Charlie sighed. "I just wonder if anything lasts. You know, no one really stays together."

I folded my comforter down and sat up. "Babe. That's not true. Lots of couples stay together. It takes work, I'm not going to lie. But it's worth all the effort when it does work. Don't be afraid to try. You are not us. When the time comes in your life when you meet someone who fills you with peace and joy and fire and accepts you with all your flaws, give it everything you've got."

He leaned his head against the door. "I don't know how I feel about Melissa."

236 | *Kimberly Wenzler*

"You don't have to know right now. You're young. Enjoy the freedom. Just have fun. I promise you will find love."

"So will you," he said.

"I know." I looked at my child, my intuitive, honest boy, who was not so self-absorbed after all. I almost told him I already found love again but thought better of it. Baby steps. And there was nothing to tell anymore.

***

I tossed and turned all night, so I stayed in bed until mid-morning. I heard Charlie get up and leave the house, probably going to the gym or Missy's. Or anywhere else an eighteen-year-old wants to go on a Friday morning in August. He left a note for me on the kitchen table. *Sushi tonight?*

We hadn't gone out all summer, thinking we had plenty of time. I took the note, hung it on the bulletin board in the mudroom, and went outside.

In the yard, I took my daily visit to the vegetables and thriving sunflower. Leaning over the small fence, I pinched the top flowers from the basil plants, which had grown taller, the fat leaves bright green and fragrant. Then I knelt and found another small mint plant growing along the fence and pulled a blade free. Sitting on the ground, I inhaled the fresh scent. I lay back on the grass, rubbing my fingers on the leaf. Maybe I can put this mint to use.

The sun heated my skin, and I sat up slowly. From the angle I was situated, I saw a patch of red on one of the tomato plants. I leaned over and moved the leaves aside to spot the first ripened beefsteak tomato of the season. With a growing smile, I gently tugged, and it let go of the stem without complaint. I rested back on the grass and held the fruit in my hand. A hummingbird flew by and hovered over me, her wings beating furiously as they held her in place not far from my face. I lay frozen, in awe, staring at her perfect tiny body. She seemed to stare back at me, and for a breath, we watched each other, until she flew from my line of sight.

I'd never seen a creature so perfect before, and certainly not so close. I felt a rush of gratitude rise within me and couldn't stop my tears.

Charlie came home at seven, and we went to our favorite sushi restaurant, a Harrison special occasion destination over the years.

"How is Melissa taking your leaving?"

"She's going back to school in a couple of weeks. No biggie."

"Okay." I scanned the menu, glimpsing the cocktail page, and my eye caught something. I smiled. Lime, mint, and rum. A Mojito. Of course.

The waitress brought two glasses of water and took our orders.

"What's so funny?" Charlie asked when she walked away.

I shook my head. "I just found a use for the mint I'm growing."

"I thought you said you didn't want it."

I shrugged. "I didn't. But it keeps showing up. I love the way it smells."

Our dinner arrived, and we ate quietly for a while.

"Remember when I needed chopstick helpers?" Charlie said.

I grinned. "Like it was yesterday."

He skillfully lifted a roll, dipped it in soy sauce, and popped it into his mouth.

"You have no problems using them now," I said.

He smiled with his cheeks full of food. I'm going to miss this kid.

"Mom?"

"Mmm?" I was focused on the serving plate, choosing what I would eat next. I aimed for a piece of tuna roll and put it on my plate.

"I called Cole yesterday to say goodbye and tell him I'll see him Spring semester."

I stopped chewing.

Charlie continued. "His mother answered his phone. She said he'd been in the hospital this summer. Getting tests."

I placed my chopsticks on my plate and forced down the food in my throat.

"She said he had a recurrence. I didn't know what she was talking about so, she told me he was sick in high school. He missed his eleventh and twelfth-grade years." Charlie shook his head. "He didn't tell me." He pushed a roll on his plate while I held my stomach as bile rose to my throat.

"That guy, Dave, is his medical counselor. Cole told me he was a friend. He slipped once and called him his counselor. I figured he might have had a drug problem. There are a few people on campus who do some pretty intense stuff, so…" He gazed at his plate, and I listened in disbelief.

"Anyway, Mrs. Prue said he's home. Well, not home. He has an apartment in Boston now."

"Did you speak with him?" My words were a whisper.

Charlie shook his head. "He wasn't available. He's not going back to school."

Cole last texted me on June 1st. Two months ago. I thought he'd found someone else. He may still have.

I stared at the remnants of our dinner as they drifted in and out of focus while Charlie kept talking.

"It's crazy. I don't know what's going to happen to him. Mom? Where are you going?"

I had pushed back from the table and stood. "Be right back," I said, though I'm not sure if Charlie heard me. The words barely came out. I ran into the bathroom and directly into a stall. Bent over, I rested my hands on my thighs and took deep breaths, in through the nose, out through my mouth, until I finally eased my shaking body and sudden nausea. I stood and leaned against the stall while my mind raced. How could he be sick? That beautiful, healthy man? What must he be feeling? Does he hurt? Please, God, make it a mistake.

I started putting pieces together, pieces I couldn't see at the time: his view on life so different from others his age. *Live for today, Heather,* he'd told me, *Don't worry so much about the future. We don't know how long we have. I'm against marriage. I must eat healthy to keep you satisfied. I'm a fighter.* The scar on his collarbone. The long scar down his calf. *I was angry.*

I went to the mirror and stared at the pale woman looking back at me. *Pull yourself together, Heather, and go back out to your son.*

I wiped the running mascara below my eyes, straightened my shoulders, and left the bathroom.

Back at the table, Charlie watched me, concerned. "Are you okay? You don't look good."

"I'm sorry,' I said. "That last roll didn't sit well."

The drive home was quiet.

"I was his roommate," Charlie finally said. "Why wouldn't he have told me?"

I stared out the windshield as I navigated the familiar road. "He didn't want you to treat him differently."

"I wouldn't have."

I nodded, understanding why Cole kept this piece of himself from me. "Yes. You would have. It's only natural."

Charlie looked out the window.

"Do you have his address?" I asked.

Charlie turned to me. "Why?"

I shrugged and kept my eyes on the road. "We can send him something. You know, a get-well card or basket."

"I'll call and ask for it."

I spent the next week in a daze, helping Charlie prepare for his trip. In between last-minute shopping and packing, I grappled with the continuous desire to pick up the phone and call Cole. I wanted to talk to him, to understand what he was going through, to tell him…Tell him what? And that's when I'd hang up the phone. Would I have stayed with him if I'd known? He wouldn't have wanted that. He wanted me to stay out of love and desire. Not pity. That's why he kept this huge secret from me. Over and over, I argued with myself about what to do until finally, the day of Charlie's flight arrived.

We enjoyed a quiet lunch and set his bags by the front door. All his paperwork was in order and secured in his backpack. He was ready.

"I'm so proud of you." I fixed his collar, though it didn't need it.

"Everyone does this now, Mom. It's no big deal."

But it was. To me.

"You'll come home in December, fluent in Spanish."

"Let's hope." He held up crossed fingers.

Damian came to pick Charlie up at four o'clock for his evening flight. Charlie loaded his bags into the trunk while we stood on the driveway.

"Why don't you come with us," Damian said.

"That's a good idea," Charlie added and shut the trunk.

"Come on," my ex said when I hesitated. "If you're with me, I'll be able to use the HOV lane on the way home."

I considered the offer and decided to grab one more hour with Charlie. "Sure."

I locked up the house, and together, we headed to Kennedy Airport to send our only son out into the world.

Chapter 24

Dear Aunt Emma,

I'm not sure if you'll remember me. I wrote to you last year in August, distraught because I thought my husband might be cheating on me after twenty-two years in a happy marriage. You suggested I confront him or ignore his behavior and hope it fixed itself.

I did neither. I did the only other thing a woman could do; I turned to my closest girlfriend. We talked about what was happening, and she assured me I had nothing to be concerned about and that there must be a good reason for my husband to be acting the way he did. Her optimism and certainty gave me solace. So, I waited.

Two months later, I entered my favorite restaurant, and what I saw cemented any doubt I'd had about the love of my life. Standing in the restaurant facing me was every person I loved in the world (and some I didn't - fodder for another letter). My husband stood beside me, perspiring and relieved to finally have all the work and planning come to fruition. He and my best friend spent months putting this wonderful life celebration together. For me. Because they knew how hard I had been taking turning fifty. Because he loves me.

I finally decided to sit down and write you this letter. Sometimes, Aunt Emma, if it walks like a duck and talks like a duck, it could merely be love in disguise.

Not everything is as it appears to be.

~Fifty and (no longer) Forlorn

The letter from Fifty and Forlorn floored me. How small-minded and unprofessional I'd been with my response to her last year. I answered not from a thoughtful, objective point of view but from a personal place inside of me. The place that fed my anxiety, pain, and betrayal. The part of me from where I'd drawn decisions for too long. I fully believed at the time that changed behavior was circumspect. If I'd received her initial letter now, I wonder how I would have answered. Today I view life through a different lens. She was right, and I needed to hear it.

I moped around the house the morning after we dropped Charlie at the airport, my mind swarming with thoughts. I didn't want to work, did not want to speak to Trish or Dottie. I paced, feeling restless, but I had no desire to run. So, I started rifling through my bedroom drawers, tossing unworn clothes into a pile. The mindless act of deciding whether to keep a shirt or a pair of jeans or donate it helped somewhat and I made it all the way to the bottom drawer without thinking of…and then I saw it. And I knew that was the reason my room now looked like it had been ransacked. I reached in the drawer and pulled out the faded pink t-shirt, the shirt Cole wore during his first visit here on Thanksgiving, the one he left for me and found me wearing when he showed up unexpected at my door last December. Eight months ago. A lifetime ago, it seemed. I brought the shirt to my nose and breathed in deeply, but it no longer held his scent.

My cell phone rang downstairs. Still holding the shirt, I went to answer it. When I reached the top of the stairs, the ringing stopped. I paused at Charlie's room, neat and empty, and wondered how I'd get through the next months without seeing my favorite person.

Then I stood at the guest room and knew my answer. I'd do it, but it would be difficult.

I closed my eyes. *Let's play a game. If today was a gift and there was no tomorrow, what do I want to be doing?*

I opened my eyes, went back to my bedroom, and pulled out my suitcase.

Outside I stood over my garden, holding a bowl. I picked the ripest tomatoes, leaving the green ones to stay for a bit longer. I cut a healthy portion of two of the basil plants, sprigs of thyme, cilantro, pulled six peppers, and five large cucumbers. I had no idea how rewarding and therapeutic a garden could be. Growing food from the ground is good for the soul, and I wasted all those years, ignorant. On my way to the car, I pulled a mint plant out by its root and added it to the bowl.

The house locked up, my suitcase in the trunk, my bowl of homegrown veggies on the seat beside me, I backed out of the driveway. I rolled down my window to let the warm August air blow through the car and headed for Boston.

I checked my phone at a rest stop. Charlie texted that he had arrived at the Seville airport, and I quickly answered him, relieved. Trisha texted me, too, asking what my plans were for the weekend. Hers was the phone call I'd missed earlier in the house. I didn't respond. No one needed to know until I decided what my plans were.

I had five hours to think of what to say, and yet, when I pulled onto his street, my mind was still as confused as when I left my driveway. I parked two blocks from his apartment. It was mid-afternoon, and the air was thick like soup. I'm sure my hair grew twice its size with the humidity. As I approached the brownstone, a man walked down the steps and passed me. He looked familiar, and it wasn't until I stepped onto the same steps that I realized it was the man I'd seen Cole with outside the diner next to my hotel near Amherst. I turned to look down the block, but he was gone.

When I finally reached the door, I was perspiring and lifted the back of my tank top from my skin to relieve myself of the heat. In one hand, I clutched the bowl of vegetables. The suitcase, with a change of clothes, was in the car. Just in case.

Cole's name was next to number 4A, handwritten on a temporary white slip, among the list of apartment numbers and residents. I read it over, saying it to myself, his name rolling on my tongue. I lifted my hand to press the button, but it froze before my finger made contact. He had no idea I was coming here. What if he'd met someone and he's inside with her now? How would he explain me to someone else? What am I doing here? I was rash, spontaneous. This isn't me. I don't even know who I am anymore. I turned to the street and took a deep breath. Okay, Heather, you drove five hours to see this man. Ring the damn bell.

I pressed the button and winced. I waited. There was no answer. I turned around again and stepped onto the first step toward the street when a woman's voice came through the speaker.

"Yes?"

I returned to the intercom. "I'm looking for Cole."

There was a brief pause, and the door buzzed. I pulled it open, but hesitated to walk in, wondering who belonged to the voice that just let me in. I suspected I knew, but a twinge of doubt entered my mind.

I almost left. I should let things lie, continue with my life as it is. All I had to do was turn around and go home, and nothing would change. But something made me keep walking. I took the elevator to the fourth floor. I am here. I am not walking away. I want to know how he is. I need to know he'll be okay. I need to know I'll be okay.

I stepped from the elevator and turned in the direction of his apartment. Standing in the hall was a regal woman with cornsilk hair perfectly coifed and pulled back at the base of her neck. Her deep green, sleeveless dress complimented her brown eyes and tanned skin. She was quite attractive, as I knew she would be. As I stepped closer to her, though, I could see the age around her eyes and on her neck. She had to be in her mid to late fifties. She stared at me.

"I'm sorry. I was looking for Cole."

She squinted. "And you are…?"

"Heather." I held out my hand.

"Oh." Her eyes widened, and she took my hand. Hers was smooth and cool to the touch.

"I'm Diana. Cole's mother. Please come in. Cole will be back shortly."

She led me into a modest room and gestured to a deep brown leather couch. The apartment was chilly, and I felt my skin respond to the severe change in temperature from outside.

I sat, holding my bowl of vegetables on my lap. Diana lowered herself onto the loveseat facing me. Cream walls and a tan area rug complimented the plush couches. I wondered if the woman scrutinizing me right now was responsible for the decorating. In the corner of the room sat a chair with thin legs and a low back.

"He insisted on buying it," she said, following my gaze. "I couldn't say why. It doesn't look the least bit comfortable, and it matches nothing."

I bit back a smile. "I love it."

She watched me closely, her eyes flitting to the bowl I held. Feeling awkward and not wanting to explain why I brought it, I

244 | *Kimberly Wenzler*

moved it to the floor by my feet. I crossed my legs, not sure how to begin.

She spoke. "As you might have surmised, Cole has told me about you. Did you know that?"

"No."

"My son has been very down these past months." She held my eyes. I couldn't turn away. "I'm sure, as a mother yourself, the hardest thing to see is your child in distress."

"Yes," I said.

"Before this summer," she continued, "Arthur and I saw a change in Colton. He was serene –more so than I'd ever seen him. He seemed...fulfilled." She smoothed her dress, embarrassed by her emotional expression of her son. "We attributed this contentment to you."

I held my breath and waited for Diana to go on, to tell me where she was going with this.

"Tell me, Heather, if your son told you he fell in love with a woman twice his age, how would you respond?"

I wanted to point out that I was only seventeen years older, but instead, I said, "I would be upset."

"Why?"

She's right. What did I expect from this woman? That she'd embrace me? I can ruin his life.

"I'd want him to be able to start a family. Grow old with someone. Connect to someone his own age." I wrung my hands. "I'd want him to be happy."

"And you think Charlie wouldn't be happy with an older woman?"

"I don't know. Charlie isn't like Cole."

"No. I suspect he isn't."

I pressed my hands beside me on the couch. Do I leave now? She watched me, waiting for my next move. I took a deep breath and lifted my hands. No, I'm not ready to go just yet. I crossed my legs. The corner of her mouth twitched, and I saw Cole in her.

"If I tell you Cole cannot have children, nor does he want any, should that make a difference to me how I feel?"

My eyes filled. She made no sign that she noticed.

"All I want is for my boy to be happy, as any mother does. It's quite simple, really. And I'm not surprised to see you here."

"You're not."

"I know my son. It was a matter of time."

I took a deep breath and wiped my eyes. I knew I would be here, too. I'd just been ignoring my heart until now.

"Did you come here to break his heart?" she said.

I studied her face as she waited for my answer.

"I don't know why I'm here. I thought I'd figure it out on the ride, but I didn't."

She frowned. "Did you know Cole was sick?"

"I just learned he was," I said. "That's not why I came."

She nodded. "We lost our daughter. He struggled with that. And then, he had his own hurdles." She paused and took a breath. "The prognosis is…" She exhaled. "We're cautiously optimistic."

I nodded slightly, unable to do much else.

"After he took his GED, he insisted he wanted to travel. He felt confined, I suppose, for so long. He was never one to stay still. We indulged him. He's experienced more than most twice his age." She leaned over and parted her crossed feet. "So, you see, we're not surprised he couldn't connect with his own peers.

"He was well for four years. Earlier this summer, he moved out. He wanted to be on his own." She gazed around the apartment. "He never said, but I believe he was preparing to go get you." Her eyes steadied on me. "Cole doesn't give up. He's a fighter."

I was mesmerized, caught up in this woman's own strength.

"In June, he appeared… we thought perhaps…" Her incomplete thoughts dissolved into the air. "We finally convinced him to be seen, and he spent some time at Boston Medical. He came home last week."

"There was a man here earlier. I saw him once at school," I said.

"David. He's a counselor. He's been a great support to Cole since the beginning. He was a rock for my son at his lowest point. They've become friends."

I took a deep breath. "Diana, why did you tell me this? Do you want me to leave or stay?"

We watched each other. I tried to understand her motive. Before she could answer, the door opened, and Cole walked in with two bags of groceries in his hands. His hair was wet with perspiration, and his arms strained under the weight of the bags. He stopped when he saw us.

Diana stood, walked to her son, and kissed him on his cheek.

"It's time I leave. Your father wants to eat at the club tonight." Without a glance back to me, she picked up her purse and walked out.

I stood, and Cole and I looked at each other. My mind, muddled with what I just learned, prevented me from speaking. Still holding the bags, he went to the kitchen. He returned without delay and resumed his position standing at the entrance to the den.

"I didn't call to tell you I was coming. I'm sorry to interrupt your visit with your mother."

"She wasn't staying."

I nodded.

"You look amazing," he said.

I wore a tank top and linen shorts. I should have put more thought into what I was wearing, but I couldn't think straight before I left.

He'd lost weight, and his eyes seemed lighter within his pale complexion. He grew his hair and wore a few days' growth along his jaw. He'd aged since I'd seen him last. Still, he was beautiful.

"Do you want to sit?" he said.

I sat back down on the couch, and he replaced his mother on the loveseat.

He crossed his arms, and we stared at each other. The last time I saw him was at the airport in Punta Cana after a week together filled with love and lust and, for me, pure happiness. That was four months ago. Since then, I learned that I haven't been lonely. I have been looking for someone to fill me up, and I let myself get in the way of that.

"How did you find me?" he said.

My cheeks felt warm. "Your mother gave Charlie your address. I asked him for it."

We sat in silence. I could look at him forever and never tire of it.

"I want to show you something," I said finally.

The corner of his lip lifted. "I've wanted to hear that for months."

I reached to the bowl by my feet, pulled out a deep red tomato and held it to him. His eyebrows lifted. "You're going to cook something?"

"I have the makings of a small pot of sauce or a big salad."

He didn't understand.

"I grew this." I lifted the bowl. "I grew all of it. In my garden. This summer."

"You planted a garden?"

"Yes."

He beamed and ran his hand through his long hair.

"I'm going to extend it next season. There are so many possibilities. I had no idea how rewarding it would be."

Cole looked up at the ceiling, working to regain his composure. I wanted to grab him, pull him to me, and hold him tight. Instead, I put the bowl onto the table between us, and he leaned forward to study it. "Tomatoes, basil, cucumbers, peppers. Wow. What's that plant on top? Is that mint?"

"I didn't plan for the mint. It just showed up, and now it's everywhere. I yank it out, and it grows back. It's relentless." I gazed at my bowl. "I finally decided to embrace it."

"It's a great herb."

"It is."

He pulled his eyes back to mine.

"Did you go to Paris?" I said.

Slowly, he shook his head. "I won't go unless you're with me."

I gnawed the inside of my cheek. I knew this already.

"It's nice to see you," he said.

"I'm not sure why I'm here. Something made me get in the car and drive."

He looked confused. "You didn't get my letter?"

"Letter?"

He tilted his head. "You're here, and you didn't get it?"

"I don't know what you're talking about."

He smiled to himself. I'm not sure why.

"Did Charlie leave for Spain?"

I nodded, and he exhaled. "I would have come anyway," I said. The look he gave was so tender, my heart thrummed in my chest. "I like your place."

His gaze didn't waiver from my eyes.

"Why didn't you tell me you were sick?"

"I didn't want you to think I was with you for the wrong reasons," he said.

"The wrong reasons? Aside from the obvious?"

"That was never an issue for me."

"I know." The age difference was my problem. The only issue I had with Cole. Otherwise, he was perfect for me.

"How do you feel?" I said.

"That's the other reason I didn't want you to know. I don't want you to see me this way. Weak."

"I don't."

He leaned forward, resting his elbows on his knees and clasped his hands together. The thin leather rope hung from his neck. I wanted to put my hand against it, feel his pulse against my palm.

"How do you see me, Heather?"

I swallowed. "I see you as the one person who knows who I am. You brought me to life."

"I've been waiting for you to come back to me." His voice cracked with emotion. "Not knowing if I'd ever be able to hold you again is worse than anything I've been through."

My eyes welled. "Please tell me. Did it come back?"

"I've beaten it before. I'll do it again."

"I wish you would have told me. You stopped texting. I figured…" I dropped my head, embarrassed.

"You figured I gave up."

"Yes."

"I could never," he whispered. Deep down, I knew that, too. "Did you give up on me?"

"No," I said. "I gave up on me."

His blue eyes bore into me. "Why did you come here today?"

Seeing him across the small room, I knew at that moment what I wanted to do. I understood with such clarity what I needed to do. "I want to be with you. I'll take care of you."

"I don't want you to take care of me."

I finally let a tear trickle down my cheek. "That's what love means, Cole. It means in good and bad, I don't leave. I'm here. You promised to show me the world. I'm going to hold you to it."

He smiled. "You love me?"

"I do."

"It took you long enough to admit it."

"I needed to understand what was holding me back. I'm sorry," I said.

"Don't be. You were worth the wait."

"So were you."

The apartment was quiet, the soft hum of the air conditioner soothing.

"I may not have as much time as you."

I swallowed my fear. "Someone once told me that no one knows how much time we have. It's what's so unpredictably wonderful about life."

He stood, and I mirrored him.

"Let's take care of each other," he said.

"Sounds like a good plan to me."

Unspoken promises lingered between us. "Come over here," he said softly. Color filled his cheeks, and I glimpsed the Cole I'd fallen in love with under an autumn sky in my yard. I stepped into his arms. He held me close. I breathed in his scent, my nose to his neck, his fingers wove through my hair, a hand on my lower back pressing me closer, our bodies touching to our knees, and I let out a breath as my eyes closed. I'm not sure how long he has, or how long we have, but I do know that however long we're given is what I'll take.

I opened my eyes and pulled back to see his face. I put my hands on his cheeks, loving the feel of his skin after missing it for so long. "I like your knitting chair."

"I thought you might."

"Let's put it to use."

Chapter 25

Dear Aunt Emma,

I've experienced more than my share in two decades. Many experiences were painful. But none as painful as having a taste of pure happiness only to have it taken away. This has been the most difficult fight I've faced yet.

I have loved one woman. She is everything I need. Everything I desire. For six months, we shared the most intimate experience two people can share, and I want to continue doing so until I take my last breath.

It's been sixty-one days since I last held her. She has pushed me away to make others happy. She has taken the most natural, beautiful act of love and locked it away in a dark room because she believes she's doing the right thing. For me. For her family and friends. For everyone. Everyone but the two of us.

Life is short, and it is hard, but it can be beautiful if we allow it to be. Please ask her to look deep into her heart and uncover what it is she truly wants. I am confident if she does this, she'll return to me, and I will spend the rest of my life making sure she never regrets her decision. We will be happy. I am as sure of it as I am sure the sun will rise tomorrow.

Love is love. It's that simple. You can't put parameters around it or enforce rules. It's there, without plan or design, between two people. It's what these two people choose to do with it that will define them. If it's right and we give ourselves wholly to it, we'll be free.

I choose happiness. I choose her. I choose freedom.

She once told me that I brought her to life. But she was wrong. She held all the power. My life began when we met.

Please tell her I will wait for her. I will wait for as long as it takes.

~ Cole

I looked out the window over the building rooftops. The sky was a promising pink, a welcome change from the bleak March month we'd just bid farewell. I rested my hands on the sill and pressed my face to the cool glass. It felt good on my warm skin. The heat from the radiator surrounded me like a thick blanket, leaving me stripped down to a tank top and underwear. A small flock of birds flew into my sight, weaving and swaying with the spring wind. Do they know where they're going? Or do they let the wind take them? I still wonder how I ended up here, so far from where I started. Sometimes I don't believe it myself. What will life be like when this is over? I closed my eyes and exhaled. Don't think about tomorrow. Tomorrow doesn't exist.

"Heather," Cole whispered from the bed.

I turned to him.

"Open the window."

Gratefully, I did, and the air rushed in like a welcome guest after a long absence. My skin prickled with the cool air, relieving me.

"Come," he said, beckoning me back to bed.

I climbed next to him and pulled him close. He rested his head on my chest, his arms around my torso. I ran my fingers through his hair, and his breathing slowed. I kissed the top of his head and hummed a familiar song.

Lately, I find myself reliving moments that took my breath away - small, significant pearls among the many days we spent over the past four years: conversations we had while hiking through meandering, gorgeous trails in Switzerland, the feel of holding his hand along cobblestone streets while he taught me the history of a town in Amsterdam and then Austria. The nights we cooked together in a villa in Tuscany, wearing little more than our hearts, impromptu dances on the terra cotta floor while the aroma of sautéed vegetables wafted around us. Whispers and songs only I could hear. And yes, we went to Paris. Hours of passionate lovemaking morphed into gentle caresses and intertwined limbs as he weakened. We held each other, whispered vows of love and dreams. Later, through extended hospital stays, we remained close, always touching, always promises. He never stopped dreaming.

Last month, Cole stopped his treatments and told his parents he was ready. He swore he wasn't afraid. I allowed them the time they asked, understanding a mother's need to be with her son, and visited Charlie at school where he had stayed an extra year. Over dinner, Charlie updated me on his post-graduation plans and his latest girlfriend, Pamela, who would be graduating as well. Then he asked about Cole, and I told him while he held my hand. At first, Charlie had been reluctant to accept my being with his former roommate, but he gradually grew to accept it. "It's nice to see you happy," he told me during one of our talks. "How can I begrudge you that?"

When I returned to Cole, we talked into the night, filling the hours with memories of our travels and intermittent sleep. I made him tell me more about his own travels before me, and I never tired of them, picturing the world through his beautiful, inquisitive eyes. I read him Dear Aunt Emma letters I received, and together we discussed how I should respond, weighing different scenarios. I learned so much during these talks.

I never cried in front of him. I wanted him to see me as truly happy as I was to be with him. And I was. More than I ever thought possible. He taught me to enjoy every day, to forget about tomorrows, for they didn't exist, and not to dwell too long on yesterdays.

I ran my fingers through his hair, now brittle from drugs and disease, and thought of how far I'd come, how much happiness I experienced because of this man.

"Hey," he whispered into my chest.

"Yes?"

"Happy birthday." He squeezed me and sang the song. Today, I turned forty-five.

"Let's play a game."

My fingers paused, and I let my hand rest fully on his scalp. I stared at his profile, the lips I could have kissed forever if allowed, the cheek with the dimple that stayed with me long after I closed my eyes, his chiseled chin. I ran my fingers gently along his jaw and thought again, as I did every time I looked at him, how fortunate I was. I knew what day this was. I could feel it. He did, too. For as long as I draw breath, I will remember this as the best day of my life. And the worst. I inhaled deeply, feeling significant pain and calming peace. How did he do that?

"Let's play a game," he said again.

I closed my eyes.

Chapter 26

Two years later

I walked through the hotel lounge, past congregated groups of unfamiliar people, new faces that have replaced the ones I knew, those I lost touch with while I'd been gone. I paused to view the bar, craning my neck toward the corner seats, and then I saw my old friend, John, who I'd come to see. He was in conversation and didn't notice me walk up to him.

I tapped him on the shoulder, and he turned around. His eyes widened, and his face broke into a smile.

"Heather."

"Hi, John."

He stepped from the stool, and we embraced. I was so happy to see him and knew it was reciprocated. He excused himself to the person he had been speaking with and asked me to sit. I did.

"Can I buy you a drink?" he said.

"Seltzer for me. Thanks."

He ordered and slapped his palms on his thighs. "Well, I'll be. I didn't think I'd see you again. What's it been? Four years?"

"Almost five."

"Five years. And not a word. You just dropped off the radar."

"I'm sorry. Things got a little intense for a while. But…well, here I am."

He shook his head and rubbed his chin, watching me. "You look terrific."

I inhaled deeply and let it out. "I feel good. I'm in a good place."

"Yes," he said. "Good for you."

I sipped my seltzer and looked around. "Some new faces, I see."

"Some of the old group, too. They'll be coming in tomorrow. How long are you here for?"

"Not long," I said. "I'm not here for the conference. I'm not sure when I'll be ready to return to them."

He watched me.

"I came here to see you."

John pointed to himself. "You came to Seattle to see me?"

I nodded and laughed. "I do that now. Spontaneous, crazy things."

"I'm flattered." He signaled to the bartender for another drink.

"How's your wife?" I said.

"She's well. I have to show you something." He pulled his phone from his jacket pocket and held up a picture of his wife holding a baby. I grabbed the phone and enlarged the image with my fingers.

"Your daughter had a baby!"

He nodded. "Turns out, it's not so bad to be a grandfather. In fact, it has its perks."

I kissed him on his cheek. "I'm happy for you."

"Thank you." He gazed at the picture a moment before putting his phone back in his pocket. "How's Charlie?"

"He's great. He got his Master's, and he's back in Spain until Christmas."

John sipped his drink.

"Congratulations on the book. I read it. It's wonderful."

He blushed. "I wasn't sure if you knew."

"Of course, I do. I make sure to keep up with my friends. I have something for you." I opened my pocketbook and took out a box. I placed it on the bar and waited.

John's eyes switched between me and the gift, and finally, he took the cover off and looked inside. "Humph." He pulled out a small replica of the Eiffel Tower, made of delicate steel.

"Check it out," I said, flipping a small switch underneath. On the bar, the figure lit up, and lights flickered on and off along the entire piece. "You should see this in person. Every night at sunset, it lights up against the dark sky. Pure magic."

We stared at it, and John took my hand.

"I wanted to bring a bit of Paris to you until you get there yourself," I said.

"You've been to Paris?" he said softly.

"I've been everywhere."

I left John shortly after and re-traced my path through the lounge to the lobby, feeling a surge of hope. My future lay before me, and I looked forward to it. I stepped into the elevator car and smiled as the doors closed me in.

I'd just pulled my suitcase from the luggage belt at JFK when my cell phone rang.

"You'll never guess where I'm going," my sister said when I answered.

"Let me think." I smiled as I wheeled my bag toward the airport exit.

"Forget it. I'll tell you. Santorini! Adam surprised me for our anniversary. We're going in April before the girls get home."

"You're going to love it," I said, wondering if Adam chose the hotel I'd recommended.

"I know. I can't wait. All I got him was a watch."

"Which I'm sure he loves."

"Whatever. I'll make it up to him. Are you home yet?"

At the curb, the driver stepped from the car to take my suitcase from me as I climbed into the back seat. "I just landed. Heading home now."

"Okay. I'll call you tomorrow. Let's have lunch and catch up. I'll bring the seltzer."

I laughed. "Sounds like a plan."

An hour later, we pulled onto my street. I sat in the back seat and wrapped my fingers around my wrist, covering the inked word along my skin, *Today*, whispering to myself my mantra, a daily message of love and gratitude, and with a smile, stared out the window at the gorgeous foliage. Thanksgiving was only a few weeks away, followed soon after by the bareness and cold felt in a New York winter. But for now, the world was a palette of red and orange and the air so crisp and clear, every breath rejuvenated me.

From my driveway, I watched the Town Car back up and leave. I went through the front door of the house, dropped my suitcase in the kitchen, and walked straight out into the backyard. Pulling the rake from the shed, I worked, perspiring under the weak sun, until I had a large, deep pile of leaves. I tossed the rake to the side and took several steps back. With a smile and happy tears, I ran and jumped in.

What My Garden Taught Me

by Heather Harrison

I planted my first garden in my yard on a balmy spring day in April. I was forty-one years old. It was the year I fell in love with someone unexpected.

In a ten by ten square, in a sunny spot, I planted various infant vegetables and herbs known for their resiliency and ease of growth. For the next months, I did everything to make sure they thrived. I pruned, hydrated, weeded, and watered.

What surprised me most was the joy it brought me.

It wasn't as hard as I thought it would be. If you listen carefully, the plants speak to you. They talk through the wind while they flow gracefully, content, ask for water with their withered leaves, smile into the warm sun when they're happy. They bear fruit and say, thank you.

There was, however, one plant that wouldn't grow. The stem remained thin, the leaves were perpetually drooped and brown, the minimal fruit, small and hard. There was no rhyme or reason to why it withered in the same spot where other plants grew big and strong. If a seed has everything it requires, it should very well survive. Still, there are exceptions. A once-healthy plant can become afflicted with an unforeseen disease, and all the sun and soil, and attention in the world won't save it. Without apology, life goes on.

Sometimes, an unplanned plant emerges from a neglected patch of soil, or through a crack in cement, and it grows where it's not meant to. Despite a harsh, unwelcome environment, it takes root, holds on, forces its way up through the surface, and reaches for the sun. It defies all odds and flourishes.

This happened to me. Against the cement wall near the foundation of my house, in dry dirt I ignored, grew healthy, vibrant green mint. When I tugged it out, roots and all, it returned. It was relentless. I pulled it, and it grew. As I did, I started to enjoy the scent of the leaves more and more. Why was I trying to eradicate something so delicious? Because I didn't plan for it?

I learned to love mint. And I learned to make mojitos.

So, dear readers, if you've wanted to try something new but haven't, I implore you not to wait. There is only today. Life is short. Do something as simple as plant a garden. Take time to watch it grow. Experience the unparalleled joy of touching a petal that is softer than the barest silk. Breathe in the scents of the wild. Dig your fingers and toes into cool, fertile, supple soil and know that life begins and ends there. Take out your earphones and let the music of nature serenade you. The orchestra of bees and cicadas, harmonious with birds and wind, can be just as fulfilling as Mozart or Bach or Taylor Swift. Sit on the soft grass, eat a tomato off the vine and let its juices run down your chin.

I did, and this simple garden not only taught me valuable life lessons but introduced a wonderful person with whom I fell in love. Me.

Acknowledgements

Along with my family and friends, who fill my life with joy and laughter, I offer my deepest gratitude to the following people:

My editors: Karli Jackson, Gina Ardito, and Jen Gracen. I learn so much from you and appreciate your help.

Suzanne Fyhrie Parrott, of First Steps Publishing. You wear many hats for me: cover designer, writing partner, beta, and proofreader, but the one hat that covers all the others is, friend. We've been together from the beginning. Thank you for your continued support and patience.

Suzanne McKenna-Link, I am so grateful we met and that we're now going through this crazy journey together. Thank you for continuously talking me off the ledge, for your constant input, and your friendship. I hope we'll share bad pancakes through many more books.

Mom, my first and favorite reader, thank you for reading new drafts over and over until you finally said you liked it.

Monica and Katie, friends from the womb (almost), thank you for your constant support through the years, with everything.

Sue Guacci, my dear friend, and creative companion, who went through this story with me many times, offering invaluable input and advice. I don't know what I would do without you.

Booked For Drinks — book club extraordinaire — who came through for me again: Sue Moran, Liz Tompkins, Mara Kelly, Patty

Maletta, Kerri Messina, Eva Rizzi, and Deb Luoni. Thank you for not only taking time to read my stories, but for continuously welcoming me to your gatherings, and entertaining me with amusing tales of your lives. I can't wait for the next one.

Valerie Dietrich, Linda Michaels, Cathy Michaels, Nora Katz, Janice McQuaid, Joanne Kalfas, Tracy Bianco, and Aunt Terry Alexander. I can't adequately express my appreciation for you all. So, I'll just say *thank you* for reading early drafts (sometimes more than once) and for your friendship, input, and support.

Eileen Nieves, Kristina Shields, Cristina Tagliaferri, Suzanne Kelly, Carrie Logan, Ann Marie Maud, and Shari Feuer – my new betas! Thank you for the time you gave me to read my manuscript, and so generously answer my questions. I hope to meet you soon.

My uncle, James Granauro, thank you for your input. I love our private book club and the random texts I get at all hours.

Zach & Alex, my loves, who are working hard at school, and adapting to this crazy world with grace, I am so proud of you. Steve, thank you for not minding when I disappear for hours to stare, bleary-eyed, at the computer screen, and for occasionally popping your head into the office to say, "So, tonight...cereal for dinner?" I didn't think it was possible, but I love you more every day.

And thank you, dear reader, from the bottom of my heart, for spending some time with me. I hope we meet again.

~Kimberly

About the Author

Kimberly Wenzler, author of *Both Sides of Love*, *Letting Go*, and *Fabric of Us*, was born and raised on Long Island, New York. On her website, she uses humor to share her personal views of life, writing and reading. She's currently working on her next novel.

www.KimberlyWenzler.com

www.facebook.com/kimberlywenzler

Made in the USA
Middletown, DE
14 June 2020

97504961R00156